M000073364

CHECK YES, NO, OR MAYBE

CHECK YES, NO, OR MAYBE

STORMIE SKYES

4 Horsemen
Publications, Inc.

Check Yes, No, or Maybe
Copyright © 2021 Stormie Skyes. All rights reserved.

4 Horsemen Publications, Inc.
1497 Main St. Suite 169
Dunedin, FL 34698
4horsemenpublications.com
info@4horsemenpublications.com

Cover by 4 Horsemen Publications, Inc.
Typesetting by Autumn Skye
Edited by Amanda T. Miller

All rights to the work within are reserved to the author and publisher. No part of this publication may be reproduced, stored in a retrieval system, or transmitted in any form or by any means, electronic, mechanical, photocopying, recording, scanning, or otherwise, except as permitted under Section 107 or 108 of the 1976 International Copyright Act, without prior written permission except in brief quotations embodied in critical articles and reviews. Please contact either the Publisher or Author to gain permission.

This book is meant as a reference guide. All characters, organizations, and events portrayed in this novel are either products of the author's imagination or are used fictitiously. All brands, quotes, and cited work respectfully belong to the original rights holders and bear no affiliation to the authors or publisher.

Library of Congress Control Number: 2021951153

Audio ISBN: 978-1-64450-442-0
Ebook ISBN: 978-1-64450-443-7
Print ISBN: 978-1-64450-444-4

CONTENTS

CHAPTER 1

Y ou know that opening moment in comedy movies when the main character wakes up screaming? The frame freezes, revealing that stupefied face—mouth agape, eyes wide—once they realized they'd done something stupid in a drunken binge. Sometimes the director wanted to give the audience more chances to revel in their humiliation, so he has them pull the sheets to cover themselves. Sometimes they see their mysterious partner and fall out of bed.

You get the picture.

That was me after realizing I wasn't in my apartment in yet another, probably humiliating, line of horrible relationship/hookup decisions. I didn't fall out of the bed, but it took all my willpower to replace the horrified scream with a gasp. Don't misjudge. I didn't make a habit of going home with strange men, letting them sex me into a stupor, then waking up wondering what the hell I did—or let happen to me—the night before. No one had properly laid me in almost three years. Well, the word "properly," in this case, was in the beholder's eye. Truth was, I hadn't gotten laid at all. Pathetic now that I that I thought about it. The point was, hooking up with anyone after getting royally screwed never went well. I often white rabbited—yes, I made that a word—any time someone showed the slightest interest in me.

1

Okay, okay, don't panic. Hasty breaths raced from my lungs. Sweat beaded on my temples. My hands ran through the mid-cut waves of deep auburn—almost black—hair as I jerked my head to survey the room. *Let's step back and start with figuring out where the hell I am.*

I took a quick glance around the room, noticing all my cheap furniture had been replace that expensive modern furniture. You know the kind. Sleek, black, often with no cushioning at all. *Why is it always black? And leather?* Silky sheets cradled my ass. The pillows and duvet probably cost more than my car. *At least the bed is nice.*

I know what you're thinking, and you're right. I didn't drive an Audi or Aston Martin. But why replace a working vehicle when my college tuition was at stake? I barely made enough to keep ramen noodles in my pantry and my dog fed. *Not important right now.* I shook my head.

I couldn't remember how the hell I got here. My head throbbed with the worst hangover I'd had since my boyfriend broke up with me. I remembered going out with my best friend, getting sloshed, and then it all turned into a fuzzy television screen.

What the heck happened last night? I stared at the bedside table and saw a bottle of water and two Tylenol—*or Advil, who knows*—waiting. *At least whoever I was with cared enough to leave them there.* I swiped the two pills, tossed them in my mouth, and gulped the water. *Hopefully, there's no GHB.*

Things got more insane when I realized I was wearing nothing but my green cotton boxer briefs. *Holy crap! How didn't I notice this before?* My eyes bulged, and I fought the urge to scream again. *God, please tell me I didn't take a flying leap into some stranger's bed and let him screw my brains out.*

How embarrassing of a conversation would that be? Especially in a work environment like mine where gossip ran rampant.

"Hey, Aaron, how was your weekend?"

"Oh, you know, went home with an utter, hopefully hot-as-hell, stranger—nothing too eventful."

Josh wouldn't let me live it down, and Frankie might fall out of his chair belting laughs at the top of his lungs. *Either way, my work reputation is officially FUBAR.*

I smacked my forehead, regretting it immediately.

My mind shifted to the defense mechanism I'd had since I was seven. I placed my palm on my eye socket, clenched my teeth, and tried to ignore the throbbing in my ears. *Out at the cocktail bar with Elliot? Yes, that sounds about right.* It was Friday. My ex had pissed me off by calling again … definitely. *Everything else is blank! Completely blank!* A low growl rumbled in my throat. *How could Elliot do this to me? I'm going to kill him.*

Somewhere in the distance, rushing water buzzed to life. *Is that a shower?* I threw the sheets aside and stood, using the bed to stabilize myself as I staggered a bit. *My fricking head!* I had no time to waste. I had to get out of there. If I ran into whoever owned this swanky place, my face would burn.

It wouldn't be the first time a bout of humiliation ruined my life, leading to endless spewing of apologies and awkwardness. My reputation for landing in horrible relationships should earn me a medal. If screwing things up was a sport in the Olympics, I'd be the founder. I was the sad case who would actually cry in any reality show I starred in where the main character pretended to sob while calling their ex a selfish asshole.

Besides, not like I'd ever see the guy … or girl. A strong smell of musk struck my nostrils. *Definitely a guy.* At least I got that right. *It doesn't matter. It was one night. One ... frustratingly vague, alcohol induced, most likely horribly decided night...*

Like a cartoon, I stumbled around the room trying to find every article of my clothing and tripped over my jeans while putting them on. Time was my enemy if I planned on avoiding my mystery "night lover" before he finished his shower. Being frantic didn't help. I stubbed my toe on a fancy wooden chest of drawers.

"Shit," I muttered under my breath. Tying shoes became another hassle, then I got my shirt and hoodie, hauling ass downstairs.

Woah. I froze upon seeing the spectacle in front of me.

The paned glass offered a beautiful bird's-eye view of Manhattan. Honking cars and taxis filled with impatient morning people looked like kids' toys. It was audible from here because the buildings acted like huge, empty walls. Everything echoed! Giant billboards advertising the latest fashion sensation and upcoming blockbuster flashed on both sides of the streets.

I recognized the place as one where the elite live. I was in a Park Avenue condo with the largest living room I'd ever stood in. The furniture continued the boring, monochrome, modernist feel that the rooms upstairs completed with leather sofas with white pillows. A glass coffee table sat on a white— *why is it always white?*—sheepskin carpet. Everything faced a large, mounted entertainment center made of sleek, black wood shelving on both sides that took up the same space as a large bookshelf. And not the small ones either. Hell, the guy had speakers mounted in all four corners of the room. The weirdest and most out-of-place thing that resembled a normal house was the electric fireplace.

The entire far glass wall opened to a balcony adorned with palm trees, folding sun chairs, and ... a jacuzzi and a pool?

Man, who is this guy?

The shower stopped, and I was reminded I needed to keep hauling ass if I didn't want a confrontation. *"Hi, Mr. Unknown, I'm Aaron Cambrian. Look, I have no idea how I got here, but would you mind telling me what happened last night?" How awkward would that be?*

I grabbed my cell and wallet from the kitchen counter, carefully opened the door, and snuck out into a hallway that was as fancy as the condo. Floral wallpaper decorated with expensive paintings lined both sides. Plush, red carpet led the way to bronze elevator doors.

I am REALLY out of my element here. I walked to the elevator and jabbed the button multiple times with my thumb. *Like that ever speeds things up.* A quick check over my shoulder told me my bed mate hadn't followed me. *That's good.* I sighed heavily, eyes on the ceiling.

The doors finally opened, and I repeated the manic button pressing inside the elevator, watching the door at the end of the hallway. *Please don't come out. Please don't come out.* No one did, and I was free to forget—*or try to remember*—what happened.

While waiting to reach the lobby, I checked my phone to see if Elliot had texted. He hadn't, which led me to believe he was busy getting his ass pounded or dealing with a hangover. *Karma, please be on my side and let it be the latter.* Either way, I was going to have my own words with him. *What kind of best friend lets this happen?* Whatever *this* was.

I shot him a quick text once I exited the spinning glass doors leading to a doorman hailing taxis for his rich patrons.

[Aaron: Elliot, you asshole, you better call me when you get this.]

"Morning, sir," the doorman greeted, beaming. "Get you a cab?"

He reminded me of Dr. Watson with his round belly, full mustache, and wiry beard. Gold tassels dangled from a button up suit. On his head was a hat like a chauffeur wore. *Not that I would know.*

I shook my head. "No thanks. Think I'll walk." Confused, I glanced one way then the other. *Now that I think about it, where the hell is my car?*

Cold breezes reminded me to put my hoodie on if I didn't want to die of hypothermia. I shivered and pulled it on quickly. I'd always hated the cold. Frigid weather always reminded me of the multiple days my ex stood me up when we planned holiday dates and I was left standing on the frozen sidewalk without a ride. I had to call Elliot to come get me. Why I ever thought I loved that dick remained a complete mystery. A quick glance at the sky said we were looking forward to the first snow of the season or another freezing rain.

With my hands pocketed, I strolled down the crowded street. People on their cell phones shouldered past dog walkers taking care of too many dogs at once. Vendors started up their carts, readying their various foods for patrons looking for quick breakfast food choices. The mingling aromas both confused and excited my rumbling stomach.

A woman with large breasts ran into me. She stumbled on her bright cherry stilettos, almost falling.

"I'm sorry," I said, though I didn't really mean it. She shrugged it off with a "no problem" accompanied by teasing eyes. *Too bad for her. I prefer cocks.*

6

I stopped by my favorite coffee shop to pick up some food. As the sign featuring a small white bird came into view, my mouth practically drooled at the scents of coffee, cinnamon, and sweet treats. I held the door open for a family—Mom, Dad, and two kids—then quickly joined the line, shoulders dropping at the length. *How early do they get up to be here so soon?*

I was reminded of my headache, and I drew my shoulders to my jaw. *Geesh, why aren't those painkillers working yet?*

While waiting for my turn, I tried again to go over the previous night's events. *Jesus, how much did I drink? I can't even remember his face.* What if I went home with someone "less than desirable?" *Yeah, that would add to the humiliation. An ugly, rich, fat guy.*

"Next!" The cute blonde cocked his shoulder, looking me over. "Well, well." He appeared to think. "Aaron, right?"

I nodded, wincing. "Yeah. I think so."

The blonde hissed through clenched teeth. "Damn. Looks like you had a rough night. The usual?"

I rubbed my head. "Sorry, but do we know each other?"

He placed a hand on his hip, the other on the counter. Aiming a raised brow at me, he said, "Wow, am I really that forgettable? I used to work at the Early Bird right down the street from your apartment. We almost went out a couple times."

Maybe it was the headache. Or the fact I reeled from embarrassment at the night before. "I'm sorry. I don't—"

Cutie raised a hand. "No problem. Hangover brain does that to the best of us. I'm Cameron." He held out a hand. "Nice to re-meet you. The usual?"

I nodded, taking his hand, and shaking it, thankful he didn't need me to think much more.

"Cool," he said, then called out my order and took payment. "It'll be a few minutes. I'll get your muffin. Want it warmed?"

I shook my head. "Not this time." *I remember that detail, at least.* "Just starving."

He handed me my muffin, and I walked to the back and sat at a round table. Old Blue Eyes' "Fly Me to the Moon" came on over the speakers, and I found my foot tapping at the beat. *No New Yorker worth their salt doesn't like Sinatra.*

I pulled out my phone, checking all my texts. Still nothing from Elliot. Thankfully, it was the weekend, so I didn't have to worry about work. *And I didn't give Mr. Mystery One Nighter my number.* I raised my eyes, puffing my cheeks and blowing air out. *Thank God.*

Cute blonde delivered my order personally. "Now get yourself home and sleep that off," he joked.

I gave him a tight-lipped nod, stood, and left. *One thing down. Now for a certain "friend" and to find out what the hell happened last night...*

CHAPTER 2

Getting to my apartment from the coffee shop was too far, so I grabbed a cab. After a few puddle splashes added to an already "wonderful" day, I finally got lucky. *Or maybe not.* The cabby looked like he belonged in a serial killer film or an episode of *Law & Order.*

"Where to, pal?" he asked in a raspy voice.

I gave him my address and got comfortable—arms crossed, legs spread—for the long ride. *That's what I get for being on fricking Park Avenue.*

Damp clothes made me shiver, and I curled up further in my hoodie. My head pounded in time with the theme music of the radio show the cabby played. The plate on the back of his brown leather seats told me his name was Ernie Beckett. His photo reminded me of a mug shot.

Yep. Definitely done time.

My phone vibrated in my back pocket. I struggled against the seat belt that gripped me like a python to grab the damn thing. *God, can something please go right today?* I wondered if I'd done something horrible, and karma was blasting my ass with interest.

Elliot's name flashed along with a selfie of him puckering his lips in a pouty kiss. His glossed lips shimmered in the light, accentuating his dark hair. When the hell did he take that? And why was it his contact picture?

9

"Elliot," I grumbled.

"Hey, babe!" he replied in a singsong, perfectly put together voice. *So much for karma being my ally.* "How *was* he? And don't you leave out a *single* detail! Oh, please tell me the sex was as hot as his looks!"

How was the sex? "That's a brilliant question," I groaned, squeezing the phone, rubbing my head. "Look, asshole, I don't know what stunt you pulled last night, but I need you to fill me in."

Heat filled my cheeks with the rising embarrassment. *Or maybe it's the lingering alcohol.* Either way, I had to know what I did. Since Elliot sounded fresh and sober, he probably manipulated me into another of his stupid dares.

A brief silence. "What do you mean?" The canary voice changed to "Serious Elliot," his tone so deep you wouldn't recognize you were speaking to the same guy. "Oh. My. God." The sound of a hand slapping against a forehead came over the phone. "Did you *seriously* drink so much you don't even remember? Christ, Aaron, the once-in-a-cosmic-miracle time you drop your checklists, and you can't even remember *doing* a guy that sexy?"

My checklists. The one flaw Elliot had tried to "free" me from for years. Sometimes almost daily. I'd put them into place to avoid falling into bed with the wrong super dick—among other things like drinks, clothing choices, professions, etc. Each time I faced a choice, I mentally formed a piece of paper with "yes," "no," "maybe," and sometimes other categories to help me decide. They were the only things I had to keep control over my dumpster fire of a life. But it drove El nuts, and he'd made it his life's mission to get me to let the lists go.

Glad he remembers Mr. Apparently Fine. "I guess not," I snapped, thanking God the glass between me and the cabby was closed. "Remind me, El. Remind me why I woke up almost naked in a Park Avenue condo."

A loud "ugh" droned on. I tapped my finger on my knee, waiting for the drama session to end.

"Aaron, Aaron, Aaron," Elliot chided and breathed out an extended, overly exaggerated sigh. "What am I supposed to do with you?"

Do with me? "Are you nuts? How about answering my question? I'm not kidding, El. I'm fucking humiliated! Oh, and while you're feeling giving, try telling me where my damn car is."

A brief pause ensued, giving me ample time to debate how hard I was planning on hitting my "friend" when I saw him. We'd known each other since community college. Elliot kept in touch after he left for beauty school. After finding out we both lived in Manhattan, we kept a weekly get-together. Elliot spent most of that time keeping me from crawling back to the dick responsible for my latest breakdown.

Hence why I'm sitting in a cab...

"That's easy! You didn't have yours. We took mine." El popped his lips. "Listen, I'm still at Brandon's apartment—"

"Who the hell is Brandon?" I almost shouted.

"Easy, babe. You aren't the only one who had his ass pounded last night." He paused again. "In your case, *hopefully*, got pounded. Anyway, it'll take me a bit to get this hot mess fixed," *I did NOT need that mental image,* "and then I'll meet you at your place to catch you up. Around five sound good?"

Do I have a choice? "Yeah, sure. See you." Elliot made his kissy sounds, and we hung up just as the cabby arrived at my apartment building in lower Manhattan. The building's brown bricked form overshadowed the small community center on the other side of the street.

"Take it easy, mac," the cabby said.

I smile falsely, handed him my fare, and waved as he drove off. To add to the crappy morning, the cab's tires splashed mud-mixed rain onto my jeans.

"Shit!" I raised my boot and shook it like doing so would help the denim. "Can this day get any worse?" The answer to that question lay with whatever El had to tell me.

Kids playing basketball stopped and waved, bright smiles on their faces. My neighborhood wasn't the safest or swankiest place, but we got along well and did what we could for each other. I returned the gesture, cursing when my ear pressurized and started ringing.

I pulled my keys from my hoodie, turned the lock, and marched through the dilapidated door, greeted by the raunchy landlady. She wasn't as bad as some other tenants—namely, the partiers—made her out to be. Curlers held what was left of her white hair up. Loud meowing from her apartment took her attention from my smile and warm greeting.

Unlike the condo, my apartment building didn't have shiny elevators or plush carpet. Hell, I didn't think there was any "plush" left beneath the dirty brown carpet under my feet. Years of wear and tear caused the edges to fray and pull from the nails and moldings. Dust particles flew through the air, and the faint smell of mildew came through the vents. Not the best place, but it was the only one I could afford with my meager wages and tuition costs.

I don't care how "hot" he or the supposed sex was. Anyone who lives in a condo is definitely a no. I made the mental check in the "no" category. *Rich people. They think they're so entitled.*

At the end of the hall, overlooked by a single rectangular window, my apartment provided me with enough privacy that I didn't worry about nosy neighbors or police knocking at ungodly hours. Like it did every time I tried to unlock the door, the key fought me. Eventually, it lost, and I kicked open the door, entered, and kicked it closed.

My shoulders slumped, and my back hit the door, head directed at the ceiling. The throbbing had lessened thanks to the coffee and Tylenol roaming through my system. Rumbling in my stomach brought about a wave of nausea, and I felt like vomiting. Thankfully, I didn't, and I pushed away from the door, shed my hoodie, and hung it on the mounted coat hooks.

"First things first. Roxxie! Here, girl!" I waited for my Aussie Shepherd to saunter around the corner. She sat, uttering a soft whimper. I knelt and petted her silken fur. "Hey. I know. I missed you too."

Roxxie bumped my leg as I reached for the recently dropped mail. I turned to see her raise a paw and bring it down.

"I know, I know. You think I expected to stay out all night?" I grumbled and went to rummage through the cabinets for a pan, thinking about Elliot coming over and the run I needed to shed some frustration. "Aha!" I raised the cast-iron skillet. "Told you I'd find one."

Roxxie's head angled right adorably, her ears flopping and her eyes growing large.

"I'm sorry, Rox," I said with a sigh, turning on the stovetop. "Last night didn't really go like I planned either." *I guess.* A cheesy grin curved my lips. "If you want to, blame Elliot. He's coming over later, and I have no problem with you getting your revenge by drowning him in drool."

To this, Roxxie yipped a bark. *Finally, karma works for me.*

While Roxxie's meal cooked, I pulled the juicer from the lower cabinet, eyeing the dog lying on her stomach and covering her face. *Seriously? It's like she's not even a dog sometimes.*

"What? Just because you don't like to eat healthy—" I didn't bother finishing the sentence over the juicer's roaring. *You'd think they'd mute the sound. No wonder Roxxie whines when I use this.*

She rolled onto her side, sighing heavily.

I finished assembling my smoothie. "Impatient much? It's almost done. Get your bowl."

Roxxie was on her feet in seconds. Soft clacking of her claws on the wood echoed as she retrieved her bowl. It usually waited next to the island. Plastic clanking against the wall told me Roxxie had transported her bowl near the front door. I wondered if she romped around the apartment with it in her mouth when I wasn't home. Wouldn't be the first time she'd done it.

She eventually returned with the bright red bowl featuring her name, placed it down, and sat, tail wagging.

Laughing, I spooned the food into her bowl. She was on it immediately, gobbling it down like I hadn't fed her in ten years.

"Drama queen." I huffed a laugh, sipping my smoothie and searching through the mail. "Nothing but bills, loan pay off offers, yada yada." I took the relevant stuff and recycled the rest.

There was not much for me to do until Elliot got here, so I dressed in running clothes—shorts, phone and ear buds, muscle shirt, and the same hoodie—and called for Roxxie. She eagerly jumped and pawed at the door. I grabbed and pocketed my keys before we headed out into the morning mist.

CHAPTER 3

R unning always helped calm me. In the chaotic labyrinth of my mind, sometimes thoughts of what needed doing crowded out the present moment. Sounded confusing, but for someone like me, it was a fact of life.

Throughout our run, I periodically stopped and checked my phone. Almost like I was expecting the guy from last night to text. Why he would, I had no idea. *Is my subconscious mind remembering something I'm not?* Or did I want him to text so I could tear his ass up for taking advantage of a *clearly* volatile situation?

Despite Elliot and his likely-what-got-me-screwed-in-the-first-place dare, why hadn't my mystery man said no to whatever stupidity I'd pulled? *Get over it, Aaron. You're expecting too much from people again. Not everyone thinks like you.*

Roxxie and I were rounding the final stretch on our way home when I slammed into Elliot getting out of a cab.

"Ack!" El shouted, backing into Roxxie who yelped, and we both hit the ground. "Christ, Aaron!" Elliot groaned beneath me. "You could've killed me, you muscle head!"

He acted like a prima donna. I was lean at best, built like a runner at most.

I panted, pushing off the ground. "I'm not that big, moron." El rolled his eyes, extending his hand. I pulled him to a stand. "Besides, I didn't expect you until five. It's only three."

El dramatically shook his dog-dirty hands. "Ugh, you are so paying for this. These clothes are some of the cutest and so expensive."

Such a prima donna. "You can use my washer. Happy?"

Elliot scowled. "No thanks. The thought of washing my clothes with your sweaty mess gives me chills. I'll do what I can with towels and water." His perfect hair fell to one side. "Looks like I'll need to fix my hair too."

Anyone in Elliot's circle—including himself—knew how pretty El was. But I'd witnessed how long it took for him get the way he currently looked. Gloss caused his lips to glisten, and deep eye shadow brought out the cerulean of his eyes. If we weren't friends, I might—emphasis on might—have considered dating him. The guy had men lined up to take him to bed, but he wasn't known for getting involved with any of them.

"Anyway, now that you've completely ruined me, can we get out of the mist?" He cocked his hip, propping a fist on it. "It'll destroy any hope I have of repairing this mess." He directed his free hand to his body.

I rolled my eyes and nodded. "No worries, princess. I'll make sure you have the run of the master bathroom for ten hours."

"Haha, cute," he mocked. "Just because *you* don't like looking fabulous, doesn't mean I don't. Which is a shame, because my dear, you are super sexy when you want to be."

Another eye roll and I opened the door, mock bowed, and followed him into the building.

Elliot made himself at home in my bathroom while I waited on the bed twiddling my thumbs, leg tapping rapidly.

Throbbing beats and rushing blood caused my ears to heat. We spoke briefly about the night before in the elevator. Wasn't much considering I didn't remember anything.

"So, what can you remember?" Elliot yelled. His voice was a bit muffled. He was probably reapplying his gloss. "And don't say nothing because," a brief pause and a lip pop, "I will hit you."

My hands ran through my hair to the nape of my neck, eyes aimed at the ceiling fan. *Give me strength.* "I only remember what I told you. We went to the bar, I got shitfaced drunk, and the rest is white noise. Like late night TV ending snow."

"Hmm. Guess it's up to me then." His voice grew louder until he stood in the doorway. My jaw dropped at how fast he managed to put himself right. "Honestly though, babe, that's both a good and a bad thing."

I really don't like how he said that. "What do you mean?" I jerked my eyes to his. They were lowered.

Elliot slowly raised his head, sighing through his nose. "Because Dicklan was the one who caused all of it."

My teeth gnashed, and I closed my eyes tight. *Of course. It's almost always him!* "Tell me, El. All of it."

"What does it matter? This is Manhattan! Not like you'll see the guy again." El's voice was high. He'd crossed his arms, gripping both biceps, face distorted.

Elliot only did that when he was afraid the truth would wind up hurting me. He was right, but I still wanted to know.

"Because you know I don't do things like that." I lowered my eyes. "Truth is, I feel betrayed, El. I know Dicklan probably started it, but I know you had something to do with what ultimately happened."

Hurt welled up inside. That was why I wanted to know. My heart felt like a toy some kid played roughly with.

El joined me, covering my hand. "I'm sorry, babe. I had no idea. I'm just so sick of seeing you hurt. I'll tell you everything. Just be ready."

I couldn't blame him. Dicklan—our nickname for Declan Bradshaw—had hurt me bad. And what made it worse, I let him do it multiple times. Each time we broke up—after ranting and crying to Elliot—I swore I'd never fall for the same trap. Declan put his cock into every willing hole in high school and college. We hooked up only when he went through dry spells and wanted an easy fuck. Made me cringe to think about. *Hello, desperation, my old friend*. Since the final break-up, El stepped in and did what he could to keep me from falling all the way apart.

"Your horrible day started at work," El began with a sigh I took as pity. *Tell me when I have a "good" workday.* "Travis was, well, being Travis, and then Declan called you. Aaron, you called me out of your mind with grief ... again." *Gee, thanks for making my train wreck sound more pathetic.* "I couldn't believe everything he said to you. I won't tell you, though you can probably guess."

I could, and I was glad Elliot didn't repeat it. Knowing Declan, he probably laid the charm on thick—told me he loved me, how wrong he was, and how he would change. Or he went the other way and told me how sad I was and how no one would want me because of my "condition." Not exactly what I would call those mental checklists, but he made a habit out of making fun of me for them. *I lean toward the latter. Probably got off on it later.*

Elliot continued droning on, interrupting the noir narration of self-loathing ravaging my brain. "And we went to our favorite cocktail bar—"

The more he spoke, the more I questioned whether I wanted to know. Whatever happened that sent me into a mystery man's bed had to be horrible.

Instead of voicing what my inner critic said, I hunkered in, letting Roxxie leap onto the bed and nestle into my lap. I loved how she always seemed to know what I needed when I needed it. *Like she's the only one who really gets me.*

"When we got to the bar, we picked a seat close to the back." Elliot's mouth flattened, his nostrils flaring. "That's when things went ... weird..."

Flashes of memory slowly returned as Elliot carried on.

The dim lights in the White Rabbit, Elliot's and my favorite cocktail bar, illuminated the crowded tables. Each had a single lit candle to give the patrons sitting at them a relaxing ambience perfect for Friday night romance, closing a busy week, and general get-togethers. Elliot and I came here mostly to catch up and—on some occasions—find our weekend hookup. Most of the time I sat at the bar drinking my shitty job away and wishing I had the balls to stand against my boss.

This time, I'd hit rock bottom. My eyes were still red from the all-out breakdown I had after my ex called. Like always, Declan did what he could to torment me while simultaneously trying to score an easy fuck. This happened more in the past few months than it did in three years. It was like Declan wanted to prove he'd imprinted himself on my brain so deeply I couldn't move on, waiting for him to call. Sick as the thought made me, sometimes he was right. Despite everything he did to me, I suffered rare bouts of weakness where I nearly gave in. It wasn't until I heard the chuckling of his friends in the background that I finally found my balls.

Not this time, I swore to myself and told the bastard off.

To save face, Declan resorted to every dirty trick and word he could think of, ending the call by hanging up on me. I was proud of myself for finally ending the vicious cycle, but damn, it hurt! It felt like I'd severed the only tie I had to any kind of relationship. No matter how bad it was.

Guess that's what Mom meant by victim. *Only after freeing myself, did I realize I had the worst case of Stockholm Syndrome I'd ever seen!*

"Don't worry about it, babe," Elliot assured me, patting my back. That's when I realized we'd sat down and ordered our first round. "It's his loss, not yours. The fact he said all those things to you only affirms what I've thought. He has no balls, and this," he held up a pinky, bending it and grinning like a madman, "doesn't satisfy the man-sluts he beds. His trash mouth is all he has going for him."

That brought a smile and a small chuckle from me. I hadn't thought about what happened like that. Good old, El. Always knows what to say.

I still only wanted to drink the day away. Our senior partner, Howard Kimball, passed away a few weeks ago, and Travis struggled to find another partner. Law cases piled up at Kimball and Marks law firm, leaving poor Travis to handle them all, including Mr. Kimball's unfinished cases. We had to pull in temporary partners to keep up. The heavy loads pushed Travis to be more of an ogre than he already was. Add in Declan, and I was about to explode!

I sipped from drink four when Elliot said, "Tell you what, why don't you get that hot little ass of yours off that stool, go out there, and ask the first guy who catches your fancy for a drink."

If I rolled my eyes anymore, they'd become bowling balls. Rolling my current Scotch in my fingertips, I shook my head. Like most choices I made in life, I closed my eyes and formed a mental *checklist.* Let's see: random guy meets drunk, heartbroken guy. Hot sex ... very likely. *Nothing was better than non-committed sex.* Ties: Nope. *I wouldn't want them anyway.* Big mistake ... most likely. *Especially when I didn't usually jump at the first cock to crow at me.*

"Don't think so. That's only asking for trouble," I replied.

"What? But you've done it before!" Elliot smacked his head. "Dear God, you just did it again, didn't you?"

Deciding to play dumb, I raised a brow. Because why wouldn't I when I was about to get chewed out for something I couldn't control? It wasn't like I wanted to have a cartoon Aaron running around in my skull, pointing at three columns with a baton and telling me how nearly everything that sounded fun was a bad idea.

I directed my eyes to the ceiling, mentally counting down from three ... two ... one...

Elliot held two straightened hands out, palms up, directing them at me. You know the kind. The ones people often use when they're about to say, "You did this when you should've done that," in any given scenario.

"The checklists. You did it again." *I heard the disappointed sigh in his words.*

And there it was.

I thought he planned to jump out of his seat or at least slam a hand on the table during his upcoming tirade. "You have to stop doing that! Life isn't a checklist, Aaron! You can't control everything. You'll wear yourself out. Especially when it comes to things like love."

I shrugged, taking a sip of Scotch. The warm liquid didn't take the typical path down to my stomach. Instead, it raced to my brain, slowly hindering my ability to give any more fucks.

Fed up, feeling the buzz, I set the glass down harder than I meant to. My head started throbbing; I was still upset and not wanting to deal with any of this bullshit. To keep from hurting El's feelings with my completely justified internal rage, I almost left. Then the worst possible thing that could happen during my already fragile state happened.

CHAPTER 4

D eclan walked in, tailed by three of his office buddies. Each had a stupid smile on their face, laughing at whatever remark their pack leader made. That was Declan. Charisma, sex, and sophistication rolled up behind a veil of narcissism thicker than the sludge comprising his soul.

Wonder which one he's fucking. Probably all three, knowing Declan. He'd made a career out of the high school and college game involving jocks and how many lays they got in a single week. Declan's popularity with both males and females wasn't a secret. God only knew how many of his marks included my desperate, attention-seeking ass.

They didn't see me, though Elliot followed my line of sight to them as they sat at an elevated corner table. My friend's eyes bulged to the size of dinner plates—all white, little pupil.

"That arrogant son of a—" Elliot snarled, his hand strangling his martini glass to the point I swore I heard it screaming for help. "He has some nerve!"

"Relax, El. Any more choking and that glass is going to file a restraining order," I replied, trying to lighten the mood. In my brain, I tried talking myself into going over and slugging the asshole in the face. "Besides, Dick's not worth it."

"Still," El said, a bit lower. "It's not like you didn't spew about how much you liked this place."

Again, thanks, El, for making my already ridiculous train wreck worse.

Truth was, Elliot was right. I'd had enough. Declan knew what he was doing. I'd slipped and told him where I liked to go on Fridays during one of my low points. But he didn't get to show up like this, tell me what a worthless twink I was, and walk away gloating about how much he hurt me. Not this time.

My turn, you stuck-up asshole. *I gulped the last of the Scotch for liquid courage.* "You know what, El," *I said confidently. The alcohol in my system told my checklists to go eff themselves.* "What was that dare again?"

If "Cole" *wanted to prove how* "easy" *a lay I was and how nobody else would want me, I'd prove to him how wrong he could be. I could get laid. After all, I wasn't bad in the looks department. Guys dig dark hair and blue eyes. I could do this.*

Elliot beamed victoriously. "Get that sexy little ass up, go find yourself a guy, and ask him to buy you a drink." *He scooted close, throwing an arm over my shoulders.* "And that delectable thing," *I followed the manicured, freshly painted fingernail to a man at the opposite end of the bar,* "has had his eyes on you all night."

I didn't remember the exact details, but I did remember the guy's good looks. Maybe some hipster glasses and sideswept dirty-blonde hair? Who cared? My liquid courage had my ass getting up and strutting to Mr. Sexy Thing. His eyes followed each move I made, inflating my ego the closer I got.

Heat hit my cheeks, cock standing at attention when he took a drink, staring over his glasses' frame. Those eyes were wild. Hungry. And I was the lucky fucker getting devoured by them.

Damn, he really is watching. *I nearly stopped and returned to my seat. Through the haze, I remembered thinking I'd never been looked at like that.* Should I really be doing this? *I glanced at*

Declan who'd found me and glared like he was daring me to keep going. Confidence renewed, I picked up the pace.

"Hey there," I said, leaning a hip against the bar.

Mr. Mystery raised his eyes to meet mine. "And hello to you, too." Even through the fogginess, I recalled the timbre of his voice.

Holy shit, and I thought Declan had a hot tone. Compared to this guy, Declan ... well, didn't compare. This guy blew my ex's sophistication and cockiness away with only one sentence!

Before I lost my nerve, I asked, "So, you come here often?" Did I really just say that! "I mean..." Oh, come on, he only said hello! Get a fucking grip!

"I know what you meant," he said with a laugh. "No, I'm just visiting." With the grace of a wildcat, he turned his attention back to his drink, tongue teasing the liquid on his lower lip. "Why? Do you come here often?"

"What? No. I mean..." My heart pounded in my ears. I wasn't sure if it was his mocking or the sexy way he looked me over, but the confidence I'd built up slowly deteriorated. I was in "quit with the small talk and fuck me" mode in two seconds. How had he turned everything around with only a few words? "If you aren't from here ... where ... are you, um..."

God, what is wrong with me?

"Miami," he replied. "Why don't you join me? Perhaps allow me to buy you a drink to calm your nerves?"

I did what Elliot dared me to, but I wasn't ready to let Mr. Hipster Frames charm me out of my jeans.

Time to take back over. I sat and leaned on my forearms, gingerly letting my knee brush his in an "I'm open for business" manner. "Sure, but only if you play a game with me. Win and you can buy me a drink."

"And if I lose?" he replied, clearly enjoying the challenge.

I shrugged a shoulder. "Then I walk."

"Hmm." A devious smile curved his lips. "Sounds good." The glasses came off. I watched him close them, set them down, and turn to face me. Thick lashes and dark green bedroom eyes pierced through the Scotch-induced amnesia. "But, how about we up the ante? How about if I win, I buy you a drink and get you to come home with me?"

A gasp escaped me, piercing my lust-addled brain. It was like he read my mind—or maybe my actions, I wasn't sure at that point—though I was too nervous to ask him for the last part. "O-okay. If you lose?"

The devious smirk widened. "I let you use me to make who-ever is sitting at that table," he gestured his head and eyes to my ex, "incredibly jealous, and you can walk. Deal?"

Is he for real? He knows what I am up to and doesn't care? *I can't put this guy in any category on my checklist so far.*

Every alarm, red flag, and warning sign went off in my brain. The last thing I

remembered was telling him he had a deal.

"Oh my God," I said, letting my head thunk against the couch cushion. Roxxie whined, tilting her head curiously while placing her paw on my groin. The events Elliot told me about—plus a few more—cleared up the maze that was my mind. I hissed, suddenly aware of the painfully hard erection the memories brought springing forward. *Great, not what I need.* "And you just let me do this? Without so much as an 'Aaron, are you sure?'" If the ache in my balls was any indica-tion, I *definitely* didn't get laid last night. That made the situ-ation more embarrassing.

He nodded.

"Christ, El, with friends like you—" I neglected finishing the overly used cliché in favor of more coffee. He got the picture. Letting your distraught friend drunkenly flirt with a hot stranger was the worst thing you could do. "What happened next?"

A grin capable of making the most mischievous demon blush shamefully crossed El's face. I couldn't decide if I wanted to ignore it and listen for the next set of embarrassing events or brush it off and bask in the bliss of utter ignorance. Either way, I was screwed if anyone I worked with found out. Gossip already ran rampant, and Travis was looking for any means to terminate my ass. That was another can I preferred to leave sealed, thank you very much.

"You both left, babe." El made a "whoosh" motion, complete with sound effects. "He won the bet, kissed your brains out while feeling you up, and the two of you disappeared faster than a New York breeze. No idea what happened then."

In many ways, I guessed I should count my blessings coming to me in the form of blurry memories. Otherwise, I wouldn't be hearing the end of the questions regarding how big Mr. Hipster Frames was, if I did in fact "scream his name" when I came, blah blah blah. If El was anything, it was nosy when things involved my love life.

El shot up quickly, startling me and Roxxie. "I should get going. As much as I adore that pouty lip thing you do when you're brooding, I have a hot date with my new beaux."

I tsked, eyes averted. "No one says 'beaux' anymore." *Thank you, fate, for intervening and getting him distracted.* "When am I gonna get to meet this new guy? Brandon, wasn't it?"

Another coy smile got tossed my way. "Come now, darling. Just because you can't get laid doesn't mean I can't."

"What does that—"

"Yes, it's Brandon," El cut me off. "And I'm keeping you two far apart as long as possible." He blew a two-fingered kiss at me. "Take the day. Do something nice with the four-legged love of your life." Roxxie licked El while he ruffled her ears. I followed him to the door, Roxxie hot on my heals. "And for God's sake, get over the checklists. I hate to see my friends sad, and you, Handsome, have so much to offer the world. But only if you get out and see it. Ciao!"

With those last words, El vanished through the door. Between the short time he left and however many steps, El had pulled out his phone and playfully shouted "Hey" to who-ever answered. *Must be Brandon.* I listened to him chatter until it faded down the hall.

I have something to offer the world. I laughed, letting my forehead thunk against the door. *Funny. If I have something to offer the world, why do I screw up every relationship I get into?*

After Elliot left, I spent the rest of Saturday picking up my mess of an apartment. Okay, maybe it wasn't a total disaster zone, but when you were someone who couldn't stand to lack control over anything in your life, even a pair of under-wear out of place is anxiety inducing. Roxxie lounged on the couch, drifting between consciousness, and snoring while I worked. My mom had called multiple times. Elliot probably contacted her—or she bothered him—and let her know about my crappy condition. While I wanted to strangle him for a possible two things now, I was grateful he kept my best inter-ests in mind. Roxxie and I took a break from chores for dinner and some television before I opened my laptop to check next week's online college work as Roxxie eventually fell asleep on the couch.

Sunday was like it usually was—slow and uneventful. My professor emailed the class letting us know our culinary essay deadlines were fast approaching. With everything going on at work—like Mr. Kimball's death and Travis's repeated outbursts—I hadn't had time to decide what topic to cover. Even though I *really* didn't want to, I decided to call my mom before she had a heart attack worrying how I was. The phone rang a couple of times followed by the boisterous call of Polly Cambrian.

"Oh my gosh! Aaron!" As usual, I had to pull the speaker away or risk going deaf. "Where have you been, Tonka?" *Oh no. Not that...* "Elliot called!"

Taking a deep breath, I stared skyward, at Roxxie, then back. "I'm fine, Mom. I had a feeling El called you. Or did *you* call *him*, Mom?"

An insulted gasp hissed through the speaker. "I am appalled! How could you think—"

"What time did you call?" I interrupted.

"About 7 pm," she admitted. "But I was only worried because you didn't answer your message things."

"They're called texts, Mom. And I'm fine. Things at work and school have been conflicting a bit. Nothing too insane." Telling her the blunt truth sounded like a bad idea. She already seemed prepared to hop a plane from Indiana to New York.

She knew I lied. And I knew she knew. While my sisters and I grew up, my dad's professional chef job kept him away until late. Sometimes we didn't see him for days on end. Mom had to quit her career in marketing to watch over us. She knew all of our tells.

Mom made that disappointed I-know-you're-lying-to-me-but-I'm-not-going-to-push- it noise. "Just promise me you'll take care of yourself, baby. You shouldn't have to work so hard. Especially in your career path. Find a decent man, settle down, and relax a bit."

Telling her I chose my current career path to avoid "settling down" seemed cruel. How could a son tell his mom he was such a massive screw up that he couldn't "find" or "hold onto" a decent man? Knowing her, she'd think she did something wrong.

"I will, Mom. Gotta go, though. Need to find my research topic before work tomorrow so I can get that started." Man, my tone sounded pathetic even to me.

We hung up, and I took Roxxie for a walk, fed her, and settled in to do some research. Worrying over what happened Friday, and with whom, took a back burner. This city was huge, and Mr. Hipster Frames had said he was "just visiting" from Miami. What did a one-night stand mean? Not much, really.

For my research topic, I pulled up a blank document, created a checklist and divided the paper into "Yes," "No," and "Maybe." In each column I added possible choices, narrowed it down, and eventually landed on the evolution of Creole food since it was my cuisine of choice.

I smiled, thinking about the rare moments Dad and I cooked together. He outlined different spices, taught me how each married with another, what didn't work, and—my favorite—how food was a gorgeous mix of chemistry and art. Cooking was the only thing we bonded over and remained the only thing we had that none of my sisters shared with him.

Thinking about those memories brought a scowl to my face. They were a double-edged sword. My mom ended things with my dad after he chose his career over our family. Things ended amicably, but divorce was never easy to deal with.

The only reason I knew anything personal about my father was through his interviews on food contests, magazines, and his upcoming cookbook. *Thank God Rebecca went into law.* She kept the paparazzi off our family with airtight contracts. Good news for me too since I tended to screw things up so much. Nothing that landed in the tabloids, thank God. But I won't go there.

Shaking the memories away, I fixed my research topic to make it more personal: *The Impact of a Career Chef on His Family.* The fix lasted briefly, but damn, it felt good to write.

"Evolution of Creole Cuisine" it is.

I typed the words out, hashed out a messy outline, and closed my laptop. Work clothes still needed washing, Roxxie needed to go out again, and I needed to get out of the apartment before my head exploded.

CHAPTER 5

One perk of working for a law firm: we didn't go in on weekends. I got lucky with scheduling and didn't work on Mondays, so I decided to spend the day fleshing out the outline for my essay and emailing it to my professor. He emailed me later saying he didn't think the topic was deep enough. The downside of being the son of a famous chef? Your culinary professors were fans.

I liked Professor White despite knowing why he wanted a "deeper" topic. He often asked what growing up with a famous chef was like and if I planned on covering it as a research topic. Too bad for him the topic in question was a sore one. I wound up editing the topic, keeping it to the science and art of cooking. God, help me. It wasn't quite personal, yet writing it would open some wounds.

Tuesday rolled around, bringing me back to my shitty job as a filing clerk at Kimball & Marks's law firm. Travis Marks hadn't arrived yet or alarm bells in the form of personal messages on the company's line would be buzzing.

"Morning, Judith," I greeted, wearing my best fake smile. The only response I got was a groan and a raspy humph. "Hope your weekend was a good one." Another humph. I shrugged, headed to the filing room, and clocked in.

The first of my two coworkers/friends, Josh Bianchi, already had his stack of sticky notes, jotting down his goals for the day. I liked Josh. Aside from, well, me, Josh was one of the only people at the firm who kept a level head and didn't gossip too much about his personal life. He made the worst habit out of teasing us with enough detail about his sex life that Leslie and Frankie ached to hear more, but he never revealed more. I'd admit it to no one, but I was curious, too.

Beside him, Frankie Jones, the office nerd, watched his not-so-secret-crush, Leslie Abernathy, gingerly scoop fresh coffee and put it in the strainer.

"Morning, Josh," I said with a wave. "How was your weekend?"

Josh's pen stopped scribbling, and he raised his azure eyes to me. "Pretty good." A coy smile. "I spent it in heated sexathons with my new boyfriend."

"New boyfriend, huh?" My tone rose, betraying underlying curiosity. "I didn't even know you broke up with what's his name."

"Blake." He scoffed. "Yes, I broke up with him two months ago. Way too clingy for my taste. And so fucking demanding." The chair creaked when Josh leaned back, folding his arms behind his head. "Know what they say. Give an inch..."

When it came to looks, Josh was beyond sexy. Not in a hot alpha male or just pretty way, like Elliot, but rather in an exotic dancer-meets-bouncer-oozes-sex kind of way. Josh's short hair mimicked the black hair of his mom, and his deeply tanned skin echoed his Spaniard father. I'd met his family at one of the firm's galas, amazed at how pretty they all were.

Like I said, beyond sexy and probably one of the best bed partners anyone could ask for. I once had a crush on him, changing my mind when it turned out he had Blake. Bitterness definitely niggled at me for a short while.

"Gonna bring this one around?" I teased, receiving a tsking and waggling finger as an answer. "Why not?"

"You know me, Aaron. I like to keep my personal life somewhat quiet here." Blush tinted Josh's cheeks. "Besides, he has a friend he thinks might be a bit flustered by us. Asked me to wait on coming out until he has a chance to think and talk with said friend."

I could respect that. Coming out as gay to my mom and sisters terrified me. Their conservative ways made me worried that Mom might throw me out when I came home with my first boyfriend. Luckily, Mom didn't. She'd done the opposite. She squealed and announced how happy she was that I finally found someone who cared about me as much as she did. *Love my mom.*

Focus shifted from Josh to Frankie, who, like always, watched Leslie's every move. Frankie's "massive secret crush" on Leslie hadn't remained secret long. He stuttered every time she spoke with him, froze when they stood in the breakroom together, and lost his nerve when Leslie came out of Travis's office crying her eyes out. *Who could blame him?* If Travis learned too much about Frankie's feelings, the upstart jerk would fire Frankie on the spot. We all knew what Travis had the poor girl behind closed doors. Without Mr. Kimball to defend her, Leslie became Travis Marks's latest office secret. I'd often wondered why Leslie refused to report Travis.

"You still haven't asked her?" I finally questioned. Frankie sighed, shaking his head. "Jesus, man. This is getting pathetic." *Open mouth, insert big, fat foot.*

"That's what I told him," Josh said, a grin curving his lips. "Wait until you hear this week's excuses. They're doozies."

Frankie shot a you-can-both-die-now glance our way. "It's not that I don't want to! I just don't know how!" Dreamy eyes went back to following the bouncing blonde presently walking into Travis's office, cradling files in a way that did nothing to hide her breasts. "Besides, you know Travis has his hooks in her."

Yeah. I scowled at Travis's door. One of the darker sides of our little firm was the sickening fact that Travis Marks took advantage of his female co-workers in the worst possible ways. Leslie excelled at her job and wanted a promotion. To get it, Travis offered an unseemly deal. That was a year ago.

"Who cares?" Josh barked. "The guy's a dick. What's the worst he's going to do? Fire her? Better off if he does. She's smart and will find a better job."

Message boxes on every computer in our office pinged.

Dracula spotted. On elevator. Gird your loins everyone!

"Looks like it's game time," Josh said.

Looks like. "We better get going, Frankie," I said.

Frankie and I departed to our desks in the filing room at the end of the hall, waiting for whatever hellish tantrum Travis Marks brought with him to work that day.

"What do you think he'll do to us today?" Frankie asked.

My chair whined as I pushed it across the well-worn mat. When I sat, I partially shouted, grabbing the edge of the desk to keep from going back on my ass. *Damn I need to replace this thing.* "Who knows," I said with a sigh. *Maybe he's pissed he's having to do some actual work around here.*

Being 6' 4" with long legs made fitting under my desk a struggle. Each plea I made to Travis justifying our need for up-to-date computers and ergonomic desk chairs blew up in my face. *Had Mr. Kimball known, the problem would've disappeared by now.*

I avoided Travis most of the morning upon learning he spent it handling Mr. Kimball's unfinished cases. The intense load made transferring some files to temporary partners necessary. That set of trips wasn't fun, and something I'd rather not repeat anytime soon. Things worsened when knowledge that Howard had no intention of making Travis primary senior partner came out. I still remembered the rant Travis went on over the phone to someone after finding out. *Likely another lawyer willing to fight the ruling.*

In some ways, I couldn't blame the guy. He'd worked alongside Howard for almost a decade, appeared at every major client event, and helped raise the law firm to one of New York's most prestigious firms—thanks to a big win against a corrupt construction company poisoning groundwater at the local park. Bit of a nightmare for the filing crew—both before and after.

I hadn't stepped a foot in the office before Frankie's clench-teethed panicked face met me. "Run," he whispered behind a straight hand. Unfortunately, I didn't catch on and ran into the office troll.

"Cambrian!" Travis shouted as I rounded the corner to my small cubby hole.

Perfect. "What can I do for you, boss?" I asked through a false smile, raising both hands defensively.

Travis made a "feh" sound. "You can make my life easier by doing your job." He poked my chest while saying the last three words. Our height difference made him look like a hobbit standing next to Aragorn.

"You know how much I love my job. Whatchu need?" Kissing ass wasn't a habit I got into, but I needed to keep my job long enough to pay my tuition.

Travis ignored my sarcasm. "There's a pile of files littering the left side of my office."

"Finished cases or—"

"Finished," Travis interrupted. "Get all of them in here and filed away properly!"

I wanted to roll my eyes. People called me many things—control freak, perfectionist, etc. etc. etc.—but one thing people couldn't call me was "lazy," "sloppy," or "unable to file mountains of paper properly."

I mock saluted and followed Travis down the hall to his office. The offices of Kimball and Marks were much larger than you would think when you entered the place. Judith, the crotchety secretary, was the first face clients saw upon entering. Behind her, on the cliché wood panel wall, were the owners' names in huge, bronze French script. Travis's office was off to the right, nestled back in a pocket large enough to contain a PA desk where Leslie sat and took Travis's calls all day. The other—currently empty—office sat at the opposite end of the reception area and was much the same, only larger and connected to the breakroom.

Upon entering Travis's office, my jaw nearly hit the floor. He hadn't lied. Files piled on the desk's edge in two columns took up the left side. I swallowed hard, looking anywhere for one of the two carts we used for transportation.

"Um?" I muttered. "Cart?"

Travis stood behind his desk, eyeing a file. "There aren't any available. Josh took one for mail; the other is on loan." I swore a sarcastic grin crossed his lips. "You might have to do this the old-fashioned way."

Wait, what? I'm supposed to what? If my eyes bugged any farther from my skull, they'd pop free. Clenched fists grew clammy, trembling subtly.

As if noticing, Travis eyed me briefly. "That's not going to be a problem, is it?"

"Problem? Oh no, no problem at all. Unless you count for how much pain my back'll be in after waltzing up and down the stairs multiple times carrying heavy as hell files!" was what I wanted to tell him, adding in a few four-letter words.

Of course, that's not what came out of my mouth. "Nope. Not a problem at all." *After I'm done, I'm going to strangle the little troll!*

To keep from saying something stupid, I picked up the first layer and began the repeated torture until all the files made it to the filing room.

As I thought, my back burned—and not in the damn-that-was-some-hot-and-kinky-sex way—all the way from my tailbone up my shoulders and around to my collarbones. My body felt like an anvil, forcing me to drop my deadweight into my chair. *God, this is humiliating. Where in my life did I screw up so badly to earn punishment like this?*

"That looks like it hurts," Frankie said, standing above me. He glanced at the two file piles. "He made you carry those?"

I nodded. "Yep. Mile high piles. My back feels like it's about to pop out of me in protest."

Frankie hissed, fists clenched, shoulders raised. "Damn, he really is a jerk. Hope the new partner isn't such a douche."

Christ, me too. Otherwise, I might have to walk out or risk premature death at twenty-eight. "Hang on a second. New partner? Do you know anything about him? Or her?"

Frankie shook his head. "Nothing yet. Only rumors. Whoever he is though, he has Travis on edge. Leslie's been cleaning Travis's office all morning. Josh has straightened the spare office, and then there's these." He gestured at the piles.

"Guy must be a neat freak or some big shot. Either way, there's no way I can survive another Travis."

Could any of us survive a Travis clone? Ever the lover of rumors over mindless cellphone scrolling—*What? Like there's anything else to do in a room full of paper!*—I said, "Let me in on some rumors. I need something to distract me while I'm putting these away."

CHAPTER 6

I listened to Frankie prattle on about the new partner well into the two or three o'clock hour. Wasn't sure which. According to Frankie, the new partner was some big shot coming out of Florida. Frankie didn't know where or any details to what constituted a "big shot." All we knew was our mystery guy had a well-known family name and was in a currently just-as-mysterious location doing who knew what. *Can this guy be any more obscure? Does Travis know anything about him? Or was he Mr. Kimball's ace in the hole after hearing he had cancer?*

Whoever the man was, Travis definitely had his reservations about letting some newcomer take his place as senior partner. I didn't think any of us heard the troll yell at so many clients only to apologize profusely to save the richer accounts.

I walked into the reception area to find Josh and Judith chatting—rather, Josh was telling Judith knock-knock jokes and riddles, confusing the older lady—when the phone rang. "You two gonna pick that up or what?"

Neither one acknowledged me, leaving me to sit in the swivel chair and play receptionist.

"Kimball and Marks law office. How may I help you?" I'd heard Leslie do this more than enough to memorize the line.

"Well, good afternoon." The deep timbre sent shudders through me.

"Uh, afternoon," I stuttered, suddenly aware of the familiarity of this voice, yet not able to figure out from where. *Come on. Don't sound like a moron. Talk!* "To whom can I direct your call?"

That voice rumbled a chuckle. "Aren't you polite? I'm looking to speak with Mr. Travis Marks. Might he be around?"

What is that accent? English? I shook my head, trying to think of any way to keep this man talking. "He's with a client presently. May I take a message?"

"Yes, please tell him Mr. Waylan called." He left me his cell number. "Make sure he knows I'm very busy and will be out starting at 6 pm. I'll need to speak with him before then."

Anything you want, I mused, imagining all kinds of dirty things I'd love whispered by this voice. "Sure. I've got the message. I'll give it to him."

"One more thing," Mr. Waylan purred. "To whom do I have the honor of speaking? You're quite professional."

Words caught in my throat in a tight ball of nerves. *What do I tell him? "Hi, I'm no one special, just the file clerk. Nice to meet you."*

"I'm Aaron," I said, cheeks heating. *Hope Josh doesn't notice.*

"It's a pleasure to have spoken with you, Aaron. May we speak again soon." He hung up.

Fuck, I hope the body belonging to that voice is as sexy as he sounds.

I placed the phone down. Thundering beats rang in my ears. My skin grew clammy and hot from the onset of the boner crowding the zipper of my work pants. *Shit, this is not the time for this! Turned on by a voice—an intense, sexy with a hint of an exotic accent voice, but still.*

"Running to the bathroom, Josh. Be right back!" I didn't wait for his answer, speeding around the half-moon desk to the hallway and straight into the restroom.

Travis yanked the paper away, almost tearing it. His eyes bulged to the size of saucers. "Who was on the phone?"

Confused, I blinked a few times. "He said his name was Waylan." Thinking back on the short exchange, I tried to hide the blush creeping over my cheeks. "Is he ... a client?"

Travis's answer came in the form of a not-so-subtle you-can-die-now scowl and a hard slam of his office door.

"He really needs to take a sedative, maybe do some aromatherapy," Josh said later, leaning against the desk. "I swear, the guy's gonna croak if he keeps stressing like every day's Ragnarok."

Chuckling, I replied, "Travis on CBD. Can you picture that?" We both laughed.

A brief pause ensued, followed by the question I feared.

"What was with your dash to the bathroom?"

I gnawed my lower lip, overcome by another bout of embarrassment. "Cafeteria meat. You know how that stuff tears up the old insides, leaves a coppery taste."

"Ugh." Josh tilted his head to the right. "Say no more. Stuff's like motor oil. No idea how the FDA hasn't shut the place down."

Not all the cafeteria food had questionable ingredients. The problem was, the woman in charge had a strange understanding of what constituted as acceptable vegan cuisine and had a hard time remembering many of us still wanted to indulge in actual meat. It was not that I wasn't open to trying different things. Hell, I worked with all types of food. It was just after having a bad experience—aka massive vomiting for a few hours followed by debilitating nausea—while out with Elliot and his now-ex, I tended to err on the side of caution.

"Speaking of lunch," Josh said as we walked to punch out for the night. "Don't quote me on this, but I think Frankie actually invited Leslie to have drinks with us tonight."

"You're kidding!"

Josh shook his head. "Nope."

I'll be damned. Looks like the guy's finally found his balls.

Going for drinks on Tuesdays became a tradition after all of us realized how much we hated Travis and honored Howard Kimball. All the firm's employees—minus Leslie and the rarely talked about Dudley Crosley who worked in the basement filing room—walked across the street to the Rabbit Hole Sports Bar, sat, and proceeded to indulge in liquid courage.

Frankie made things more interesting when he started doing his Travis the Troll impersonations. "I shit you not," Frankie said, slightly slurring. "He stormed into the office after Aaron gave him the note from Mr. Waylan shouting 'Get off yer arses! Time to clean!'"

We all burst out laughing. I almost spewed my beer into Josh's face. Travis rarely let his Irish side out unless he drank like his ancestors.

"How horrible is that?" Josh barked. "Forced to clean despite having a janitorial department! I barely kept up today." He took a deep swig of his Blue Moon. "Who is this Waylan guy, anyway? Some rich bastard with a silver spoon pedigree? I swear I've never seen Marks crap his pants so bad."

I thought back to the voice on the phone. *The guy did talk like he was from some snooty, uppercrust family.* "Dunno,"

I interjected. "Never heard of him. Maybe Marks is making something out of nothing. We all know how he is."

Leslie raised her glass, smiling brighter than I'd seen in a long time. "I'll drink to that!"

Topics changed from Travis's meltdown to the mystery guy Josh was dating. As he had earlier, Josh kept the details close to his chest. By the end of that talk, all we knew was how "absolutely gorgeous" the guy was and how hot the sex got between them.

"I am not hearing this!" Leslie laughed, covering her ears. "Though, I bet that *is* hot to watch."

I blushed at that. *What is it with chicks liking to watch two guys getting it on?* I checked my watch to see the hour closing in on midnight. "Gotta go, ya'll. Roxxie's probably about to burst from needing to go out, and I have college work to do."

"How is that going, by the way?" Leslie asked, propping her chin on her hand. "I'll bet it's super easy considering who your dad is."

Something in my chest tightened. I knew Leslie hadn't meant anything, but I couldn't help being apprehensive. "Sorry, Les. You know Bex's contracts make it so I'm not supposed to talk about that."

Leslie's eyes rolled. "Only to the press. Not your friends."

My paternal meltdown had nothing to do with her, and I needed to remember that. A quickly deteriorating mood hastened my need to leave, and even though I hated that I did it, I snapped.

Adjusting my jacket, I said, "You know, I don't think that's any of your damn business. I gotta go."

No one said a word as I thrust my chair from the table and stormed out into the rain. What could they say? *What can I say?* I'd acted like a complete jerk to the only people who gave me the time a day other than Elliot.

Glancing at the sky, I let the rain drip down my face, soaking my hair. *What the hell is wrong with me? Why does it seem like I'm always screwing up the good things in my life?*

Two taxis drove by, splashing waves of water that soaked the lower parts of my pants and boots. *Son of a fucking bitch!* Both arms went out to my sides, palms down, foot raised, so I could shake them. I hadn't done much laundry lately and wasn't sure if I had a spare set of work clothes.

Keeping the scream gurgling within me, I strolled to the curb's edge, threw my arm out, and yelled "Taxi!" I didn't realize how far I'd gone into the street until the screeching taxi wheels and shouting passersby had me scuttling like a frightened raccoon back to the safety of the sidewalk. In a blind panic, I stumbled over the curb, slid, and landed on my ass.

Despite the many people coming to assist, I stood, dusted invisible dust from my soaked clothes, and brooded the five blocks to the bus stop.

The entire time, I wondered if I'd ever get a break. Or was life enjoying itself at my expense so much that I had no hope of things going my way? *At least I still have Roxxie.* I laughed, thinking about the movie featuring that actor who recently broke up with his wife, fell in love with a divorced schoolteacher and had a title about someone must loving dogs. *Yeah, I'd definitely make that a condition. Want to date me? You must love my dog.*

CHAPTER 7

"**C**an someone tell me why we're all piled into this tuna can of a conference room?" I asked with a pout, tapping one spread leg. After finally getting home the night before, freezing from the wind and rain, Roxxie greeted me with eager whining and scratching at the door. I felt bad for making her wait, so I took her for a run through the park to do her business. "Is Travis planning on running for mayor or something?"

To add injury to insult, I couldn't stop thinking about Mr. Waylan and his sexy-as-hell voice that drove my cock to level eleven. *Worst case of blue balls ever! Now this!*

Judith and Dudley sat across from me. Judith pretended to fiddle with what remained of her nails. Dudley glanced at me, only to pull away when he noticed I saw him.

Yeah. He's not giving away anything going on in his pants. Dream on, buddy. I don't put out for stalky basement guys.

It's not that I didn't like Dudley. Hell, I'd encouraged him when he came staggering into the office, hands shaking, for his job interview. If I hadn't grabbed his collar and thrust him into Mr. Kimball's office, Dudley would've run. *Maybe that's why he has a crush on me.* A fact I didn't figure out until later when mysterious letters like those you get in high school from your "secret admirer" showed up on my desk. I'd known it was Dudley and honestly thought it was sweet. At first.

From his spot next to mine, Josh shrugged. "Not sure. I got the text late last night at my boyfriend's house."

"Let me guess," Leslie teased. "Right in the middle of you two shagging or about to?"

I coughed a laugh at Judith's scandalized gasp and Dudley's beet red face. I liked this new, more confident Leslie. *Maybe Frankie is good for her.*

Frankie burst out laughing, nearly spilling his latte, while Josh shook his head.

"What's with you guys and my sex life?" Josh asked. "Just because I'm getting more than any of you—"

"This is highly inappropriate!" Judith finally said. "Honestly, where is the dignity of young people today? Chattering about what goes on in private situations! You should all be ashamed!"

Great. I locked my fingers behind my head. *Hurricane Judith and it's not even noon yet.*

Judith had been there the longest. She was Mr. Kimball's former secretary and was near retirement until her boss fell ill. Instead of leaving us alone with her mothering routine, political correctness, and lack of a sense of humor, Judith decided to double her efforts at making us miserable. Had to hand it to her though. When things got bad, Judith was quick to straighten an otherwise teetering case.

Travis finally walked in—*or shambled in?*—looking like he'd been through a tropical storm. His dark hair—typically plastered against his head with too much gel—laid shagged in loose sprigs. He'd put his tie on wrong and mismatched his suit jacket and shirt. This was the first time in a while I almost regretted giving him a hard time.

Damn, must be really bad. Poor guy. My lip ticked. *Did I just think that? About ... Travis?*

No one said anything, waiting for Travis to set his brief-case on the oval table. "I'm sure all of you got my message late last night." We all nodded. I'd gotten mine while sitting to work on the outline for my essay and checking a reminder about an internship I studied hard to get. "Well, the rumors are true. Our new partner will be arriving earlier than expected. For those who don't know, I can also confirm your theories."

Theories? About Waylan? Or Travis's denial of the top senior partner slot?

Travis stopped to clear his throat. "I won't be filling the top senior partner role..."

I glanced at Josh and mouthed, *Pay up.*

"...Mr. Waylan is from a wealthy English family basing their vast empire in Los Angeles and Miami."

Wealthy English family? That explains a lot. I took a sip from the swill Judith called coffee, wishing Leslie made it. *Wonder what kinds of enterprises his family runs. And why would Waylan choose to be a lawyer if his family's already loaded?* I wouldn't work a day if my dad croaked and left me his millions.

"He'll be here Monday," Travis said, adjusting his messed-up tie. I gasped, clenching my teeth. *Here it comes.* "That's why I want all of you to make sure your stations are spotless. Aaron, you and Dudley will work on Mr. Kimball's office." He narrowed his eyes on me. "I want it *spotless*, Cambrian. You hear me? Screw this up and I'll fire your ass on the spot, understood?"

The threat of termination didn't land harder than the news that I'd be working in such close quarters with Dudley Crosley the whole day. *Does he do this on purpose?* "Marks, I'm one of the most detail-oriented bastards in this place. You want it sparkly for your new boyfriend; I've got you covered."

I regretted the words immediately, but I wanted him to know his threat to my future hadn't done what he wanted it to.

Truth was, Travis had been looking for reasons to fire me since the first week I started at the firm. Not sure why we didn't "click."

"Just get it done," Travis growled. I smirked, saluting. "Leslie will help me straighten my office."

Sure, she will. Like we didn't see that coming.

Frankie jumped from his seat, earning everyone's attention. "No, she won't! She can help me since you set Aaron up with something that should be your job!"

Silently applauding, I thought, *Way to go, Frankie.*

Travis's bulging eyes and ticking jaw, joined by his signature finger tapping, told me he wasn't pleased. We all knew he wouldn't fire anyone close to a large shift in power. It'd look bad on him and drag his past fornication with Leslie to light if Frankie decided to fight him.

"Fine," Travis replied, pinching his nose bridge with his thumb and pointer finger. "Judith, work on the reception area. Josh, breakroom. This doesn't mean you won't have to do your jobs. We have too many cases and new clients coming in to get lazy."

Without a word, save for a few grumbles, we left the room to our *respective* assignments.

"Aaron! Wait!" Dudley's nasally voice grated like chalkboard meeting nails. He caught up with, wheezing from the combination of his weight and excursion.

"Easy Duds, what's up?" I asked, keeping it casual.

Dudley straightened, adjusting his glasses. "I know you don't like me," *I never said that!* "but I want you to know, I'm excited to work with you. The way you handle Travis is amazing." He clenched his fists, eyeing me like a kid would their hero. "I wish I could stand up for myself like that. Like you do."

Another eyeroll. If only he knew how badly I screwed things up. What I showed wasn't courage; it had terrified me the moment the words left my big mouth.

"It's not a big deal, Duds. Just stand up against the bullies. Travis Marks is a bully. He'll walk all over you if you let him," I said, shrugging and closing my eyes.

I didn't have the heart to tell the guy half the employees avoided Dudley.

"Still," Dudley said, lowering his eyes. He didn't say anything after that.

We'd arrived at our destination—the office of former senior partner Howard Kimball. My heart ached thinking about how much pain the old man had to endure every day he came in while sick. How many of Travis's complaints, fits, or difficult cases Mr. Kimball went through when he should've been in bed at home.

But Mr. Kimball wasn't someone who showed anything was wrong with him until he took a few "personal" days that turned into a week or two. Everyone liked him. He had cared about us as human beings and went to war with Marks over getting a coffee maker put in the breakroom. During my interview with him, Mr. Kimball noticed how nervous I was. He put down the intimidating yellow notepad and offered me a drink from his personal stash. Somehow, we got on the topic of my father, and although I hated talking about it, Mr. Kimball made me comfortable enough to answer his questions. He made sure to adhere to my sister's contracts, only asking about recipes he'd tried and admitting how he never could make them taste the same. I helped him with my own knowledge, and we quickly started sharing notes and holding taste tests at Mr. Kimball's massive house. Those affairs became parties where everyone in the firm was invited and thus became an annual thing on certain holidays.

My heart grew heavier as my eyes scanned the empty room, picturing all the degrees, photos of boats—he loved the sea—and other paraphernalia that used to hang on the walls. *How someone like that partnered with Travis-fucking-Marks, I'll never understand.*

"Doesn't seem real, does it?" Dudley said, pausing mid-swipe over the old oak desk. "Seems like I just talked to him a few days ago." He whipped around to stare at me. "Why didn't he tell us?"

That question bothered me too, though I knew Mr. Kimball had his reasons. My only concern was the new partner—the man whose voice wouldn't quit rattling around in my addled brain. *I know that voice. God, where do I know it from?*

Between the lingering embarrassment of Elliot's dare and not remembering the rest of that night, I wanted to put my fist through the wall.

We spent the rest of the day cleaning when we could, taking turns answering phones and showing clients into Travis's office. Our tasks were so tedious, we wanted to drag Marks out of his office and pound him.

I met Leslie in the breakroom while she clocked out. Running my hand over my nape, I sighed. "Hey."

"Oh, hey!" she replied. "What's up?"

"Listen, about the way I acted the other night. I'm sorry. I know you weren't trying to pry or anything..." *Stop stuttering, you idiot. Talk.* "It's just—"

Leslie's aloft hand halted me. "It's okay. I can't imagine what you are going through right now. You're holding a full-time job, college, and trying to outrun camera-hungry hyenas." We both laughed at that. "Honestly, Aaron, I have no idea how you handle it." She placed her hand on my shoulder, her eyes misty like she wanted to cry. "I really wish you'd do something for yourself that doesn't involve work. You deserve to be happy. To find someone who loves you for the sweet, sensitive guy you are."

Not her too. I fought the "uggggh" burning my throat. "I don't need a man—"

"Aaron, you know what I mean. You may fool everyone here, but you and I've known each other a while. I know you're lonely and sad. Think about it, okay?"

Leslie was right. We had known one another longer than anyone in the office. Outside of work, we walked Roxxie, talked, and hung out as friends. She loved Roxxie, and when I went out of town, I asked Leslie to dog-sit for me. What else could I say? I nodded. "I'll think about it."

Her reply was a soft smile and a curt nod.

CHAPTER 8

We spent the rest of the week making sure Travis looked good in front of the new partner. By the time my day off rolled around, every part of me—even the ones I didn't know about—ached like hell. The thought of sleeping in sounded nothing short of heaven.

The sound of my alarm—*is that my alarm?*—screaming woke me at a god-awful time on my day off. Growling, I fisted the thing tightly, curious to why I hadn't broken it. Frankie's name flashed in multiple text messages.

Frankie, I'm going to fucking kill you.

My thumb swiped the screen, opening the messages to see Frankie asking me to cover for him. He and Leslie apparently slept together the night before, got drunk, and now suffered horrible hangovers. In my mind, I formed a checklist with three columns: *Yes, No, or Maybe.* I listed off every possible thing I thought of for not going in. Unfortunately, when compared to the reasons why I should, the not going in column lost.

I dragged my exhausted-because-I-stayed-up-all-night-working-on-an-essay ass out of bed, showered, and got dressed quickly. The time was already an hour after Frankie should've showed up. *Of course, he'd choose texting over calling in emergency situations. You better have one hell of a pay-back, Frankie.*

53

Josh looked confused to see me walk in. "What the hell are you doing in? And where's Frankie? Travis is about to explode."

I waved him off, grumbling and shambling to clock in before returning to the front desk. "I'm covering for Frankie. Julia has Leslie covered. They finally shagged each other and got drunk at an after party."

No words were needed to accompany Josh's wide-eyed nod. I could tell we both had the same question buzzing through our minds. Why had Frankie and Leslie been stupid enough to go get shit-faced on a weekday? Josh returned to work while I sauntered to the file room, mouth dropping at how disheveled it still was despite all the cleaning.

If Travis sees this, I'm a dead man!

Muted voices—one Travis, the other inaudible—hovered down the hall. I stepped out to set some files on the reception desk for clients scheduled to come in.

"Looks like he's here," Josh warned.

"Who?"

"The new partner. He came in a few minutes ago. They're in Travis's—" He stopped when the door opened, revealing the one face I swore I'd never see again.

Bulging eyes brought about an instant headache as the same man I'd made a fool of myself with at the cocktail bar strolled in. Some details from that night were still hazy. Any attempt I made to fill in the blanks was met with hostile resistance in the mess that was my brain.

Eventually, I let it go. This was Manhattan, right? We were like Las Vegas. Anything that happened here and all that. Thousands upon thousands of people visited the city, many tourists. The guy said he was passing through from Miami. No big deal.

Boy, was I wrong.

Oh no! No, no, no! My fists clenched and unclenched, growing clammy the closer Travis and the guy I now knew as Mr. Waylan came. *Okay, stay calm.* I closed my eyes, willing the kettledrum in my chest to cool it. *Maybe he doesn't remember me. Maybe all that silver-spooning got him laid multiple more times and I was only one face in a million.*

Wishful thinking, but it was all I had.

"What's going on with you?" Josh asked. "You know him?"

Don't lie, don't lie, don't lie. "What? Nope. Nu-uh. Never seen him before in my life." *Nailed it!* "Why?"

Josh tilted his head, his eyes betraying he hadn't bought it. "Um, you're shaking for one thing. Second, I think I hear Frankie's stress buddy crying for help." He gestured his chin at the pink toy I hadn't noticed picking up.

For some reason, looking at the gag gift—which consequently looked and felt like a man's anal pleasure toy—disturbed me despite my tendency to use one on lonely nights when I didn't want to sleep with another case of blue balls.

I quickly set the poor thing on the desk before I popped the white "eyes" covering its bulbous head. *Okay, okay, calm down. Calm down.* I fought closing my eyes while taking some not-so-subtle deep breaths. *Maybe he doesn't recognize me. It's not like I don't have an "average Joe" face.*

Mr. Hot and Sexy had a hand in his pocket, hips moving like a runway model as the two of them approached the desk. Travis wore his signature fake smile—*probably with his added ass-kissing laugh*—at something the new senior partner said.

To buy myself some time to calm the eff down, I picked Frankie's buddy back up and pretended to drop it. *Time to disappear.*

From my spot on the floor, I looked up at Josh, giving him the "shh" gesture while slicing a finger across my throat with the other. He looked confused, but after my pathetic puppy "please, I need this" eyes met his, he rolled them and nodded.

They stopped in front of the desk, their shoes shuffling on the other side.

"Bianchi, where is Cambrian?" Travis asked with a lowered voice. *Not like Mr. Waylan can't hear you, moron.* Travis continued after Josh shrugged a shoulder. "I need him to show our new partner—" Travis stopped mid-sentence.

Being where I was, I couldn't have caused it. Travis never stopped talking unless he was terrified of the other person.

That was when I became aware of someone standing behind me. I stopped, hand outstretched toward the stress buddy, and looked up over my shoulder.

Deep jade eyes hidden behind black hipster frames smiled down at me. "Hello there," Mr. Waylan said in a voice my now-hardened male libido took immediate notice of.

Rising too fast, I bumped my head on the desk's edge and fell back against the spinning chair. Its wheels slid along the plastic mat into Josh, making him grunt.

Mr. Waylan closed an eye, hissing through his teeth. "Ooh. That looked unpleasant. Terribly sorry if I startled you."

Terribly sorry? Unpleasant? Who is this guy? That sexy accent didn't help ease the anger welling inside or the burning blush forming across my cheeks from embarrassment. *It's official. I'm in so much trouble.*

Mr. Waylan offered his hand, which I waved off. "I'm fine." It was a bald-faced lie but taking his hand would only add to my frustration.

"Good to hear," Travis mocked. "Now, *do* tell us why you were down there in the first place."

56

I opened my mouth to speak only to stop when Mr. Waylan cut me off.

"I don't think that's important, Travis. I'd like to see my new office as I'm under the impression you're behind on some cases."

My eyes bulged at how meek Travis became, clasping and rubbing his hands together while muttering "yes, of course" like a chastised child. *Maybe he's ... not such a smug alpha asshole?*

Mr. Waylan's attention returned to me. "I'd be incredibly honored if you would show me the way. We can stop by the breakroom and get some ice for that if you like." Adding insult, he smiled mischievously.

Nix that. He's a total prick. I rubbed my head one last time, stood, and tried to hide my disdain, failing miserably. "Sure," I said, walking around the half-moon reception desk. "This way."

Mr. Waylan offered a curt nod to me, and we departed toward the freshly cleaned office. The whole time I could only think two things: one, this guy confused me worse than that romance movie with the actress and Hugh Grant, and two, if Mr. Waylan did remember me, he certainly wasn't showing it.

Either way, I had to avoid getting dragged into the cloud of sex surrounding him, or I'd likely wind up hurting worse than I had with Dicklan.

"Cambrian," Mr. Waylan said. "Why does that name sound so familiar?"

Please don't find it familiar. I shrugged, making sure to keep my furrowing brow of annoyance.

"Any relation to the famous chef who won that contest a few years back?" Mr. Waylan asked.

And the other shoe drops. It always does. "Bingo. What of it?"

I knew I sounded like a total dick, but the way this guy spoke sent shocks of "hello, please fuck me now" all throughout my body. He made me angry and horny simultaneously—not a good combination after once again shaming myself in front of Travis.

"I was only pondering. By the way, might you be Aaron? The one who spoke with me on the phone?"

"Yeah, that's me," I replied.

A devious smile curved his lips. "Ah, well, it's very nice to meet you face to face. I'm Maverick Waylan. Feel free to call me Maverick. I like to think of Mr. Waylan as my father."

Does he do that on purpose? "O-kay. That's an ... interesting name."

Maverick huffed a laugh. "I hate it too, but it's what I have. Anyway, it is indeed a pleasure to meet you."

I'd had it, unsure why his way of talking bugged the crap out of me. Okay, so maybe I knew why, but I'd had it anyway. Don't judge. If we didn't arrive at Mr. Kimball's office when we did, I might've whipped around and demanded to know if our new partner was some prince traveling incognito.

"My," Maverick marveled at the large, entry space connecting Mr. Kimball's office to his waiting area. "It's much larger than I thought."

Yep. That's pretty much what everyone says.

"What is that desk for?" he asked about the PA desk.

"That's where Judith, Mr. Kimball's personal assistant, sat. She's the secretary in the greeting area now."

While Maverick explored his new space, I watched him like a curious puppy. The way he carried himself, never appeared to lose his cool, and subtly glanced at me lured me in. More than anything, I wondered if I'd been mistaken.

I barely remembered the guy I hit on at the cocktail bar having green eyes, dirty blonde hair, and glasses. What were the odds this was the same guy? He hadn't acted like he even met me before.

And this confuses you why, Aaron? Maverick has probably slept with multiple partners. Why would he remember you? I didn't know what pissed me off worse—Maverick not remembering sleeping with me or Maverick not being my Mr. Mysterious.

"What is it you do here?" Maverick's sudden reappearance tore me from my thoughts.

"I'm a file clerk. Office is down the stairs, end of the hall. Can't miss it," I replied. "The breakroom's the room we passed on the way here. Don't drink the coffee unless Leslie makes it." Hey, I had to try to lighten the mood, or I would go insane.

Maverick blinked a few times, barking a laugh. "Why is that?"

I couldn't stop the smile. "Because otherwise, you're going to have to schedule your bathroom times. Judith's coffee will loosen your bowels."

We both laughed. I couldn't help myself. As tense as this guy made me, he was my boss. Might as well not give off the wrong impression, right?

"I should get going," I said. "Travis might send out a search party if I don't get to my office. Especially since Frankie isn't here today."

"He does seem a tad jumpy for such a short fellow." Maverick's eyes went half-lidded, his glasses sliding down his nose. "I look forward to working together ... Aaron."

My heart thudded against my ribs, cheeks heating. *Is he ... checking me out? Nah. Just wishful thinking.* "Uh, yeah. Welcome to the firm, sir."

I whirled on my heel and got the hell outta there, hoping Maverick hadn't seen the embarrassing bulge my work pants couldn't hide. *What is with him?* I ducked into the restroom, closed and locked the door, then leaned against it. Dizziness as blood rushed from my brain to my balls almost took me to the ground. *Alright. Listen, body: Maverick Waylan is off limits. Got it? Stop with the erections.*

Sighing, I turned on the sink's water, splashing my face with it. My skull pounded with each heartbeat, agitating my budding headache.

It is him. I know it is. Is he toying with me?

Whatever was going on, I had to keep Maverick at arm's length. No matter how powerful his sexual magnetism, I had to focus on finishing school, getting that internship, and starting my career.

CHAPTER 9

The rest of the following week, I created any excuse—too busy, pretend phone call, sudden onset of sickness—and used every covert—dodging into the restroom, hiding under my desk, and even jumping into the janitorial closet—to avoid interacting with my new, frustrating boss. Say what you want. I couldn't get the idea that the guy watched my every move out of my head. Not in the creepy stalker way. More in a "I'm really curious about this person" or "look—a shiny thing" way. It was like a cat who watched you until a fly came by to distract it. The fly being the casework Maverick took over before he even settled into his office.

It wasn't such a bad thing when you consider how devoted Maverick was to his work. *Another tick in the "No" column. The guy's a workaholic.* I'd heard him on the phone with clients, in solo talks with Travis, and setting his appointments with Judith. Maverick was efficient and demanded attention when he spoke to us during morning meetings.

On the opposite end, everyone seemed to like him.

Maverick replaced the old computers we'd begged Travis to update for years. He let us keep music on—albeit only that low key stuff, got us an updated coffee maker, and replaced the filing room cabinets.

Every day I arrived, Leslie, Josh, Frankie, and Maverick were in the breakroom shortly before we opened. I didn't join

61

them. *He is the same guy from the bar. I'm sure of it.* And that was enough for me to avoid him. If Maverick knew who I was, he kept it a secret, something I didn't like because it meant he was toying with me, much like Declan did. *Whatever. Not like it matters.* Maverick was my boss. That fact kept me from acting on the physical betrayals my body fed me every time Maverick Waylan opened his mouth. *Who wants that drama?* It sounded like one of my mom's lame soap operas.

The smell of fresh coffee made my mouth water—a welcome relief to the bubbling frustration Maverick brought. *Man, I would love to go get some.* When Leslie made a pot, it lacked the tar taste that often came with Judith's coffee—or what she called coffee. Those mornings, everyone avoided the breakroom like someone was plague-ridden. Leslie's bursting laugh ceased any further thoughts.

I cradled the case files Travis had transferred to Maverick after the new partner got settled in. With how efficient Maverick was, things were becoming less chaotic, and we were functioning more like the prestigious law firm Howard Kimball always intended us to be.

With my head down, my thoughts turned to college and the looming internship application decisions. If I got accepted, I could get out of New York, go to New Orleans, and learn how to prepare my favorite cuisine from the very best.

"Aaron." Maverick's voice made heart and eyes lurch. His eyes drooped a little, brows creased in a melancholy look. That thick English-American mixed accent caused my throat to seize slightly. Did he even know how gorgeous he was? "Have I upset you?"

The tone reminded me of a hurt child looking for their father's forgiveness after their dad had a hard workday. Those moments we tension haunted the halls and every offense set the dad off, even when no one at home caused the problem. I remembered a few of those days before Dad stormed out, choosing fame, money, and living Barbie dolls over family.

I shook my head. I had nearly run into Maverick and suddenly became aware of how much taller than me he was. Damn me, I loved them taller. Maverick had to be around six-foot-five.

His waist bent slightly, forearm settling against the doorjamb of the breakroom. "Then why are you avoiding me?"

"I'm not—" My words halted as our gazes met. *How is he so damn aware of how I'm feeling?*

To distract myself, my eyes searched over Maverick's shoulder. I hoped no one paid attention to what was happening between us. The last thing I needed were office rumors about me and the new boss.

Again, my long-ignored cock wasn't listening to my brain and pressed against my pants. *No, not now,* I pleaded against the dirty images dancing across my thoughts. My throat became dry, muscles tense. *He's like a walking sex aura.*

"I've been busy." The lie was so lame, it needed a cane to walk. However, nothing else came to mind that sounded remotely believable. I guessed it wasn't a complete lie. I *had* been busy. Both at work and home.

Maverick's arching brow and disbelieving head shake told me he hadn't bought it. We had been busy reworking office things, yet not so busy I didn't have time to play white rabbit.

A long, uncomfortable silence floated between us. All I heard were the pounding heartbeats in my ears and the blood rushing from my brain farther south. *Please say something. This is so weird!*

Sighing through his nose, Maverick closed his eyes. "I hope you have a good day and a relaxing weekend. Please come to me if you need anything." One hand went into his pocket as he turned to leave. But he stopped to add, "I want you to trust me, Aaron."

Talk about being hit in the gut. My eyes widened, a breath catching in my throat. I suddenly felt like the biggest asshole in the place. Niggling in the pit of my stomach argued with me to keep my mouth shut to avoid saying something stupid. But truth intervened when I realized I didn't, in fact, trust Maverick Waylan beyond his role as my boss. *Doesn't mean he had to kick me in the balls, though.*

After our odd exchange, I continued to my office and plopped in the rickety spinning chair, nearly falling on my ass. The thing needed to be put out of its misery before I landed on a wheel and shattered—or at least severely bruised—my tail bone. I'd asked Travis multiple times after needing to visit a chiropractor because of the lack of back support. He'd denied me, of course, saying, "Quit complaining. I've had the same chair for years." Meaning, he probably suffered and wanted me to suffer too, thus continuing the I-still-don't-understand-why-he-has-it hate he carried for me.

"You okay?" Frankie asked, peeking around his computer.

"No, Frankie, I'm not okay. Feeling pretty shitty, actually," was what I wanted to say. Elliot had shot me a brief text letting me know he wouldn't make it for our weekly cocktail bar meet, leaving me alone to wallow. What I said was, "Yeah, fine. Been a hard week." I forced a smile. "Looking forward to tonight."

"Same here!" Frankie said, beaming. "Leslie and I are finally going on our first actual date!"

I smiled, really smiled, for the first time in a while. Frankie had pined over Leslie for years. Come to find out, Leslie was doing the same. But neither one knew how to approach the other. "I'm glad for you, man. Where you going?"

Frankie rambled off the names of popular restaurants, asking my opinion which was best. "She loves seafood. Especially a good lobster or crab legs. I know a place my dad took my mom for her birthday, but I'm not sure if Leslie would like it."

My foot tapped against the plastic mat my desk sat on. "Take her somewhere special. If that place with your parents is special to you, Les will love it."

"You think so?"

I nodded. "Definitely."

Frankie thanked me, and we resumed shuffling around each other, organizing files, and taking them to their respective owners.

I wound up needing to take another set of files to Maverick's office. The whole trudge made me feel like a man heading to his execution. I hadn't intended to hurt Maverick's feelings, but not knowing if he recognized me sent me into a frenzy of self-preservation. If my little drunken escapade to Maverick's bed reached Travis's ears, the troll would finally have a reason to fire me. Worst of all, I barely knew Maverick! He might want to blackmail me into doing sexual—or any kind of—favors to keep my secret.

Passing the empty PA's desk in Maverick's office, I swallowed a knot. *It's just delivering files. Like this morning. Nothing awkward needs to happen here.* I knocked, waiting for Maverick to answer.

"Come in," he called, voice lacking any lightheartedness. I swore the guy was like Dr. Jekyll and Mr. Hyde. I did as instructed, shouldering the door. When he took notice, Maverick's face loosened, his eyes gentler. "Aaron." He set his pen down, eyes wide behind those sexy black glasses. "What can I do for you?"

The way he said it stunned me. Those genuine words stalled me, making it hard to remember why I came in there to begin with.

Maverick waited, his eyes searching mine, until he finally asked, "Are those files for me?"

I blinked, our connection severed. "Um, yeah. Sorry." *Think of something. Think of something.* I looked at his empty walls, my curiosity betraying me as badly as my body. "Why are your walls empty?" *Way to be nosy. That's the perfect plan to get thrown out.*

Instead of telling me to butt out, Maverick smiled. It wasn't a cheerful smile, nor one of anger or frustration at my busybody-ness. "Again, you surprise me, Aaron."

I did what now? All I did was ask a question. *How is that surprising?* A thought struck me. Had I accidentally insulted him? Maybe I poked too far in the mysterious past he kept closer than a millionaire's riches. *Oh, no. Am I fired?* It was silly to think, though no one knew much about Maverick Waylan to make any judgement calls.

"I'm sorry," I said, hands palm up in defense. "It's none of my business—"

Maverick's hand raised, silencing me. "No, I'm glad you asked. No one else has." He stood, crossed around his desk, and leaned against it. "Why don't you come in? I've a question I wish to ask you."

I thought about giving him the files and getting the heck out of there. Heat flooded my cheeks. *A question?* "I really should get back to work, sir. I—"

"Maverick, please," Maverick interrupted. "Save 'sir' and 'Mr. Waylan' for my father. My question is simple." He stopped and closed the distance between us, the heat of his body emitting like physical waves. "Would you give me the pleasure of buying you a coffee sometime?"

Talk about unexpected questions!

"Um, e-excuse me?" I asked. *Did he really just...?*

"A coffee. I've seen you with one almost every day." Maverick leaned in close, eyes half-lidded, hungry like that night at the bar. "I'd like to get you one. And a muffin ... I believe?"

Not thinking, I lowered my head and shoved the files at his chest. Anger-mixed nausea threatened to make me lose my lunch.

"Have a pleasant weekend, Mr. Waylan." I didn't wait for the stunned expression to leave his face before turning and storming out of his office.

I had gotten so upset I briefly forgot Maverick was my boss. He hadn't even asked anything offensive like the paparazzi did. Gritting my teeth, I passed through the glass doors sporting the golden "Kimball & Marks, Attorneys at Law" into the hallway.

My fists trembled at my sides. Maverick's question buzzed in my head like angry hornets. *Damn it! What's wrong with you?* I slammed my fist into the wall, thankful for the empty hallway. My forehead fell against my arm. Shortly after, tears of confusion and hurt broke free.

CHAPTER 10

Friday night went by with little drama. I ordered a vegetarian pizza and watched movies with Roxxie, pondering the minor breakdown I had at the day's end. *Why did he ask me that? Does he think I'm some piece of office ass he can use anytime he wants?*

Thinking about it set jumper cables to my temper. I set my empty whiskey glass on the table harder than I intended, scaring Roxxie who whimpered and cocked her head.

"Sorry, girl," I said, scratching behind her ear. "It's been a rough week." I needed to vent some frustration, or I'd explode. "Want to go for a late-night run?"

Roxxie barked, jumped to the floor, and wagged her tail like an excited puppy. Her reaction brought a smile to my face.

"You got it." I quickly cleaned up, setting the dishes in the sink and changing into my running pants, shirt, and sweater.

By the time I made it to the door, Roxxie was already sitting next to it. Glass-blue eyes switched between her hanging leash and me. Each time her head moved, both ears flopped. God, I loved my dog. Sometimes it seemed like she was the only one who understood me.

I leashed her up, and we walked down the hall to the elevator. Roxxie waited patiently, watching the lights above the doors change with each floor. I checked my social media, seeing if anything had happened regarding my father. Turned out someone had seen me exiting Maverick's building the morning after I woke up in his condo.

Famous Chef's Son Has New Beau? Aaron Cambrian Spotted on Park Avenue exiting Popular Building Known to House Wealthy Patrons!

I rolled my eyes. *Would these media vultures ruin anyone's life if it got them a quick run? Not only was that weeks ago, but why is it a big deal?*

On the bottom floor, Roxxie and I exited the lobby to the parking garage. Our destination: Central Park. With the lights, sounds of rustling leaves, whispering water, and occasional marina bells, the park provided the perfect venue to think.

I enjoyed coming here at night because it was quieter. The added serenity cooled my head and gave me a moment to forget the world around me. Roxxie at my side gave security. No clouds, quarter moon, and gentle breezes completed the surreal moment as my feet rhythmically hit the concrete.

Taking off at a run down the path into the park, I reminded myself nothing my father did was my fault. My older sister would handle the newshound who dared print that headline, and I'd have nothing to worry about by morning. Rebecca held the title of top attorney in multiple areas of her profession. And in tracking down people who violated our iron-clad media contracts, Bex was ruthless. She'd sued and won against some of the largest media corporations in the country. We hadn't spoken in months.

I really need to call her.

Someone leaning against the railing overlooking the bay caught my eye. It wasn't until I saw the radiant, dirty-blonde hair and possibly the hottest ass ever that I recognized him. *Maverick? What's he doing here?*

Maverick didn't appear to notice me, staring off into the distance. He had replaced his usual charcoal grey suit with a black turtleneck and trousers. Those usually pushed back bangs blew freely in the wind, revealing thick waves of honey lowlights.

Holy shit. I swallowed, my throbbing cock standing at attention. *Can he get any hotter?* Heavy scents of cigarette smoke slapped my nose. *Wait, he smokes? I've never seen him leave to smoke.* Bafflingly, he never once took a puff, leaving the cigarette to burn down to the filter, ashes drifting in the wind.

I redirected Roxxie toward Maverick. Something about him made me want to peel away his convoluted layers and figure him out. Hate him or not, the guy was a walking, talking, sex-oozing enigma. It was a puzzle I had to figure out before I lost my mind.

Leaves crunched underfoot when Roxxie and I approached.

"Maverick?" I called then cursed internally at my tone. I sounded more like a nervous schoolboy talking to his crush than a concerned colleague.

Maverick glanced over his shoulder. Those jade eyes further tore at my resolve not to take him home and let him fuck me mindless. "Ah, good evening, Aaron," he said in that medieval English language. "What brings you out here at this hour?"

Glancing at my watch, I saw it was past eleven. "I brought Roxxie out for a run."

Roxxie bumped Maverick's leg, her tail wagging.

"Well, hello, Miss Roxxie," Maverick said, kneeling to pet the dog's head. She licked his face and whimpered. Maverick laughed.

Such a gorgeous laugh. "She rarely warms up to people like that." I leaned my butt against the railing, arms crossed. Heat flushed my cheeks, my heart a thudding mess. "So, what are you doing out here?"

Maverick ruffled Roxxie's ears once more. "I come out here to enjoy the night. Quite the change from the business of the day." He must've seen my reaction to the cigarette in his free hand because he dropped it and stomped it out. "They help calm me. I never use them, but holding one soothes the stress."

He must've smoked in his past. Hearing he didn't actually smoke calmed me down. I hated the smell of smoke. My father always resorted to smoking cigars and drinking when the day became too much to handle. That habit had resulted in multiple fights—some so loud I wound up in my sisters' rooms.

"Aaron, is something wrong?" Maverick mimicked my position, his height and nearness somehow reassuring. "Are you still upset at the question I asked earlier?"

I shook my head. "No. I acted like a complete dick. I'm sorry about that."

"No need to apologize. It was forward. And, I imagine, a bit jarring considering your actions throughout the week." He paused a moment, giving me some time to put my jumbled thoughts in order. "I can tell something troubles you, Aaron. I'd like to help if I'm able."

Troubled was an understatement. Seeing Maverick outside of work made him appear more human. And hearing him apologize for my outburst stunned me. My body became more aware of him the longer we stood together. All of it—combined with still wondering if he recognized me—swirled in my head, confusing the hell out of me.

Should I just ask? See if he knows me. How weird would that be? Asking someone like Maverick—who probably slept with whomever he wanted—if he remembered a drunk one-night stand.

"If you don't mind my asking, why did you run from me this week?" Maverick finally asked. "Seems strange—" He stopped talking.

It didn't go unnoticed.

"Seems strange? Why?" I pushed.

"Nothing. Forget I said anything." Maverick turned, resuming his earlier posture. "Strange as it seems, I'm familiar with the pressure of the media." I caught him smiling coyly. "I imagine Travis told you something about my family, yes? We're not exactly capable of hiding our reputation. Especially in the fashion and real estate worlds."

I recalled something like that. It had made me wonder why Maverick chose general law when he had millions in development and runway lights. *Better not ask. It's none of my business.*

"Yeah, heard something like that," I said. *Don't do it.* "Why's a guy who has a family like that choose general law in New York? You could have anything you want."

Maverick's boisterous laugh heated my cheeks more. I hadn't thought that was possible. "This coming from someone who has a world-renowned father. Though, I'm sure you have your reasons. Don't worry. I've no interest in prying."

I wanted to hit him. My father abandoned us for that fame. I wanted nothing to do with him or his poison-earned money. "I should get going. It's getting late, and I'm supposed to meet a friend tomorrow."

Maverick's warm hand on my arm sent chills down my spine. "I shouldn't have said that. Forgive me. I've heard what happened to you, though I'd like to hear the story from you when you're ready."

Another awkward silence grew.

To end it, I turned, whisking Maverick's hand off. "Come on, Rox."

I hadn't gotten halfway up the hill when Maverick jogged after us, calling my name. I stopped, barely avoiding falling backward when he placed himself between me and the curb.

"Forgive me, Aaron. I'm not usually this out of sorts." Maverick ran his hand over his nape. "At least, not until I met you. Seems I can't get anything right recently."

I blinked like a baffled cartoon character. I could never get things right too, especially with men I had made out with recently. But I couldn't imagine Maverick Waylan having the same problem. Especially with ... well, me.

"It's ... really okay," I said.

Maverick shook his head. "No. It's not. Let me try again. And yes, I am begging."

None of what was happening made sense. Maverick—suave, efficient, professional, Travis-Marks-scaring Maverick Waylan—stumbled over his words for someone like me? Someone who screwed up every relationship he'd ever been in? Someone who'd gotten desperate, drunk, and wound up in Maverick's condo?

"Um, okay," I replied.

Maverick exhaled a deep breath, his eyes closed briefly. "Thank you," he said, smiling that teasing smile. "You know, I know this twenty-four-hour diner nearby that serves the best pancakes. Perhaps you'd be interested in joining me?" He angled those jade eyes so they showed beneath his glasses. "Perhaps chocolate chip?"

How? "But I have Roxxie," I replied.

Maverick's mischievous eyes didn't waver. "You let me worry about that. What do you say?"

I chuckled nervously. "You never give up, do you?"

"I don't know the meaning of those words." Maverick reached out his hand. "All you have to say ... is yes."

Whether it was madness or utter curiosity that made me take his hand, I had no idea.

"A service dog?" I asked, tapping my heel, arms crossed. We'd gotten to the diner in record time thanks to Maverick's less-than-safe driving. "Really?" My brow raised.

Maverick chuckled. "It worked, yes?" Two cups of coffee steamed in front of us. "Besides, we couldn't leave our precious princess in the car alone, could we? She'd get so lonely."

Roxxie tilted her head at Maverick then me, her glass-blue eyes wide like the soulful puppy eyes of a lame birthday card picture.

Outnumbered and clearly outwitted this time, I rolled my eyes, uttering an elongated "ugh," then said, "Fine. You win."

Maverick put another packet of sugar in his coffee, watching as he swirled it. He didn't look away, seemingly in deep thought. Too afraid to ask the burning questions in my mind, I kept my mouth shut. *Why did I agree to come here again?*

Our server arrived to take our orders. True to his word, Maverick chose a hearty breakfast, complete with whole wheat toast. I went with a vegetable omelet and a couple of chocolate chip pancakes. The smile on Maverick's face made me want to slug him.

"Truth is, Aaron, I need a bit of advice."

"Oh yeah?" I took a sip of the coffee. "About what?"

Our server returned with our food, setting it down. The way she thrust her breasts in Maverick's face made me think she might offer him a lap dance to get him to look at her. His continued focus on me gave her all the hint she needed to leave him alone.

Wow. Wonder if that happens all the time. Definitely doesn't to me.

"Travis handed me a large caseload," Maverick said, taking a toast piece and buttering it. "I find myself in need of some help. Do you have any recommendations?"

I took a moment to think. Out of everyone in the firm, Judith and Leslie had the most experience as paralegals going to the courthouses and running errands. Judith was too old, however, to go as fast as Maverick probably needed.

"Leslie could. She's been Travis's paralegal until recently. People in the courthouse know her, which gives her a leg up when picking up things," I replied. "She'd be happy for the pay raise too."

Maverick locked his fingers, staring out the window. It almost looked like he was watching his reflection with that deep stare. "Hmm," he said finally. "Perhaps so. I'll think about it. Anyone else?"

I shrugged and speared a pancake. "Not unless you plan on hiring outside the firm."

A crooked grin drew Maverick's lip over his teeth. "I'd want someone I trust. Thank you, though. Please enjoy your breakfast. It's on me."

"Huh?" I answered louder than I meant to. "Uh, no offense, but I'd rather cover my half of the bill."

If Maverick planned on arguing, he didn't show it. For that, I was grateful. In the end, he agreed to let me pay for myself, and we left.

"I wouldn't mind giving you and Roxxie a ride home," Maverick said.

My cheeks flushed. The growing hardness in my pants was not helping me keep my resolve to take a cab. "No. I should be fine. I have a cabby on speed dial who doesn't mind dogs."

Maverick moved in close, giving me a chance to gaze deeply into his eyes. "It's alright, Aaron. I don't mind and would love the pleasure of your company a little longer if you can tolerate me."

I laughed. "I think I can manage it."

It wasn't a lie. No matter how frustrating Maverick could be at work, I found I enjoyed seeing this side of him. He made me curious to learn more.

Maverick dropped Roxxie and me off around two in the morning. After crinkling up his nose, asking why I lived where I did, and receiving a stern look from me, Maverick wished me a pleasant weekend and told me we'd see each other at work.

I fell asleep wondering if I'd gotten this all wrong. *Have I mistaken Maverick for the cocktail bar guy?* They both had green eyes and sandy-blonde hair, wore glasses, and had a hot accent. *But maybe this is a different guy.* Something inside me said I'd been nuts for thinking that. *Why hasn't he mentioned who he is?*

After Maverick left, I needed to cool my body—namely a throbbing cock—way down. To keep Roxxie from attacking my ... gentlemanly entertainment tool, I locked her in the hall. She often mistook certain noises for my being brutalized by my partners. It didn't make for an enjoyable time, especially when said partner didn't like animals of the canine variety.

Later, sweat dripped down my nostrils from yet another heated round of self-pleasure. I panted. *Damn it. Damn it. Damn it. Damn it.* I couldn't get Maverick out of my mind. No matter what I did or how many times I did it, that sexy, hipster glasses wearing boss of mine proved I couldn't evict him easily. Worn out and drenched with sweat, I finally collapsed into a restless sleep, only to wake pissed off at the world.

CHAPTER 11

I woke up late the next morning thanks to smashing my alarm clock and turning my phone on silent. Light beaming through my window finally shook me awake.

"Shit!" I shouted at seeing the time. I grabbed my phone, noticing Elliot had left me many text messages asking where I was. He'd gone into the salon and set aside almost two hours for me to get my hair layered. The appointment wasn't my idea. Elliot, as a professional hair stylist, served as my personal fashion police, carefully pointing out what was "last season" and when I needed to haul my ass into his workplace.

Dialing my phone, I set it to speaker and fumbled around in my closet and drawers for something to wear.

"Bitch, where are you?" Elliot screamed into the speaker. "I have a life outside of your late ass, you know?"

"Hey, sorry, El!" I said, my words muffled by the sweater I was pulling on. "I had a late night. Work's been—"

"Ugh! Busy, I know," Elliot grumbled. "By the way, how is Mr. Hot Boss?"

I didn't remember telling Elliot anything outside of my white rabbit act the last time we had a stream of texts. I certainly didn't remember mentioning how hot Maverick was or at all.

Frustrated, I picked up the phone. "El, I wasn't even talking about Maverick—" *Shit. Shit. Shit. He is so going to run with that!* I could almost feel the wide grin on my friend's face amid the silence. "Don't even think about it."

"You like him!" Elliot's high-pitched "I approve" voice was like a high school girl hearing about her girlfriend's crush. "Don't be so shocked, babe. His picture's been in the paper. Did you really think Travis would miss the chance to announce that a Waylan became *the* senior firm partner?"

No, Travis wouldn't. I smacked my head with my hand. Elliot definitely planned on running with this. *Here we go again, love life. Get ready for your schooling.*

"El, he's my boss, okay? My b-o-s-s. Even if I did—" Elliot shrieked again. This time, I pulled the phone away and gritted my teeth. "Elliot, will you stop!"

"No, I will not. Get your ass over here! I want to hear all about your 'late night' and if it had anything to do with that gorgeous lawyer." He didn't leave me time to pick my jaw off the floor before hanging up.

Roxxie came sauntering in, whimpering at me for missing her morning run. I apologized to her, promising I'd make it up, and fed her. Racing out the door, I ran to the elevator.

My stomach roared at me on the ride down the elevator and out into the street. I ignored it.

I never ran late! Thankfully, it was Saturday, and I didn't work. *Sorry, Travis. Still can't fire me.*

"Taxi!" I called, waving my hand. Like every morning, getting one took me a few tries and a near splashing of water lingering from the street sweepers. *You'd think I'd learn not to stand so damn close to the curb.*

I gave the driver the location of the Black Swan Salon and sat back, watching the passing Park Ave buildings. One of them belonged to Maverick, though I didn't remember which.

Most of the details from that night remained hazy no matter what I did to remember them.

But my arm definitely recalled what having Maverick's hand on it felt like. It was warm and sent shivers through me. I hadn't wanted him to remove it, thinking about what having him run his hands over me—*hey! Stop that right now! Boss, remember! Frustrating, secretive, talks-like-a-fantasy-character boss!* I shook my head, chiding myself.

Office relationships, no matter how hot at first, always ended badly. With my horrible luck, Maverick would fire and throw my ass out on the sidewalk within a week. *No. Off limits. Sexy, gorgeous, God-I-wish Maverick is off limits.*

With all the morning commotion, I forgot to check the news feed on my phone. Google alerts kept me aware of my father's newest shenanigans, the latest secret headline, or any paparazzo caught featuring me and Maverick's meeting. Thankfully, nothing came up at either the park or diner. *Phew.* My eyes directed skyward. *That's a relief.* Last thing I needed was another surprise of the unwanted variety like the one at Maverick's condo.

Elliot's annoying demands of wanting to hear about my "night with Maverick" distracted me. I hadn't noticed I'd missed call from my sister Rebecca flashed on the screen.

Odd. Bex didn't call unless something was going on. She stayed buried under client work the more renowned she became. I still had time before arriving at the salon, so I called my sister on my way down to the lobby. She answered when I stepped into the lobby, so I sat in a chair. Trying to hold a phone conversation on busy New York streets was a nightmare.

"Hey," I said, sinking into the chair and resting an ankle on my thigh.

"Aaron, thank God! Where have you been?" Her voice huffed like she'd sprinted a marathon.

Is everyone asking me this today? "Sorry, Bex, this morning was hectic. What's wrong?" Not sounding like a spoiled brat took more effort than I wanted. "Did Mom call you freaking out because I didn't answer a text she didn't send again or something?" I reminded myself to call my mom once I finished at Elliot's salon.

"Funny," she replied. "No. There's a problem with the family contracts. Turns out your little ... escapade at the Park Avenue condo has riled up the media. They're claiming the contracts staunch their freedom of speech."

Escapade? Christ, I knew it. Those lowlifes didn't care whose life they destroyed for a story. What made it worse was how my dad let it happen! He abandoned us, and we still had to deal with his crap!

"Bex, listen," I almost snapped, "there wasn't an escapade, okay." Shame kept me from spilling what little details I remembered about that night. "There's no scandal or 'secret' lover. Those morons are just out for blood because they have nothing else to do."

What I said was true. I had no secret lover, and even if I did, why would that need to be front page news on the Times? I didn't give anyone a public blow job. Most of my sexual "escapades" stayed behind closed doors.

"Just be careful, little brother." My sister used the soothing tone from when I used to go into her bedroom during our parents' yelling fits. Hearing it made my heart sad, yet happy. "I know things are rough for you right now, but please try to keep your head low while I sort this out. I've already called everyone, including Mom and our sisters."

Boy, was I glad to hear that. Dealing with my mom all riled up was worse than pulling an alligator's sore tooth.

"Thanks for that," I said. "I'll take things easy. I promise. How're you and the boyfriend?"

Rebecca rarely talked about her relationships to anyone but Mom. Getting those two gossiping sounded like a coop full of chickens. Bex even shared our mom's rare outbursts of laughter.

"I can't talk casual right now, Aaron. I'm sorry. My office has been a madhouse since Ashley brought this to my attention. Thank you, though. I'll see you for Thanksgiving and answer texts when I can." She sighed, making my heart turn to lead. As much of a pain as Bex was sometimes, I still missed her. Hell, I missed all of my family. "I love you, little brother. Hope you know that."

I nodded like she could see. Tears stung the corner of my eyes. "You too. It's always nice to hear from you, sis."

"You too. And Aaron..."

"Yeah?"

"Please be happy. Mom told me what's been going on with Cole. He's not worth your heartache. You're an amazing person who deserves a doting man." Bex hung up, leaving me stunned.

We'd always talked to each other about family business, but the idea Rebecca knew about the gruesome details of Dicklan and my break-up made me angry.

"Here's your stop," the cabby said through the dividing window. The gruff voice stalled my internal screaming.

I thrust the door open harder than needed, paid, and stomped out onto the sidewalk, fists balled at my hips. I wasn't sure if Rebecca's news about the contract fight or the break-up angered me more. *Maybe it's not either.* I squeezed my eyes closed. Maybe it was the confusion and fatigue from last night's events. Whatever the circumstance, I needed to get into the salon, or Elliot would skewer me.

This whole thing with Maverick could quickly turn into a bubbling geyser. I needed to get a handle on things.

The media already hadn't only blown up my story, but my younger sister's, too. Unlike me, Bethany, and Bex, Polly didn't care who caught her on camera. She'd been in and out of rehab multiple times and was going viral for strip dancing in another drunken stupor. Polly's damaging reputation was another reason Rebecca pursued the contracts—something they got into many heated arguments over.

Great. Knowing Polly, I'll get a call about how Bex was over-reacting again. It'd happened before, and I had no reason to think it wouldn't again.

I scrolled further down. *Shit!*

My eyes bulged at what I saw. Someone had seen Maverick and me at the diner, but they hadn't captured his face. *Does he know? God, what if he does? How much trouble am I going to be in?*

I wanted to ask the cabby if he'd consent to getting paid to kidnap me for a few days. I barely knew Maverick, and he already landed in another Cambrian family media war! *Would he care? I mean, he said his family was famous, so ... would he?* The more I thought about it, the more appealing the kidnapping idea sounded.

I needed to tell someone or go insane from the spinning madness. I still didn't know what to think about Maverick, the ordeal with the media, or Cole dropping in unexpectedly at the worst moments.

Can I please have one fucking normal day? My internal scream went unanswered, and I walked through the door to Elliot's workplace.

CHAPTER 12

E lliot stood with his foot tapping, arms crossed, and one brow raised. His hip was cocked like a supermodel, clad in leather skinny jeans and a cherry red turtleneck. Both azure eyes shone beneath the kohl shadowing his eyelids.

My hands went up defensively. "Look, I can—"

Elliot halted my words with a raised hand. "Nope. Don't wanna hear it." He grabbed my forearm and dragged me across the black and white floor to the back. "Get this on," he said, shoving a smock at me.

I did as he said, trying to get a single word in edgewise. "El, I really need—"

Elliot pointed a finger at me then at a chair with an attached washbasin. "You need to get that cute ass of yours in that chair before I kick it." A smile crept across his glossed lips. "Then we can talk gossip because I *know* you have some juicy stories to share."

Screw it. I sat and leaned back. El was great at his job and did wonders when my hair got too long. Sounds of cabinets opening and Elliot humming to himself showed he was ready to start.

All my cares slipped away as fingers massaged my skull through the warm water. The euphoric feeling brought a smile, and I felt myself relaxing into the momentary pampering.

Every tight muscle released, letting me slide further down the chair.

"You always know how to make me feel better, El," I said, practically purring like a satisfied cat. "I'm really sorry for—"

Another headshake stopped me. "You want me to forgive you for being late, bitch? Tell me all the delicious details about last night," Elliot demanded. "I want to know more about this gorgeous new partner of yours."

I blinked nervously, face heating. "He's not my—" Two fingers shushed me. *That's getting annoying.*

"Whatever. Spill it," Elliot snapped. "Or I'll use the cold water."

I relayed everything that happened with Maverick at the park and the diner, including how Roxxie reacted upon meeting Maverick for the first time. That was a mistake.

"See? Even she knows." Elliot rubbed my favorite shampoo through my hair then rinsed it out. "Maverick's good for you, babe. The fact he's already stumbling over his words means he really wants you. He just doesn't know how to get you."

Wish I was that confident. I laughed to make myself feel better. "I think you're projecting a bit of your own wishes there. He's probably just trying to figure out to work with an oddball who rabbits from him." *Did I just admit that out loud?* "Anyway, I don't have much to offer a guy like him. And there's my college work. I'm almost—"

"You did the list thing, didn't you?" Elliot leaned over and glared at me. I pulled my lips into my mouth, receiving a towel in my face for the trouble. "I swear!"

I stood and dried my hair the best I could. Everyone in the salon ignored Elliot's drama. They knew him and believed he should star in a Broadway musical from his antics. I'd warned them it'd never happen. He loved working with hair too much.

We walked to his station. I sat down while he rummaged through his drawer for scissors and a brush. My hair was like my mom's—thick, layered, and easily whipped into a mess. Elliot somehow played cowboy with the locks and corralled my hair.

"When are you going to accept how sexy you are, babe? I mean damn! I'm telling you, he *wants* you. Guy at the bar or not, Maverick *wants* this." He motioned at my entire body in the mirror. "Give him a chance. He's not Dicklan. Hell, he'd probably kick that douche's ass for you."

I didn't want to think about Maverick meeting Cole. Depending on which version of Maverick came to the fight, Declan might wind up in the hospital. And I didn't want anyone fighting my battles like I was some ditzy princess in a tower.

My problem wasn't wanting to give Maverick a chance. Hell, I wanted more than anything to plaster my lips against his. The guy was hot! Hotter than hot. Hotter than Cole—aka Dicklan—could ever hope to be. I'd give up my left testicle to have Maverick, even if it was for just a night. My problem was two-fold: one, I still had no clue if he recognized me or if he was even the same guy, and two, he was my damn boss! Travis would love nothing more than to fire me if he found out I dared get in bed with our new senior partner.

Thoughts whirled in my head despite Elliot's working his soothing magic on my hair. *Why can't he see this is more complicated than a "Hi, nice to meet you, wanna fuck" situation?* And with the problems my sister dealt with, the last thing I needed to do was feed the media vultures.

To get Elliot talking about something else, I laughed. "Here you are lecturing me on my love life, and you're still keeping Mr. Sex In Bed a secret." I tossed him a sarcastic look in the mirror. "Seems kind of hypocritical, don't you think, El?"

Elliot flipped me off, and the two of us remained silent. I checked my phone, waiting for the inevitable call from Polly. She'd likely want me to get Rebecca to back off. Out of all of us, Polly talked to Dad's agent the most. Miraculously, sometimes Dad actually sent a message back through his agent. Sometimes he didn't respond at all. *Guess that's all it takes to lie to yourself.*

"Something's bothering you, babe," Elliot said, pulling my tangly hair into separate sections. I winced at the short stings. "Other than the Maverick thing, I mean."

I lowered my eyes, exhaling deeply through my nose. *Should I tell him about the drama Bex is going through? About the renewed entertainment spectacle?* He was my best friend, and we rarely kept secrets from each other. Like Roxxie, Elliot watched over me. He knew everything. *Why not tell him this, too?*

I spilled, leaving out nothing. Tears misted at the corner of my eyes. *What am I thinking? I can't break down here. I'll look like a total crybaby!*

"That man really is an asshole," Elliot commented, making me chuckle. *Thank you, Elliot.* "I mean, does he even know what his shit puts your family through? If it were my old man, he'd punch the judge in the face."

Elliot's parents supported all five of their kids. We were both the middle kids, so we understood what each other went through. Especially with missing parents. El's mom died in a plane crash, leaving their now remarried father to raise the family. When Elliot came out as gay, both his stepmother and his father supported his decision. His opponents—his older brother and sister—went head-to-head against his father, wanting to toss Elliot out. The fight ended when his father told them to leave. Hearing about the decision had shocked me to my core, but Elliot couldn't have been glowing brighter.

Elliot worked like lightning, and soon, I gazed at my dried, layered hair. Smiling proudly, El took a mirror, handed it to me, and spun me to view the back.

"I doubt he cares, El," I said finally, admiring the stunning-as-usual job. "My point is the last thing I need is to—"

"Get up," Elliot said suddenly, all emotion stripped from him. I barely made it to my feet and took the smock off before he shoved me through the wash area to the breakroom in the back. Lizzie, El's closest friend, motioned him toward her.

We'd barely spoke, save for the occasional few words, although Elliot spent a good amount of time with her outside of work. From what I knew, Lizzie had a girlfriend, and they often double-dated with Elliot and his mystery boyfriend. Honestly, it irked me a little, but unlike me, El had a huge social circle.

"What's going on?" I asked.

Lizzie closed the breakroom door and leaned against it. Elliot dried his hands and whirled around. "Don't freak out," he said, holding up his hands. "Dicklan just walked in. Thanks to Sadie's interference, we got you out in time."

Son of a bitch! Really? Is there no low that prick won't steep to make me miserable? Cole likely heard about the media rant and suffered a sexual dry spell. They'd happened before and I fell for his "I'm sorry, baby" routine every time. With El's help, I hadn't relapsed in five years.

Lizzie placed her hand on my shoulder. "Don't worry. Elliot will take care of this."

My mouth felt like a desert. As if life hadn't spit in my face hard enough! The only thing I could think of scared the hell out of me—I wanted to text Maverick.

My ordeal at the salon left me shaking. Elliot had come back after he got rid of Cole. As I thought, Cole had heard about the drama and wanted to offer me some comfort. His being there at the same time was pure coincidence; he preferred getting his hair done for big press events. *How did I not know my ex came here?*

"Aaron, I swear I had no idea," Elliot said. "If I did, I'd have told you." He glared at Lizzie and Sadie. "Why didn't you two say anything?"

Sadie—another of Elliot's friends and the front desk clerk—cocked her hip and placed a fist on it. "You know how the manager is, Elliot. She couldn't care less what happens outside this place. Even if we had known, we couldn't do anything about it. Cole spends a lot of money here!"

I rolled my eyes. "It's okay. It's not any of your jobs to protect me." *This has to stop! I'm so tired of this bullshit!* "I have to deal with him. That's all there is to it."

I thanked them, waited for Elliot to give me the all clear, then left the breakroom. Cole was nowhere in sight. He'd probably went to the far back for a hair washing. Sadie got me taken care of quickly.

Elliot walked me out and waited with me while I got a taxi. "Remember, babe," he said in his "comforting best friend" voice, "it's okay to hurt. There's no getting around it, but don't let him keep you from living your life. Maverick wants you. From what you're telling me, he wants you badly." He took my hand, pulling out his best weapon. His eyes appeared to grow larger, his lips pouty. Puppies had nothing on him. "For me, please. Give Maverick a chance."

Damn him. "It's not that simple. I can't promise anything." I didn't think it was possible, but I swore Elliot's eyes grew larger. I felt like a total jerk. Closing my eyes, I huffed. "I can't promise anything, but I'll think about it."

Elliot's eyes went back to normal as he rolled them and let me go. "If that's the best I can get. At least you went on that diner date with him." A beaming grin replaced his pout. "That's how it starts, hun. You'll cave eventually, and if I remember Maverick correctly, you're in for the hottest, mind-blowing sex imaginable."

That's my Elliot. Ends everything with sex. Funny thing, though, I somehow knew he was right. Inside that work-efficient, frustration-inducing Brit lurked something bubbling. I experienced it each time Maverick stared at me. It was like he looked beyond my eyes into my soul, trying to learn everything about me, wanting to know how he could get behind my walls and find the right buttons to press. The thought made my skin break into gooseflesh and my cock throb.

What if I actually fall for him?

CHAPTER 13

The rest of the weekend passed without incident. Most of the checklists, namely various tasks around the apartment, work, and school, I had plastered to the refrigerator, bathroom mirror, and laptop all had marks in the "Yes" column. What few remained in the "No" were things I had to set aside time for in the coming weeks. I called my mom like I did each Sunday, and she, of course, wanted to know the situation with my love life. We gossiped—rather she caught me up—about Bethany and Polly. Bethany, my baby sister, was preparing to leave the nest after her boyfriend finally proposed. The news sent our mom into a fit of tears. She hadn't been alone in a long time and wasn't looking forward to it, though her pride in all of us burst from her in waves.

Later, Polly did her typical call and bicker, ending with a promise to be at Thanksgiving. That was Polly—hated many things in life but loved her family ... except for Rebecca and, sometimes, me. I looked forward to seeing everyone at the annual Cambrian family get-togethers.

I finished my college essay around 3 am Tuesday morning after changing subjects. My new concept was about how food brought people together and its role in important events like weddings. My professor loved the idea and repeated multiple times how he couldn't wait to read it. I couldn't either, hoping my subject would be enough to have me considered for the internship. Getting that position as an apprentice with a New Orleans chef would bolster my career. Especially when my main goal was to open my own restaurant in the French Quarter.

When I finally got to bed, I stared at my phone, my thumb hovering over an empty message window. Maverick's name on the address bar leered back at me, its glare like a waiting cobra. *If I go through with this, there's no going back, is there? Can I though?* Maverick didn't deserve to have his emotions toyed with—if that was indeed what it was going on. *Is it? Does he actually have feelings for me, or is he just trying to be nice and lessen the stress between us?*

I let the idea mull around in my mind, my heart sinking. *I bet that's what it is. He's feeling pressured. Probably because of how I've been acting.* By then, my chest felt like an anvil had fallen on it. If Maverick wanted to ease the strain at work, he probably just wanted to get to know me and find out why I flipped out. As my boss, he'd need to make sure no one saw our dynamic or became uncomfortable with it. *That has to be it. Right? Or am I doing what Elliot and my mom say and over-thinking things again?*

I put my phone on the nightstand. Stress tightened the muscles in my back, sternum, and lower stomach. I thought I might vomit from the mistake I nearly made by thinking Maverick's actions toward me meant more than they did.

That thought alone was enough to make me want to stay awake.

Roxxie jumped onto the bed, and her warm muzzle nestled into my arm. A soft whimper became heavy breathing as she fell asleep in the curvature of my armpit. I stroked her soft fur.

Just before I drifted off to sleep, I remembered thinking, *Either way, I'll find out tomorrow.*

Now, walking through the familiar glass doors with the large gold letters, my stomach twisted into knots at the thought of seeing Maverick again.

Once in the lobby, I placed a finger over my lips when Josh looked up from his phone. His brow arched, lips tight in a gesture saying, "What the hell are you doing?" I passed through the door separating the lobby from the back area, snuck by Judith's desk, and went to the breakroom to clock in.

So far, so good. Like a creeper, I peeked my head around the corner of the short hallway leading to Maverick's office. *Nowhere in sight. Where is he?* I'd almost made it to my office home free when I bumped into Dudley leaving the filing room.

"Woah!" Dudley said, arms waving to help him balance.

"Sorry, sorry." I jazz handed while speaking, careful to keep my tone low.

Dudley adjusted his coke-bottle glasses farther up his pug nose. "Aaron? Where are you going in such a hurry?" He blinked at me when I gestured for him to be quiet. "Why are you speaking so low?"

I smacked my forehead. *He would be the one to blast that like a bullhorn.*

Laughing sarcastically, I rubbed my nape. "No reason. Just a little fun." The excuse sucked. Hopefully, he bought it. "Can I get into my office now?"

Dudley's eyes lowered, causing his glasses to slide back down. He glanced back and forth like a nervous kid avoiding discipline. The files in his arms shifted with each clenching and unclenching of his hands.

Crossing my arms, I pinched my nose bridge. "Okay, stop. The suspense is killing me," I mocked. "Why are you acting like this?" *Please don't ask me out again. I'd hate to reject you a fiftieth time.*

"I'm afraid," Dudley said, "this isn't your office anymore."

My heart fell into my black boots. *Not my office?* Had Maverick really fired me? What had I done? Another thought struck me like Thor's hammer. *Did Travis somehow find out about the diner or the talk in the park?* If that were the case, I'd definitely sealed my fate.

"What do you mean?" I asked, trying not to let my firing nerves show.

Dudley shrugged. "I don't know. Mr. Waylan came downstairs and told me he had moved me into the main filing room." Something must've shown on my face. He quickly continued. "If it makes any difference, he didn't sound like he planned to do anything rash. He actually seemed very kind."

Kind? Yeah, I'll bet! No one would be a total dick to someone replacing their "terminated" colleague. My fists grew clammy the more I mulled over Maverick's reasoning. Yelling at the asshole would be a good idea if he wasn't my boss.

"Excuse me, Duds. Seems I need to have a word with Mr. Waylan," I said, turned, and left. My back and shoulder muscles hadn't let up since I arrived at the firm. Heading to Maverick's office, I concocted any manner of things I'd say to the arrogant bastard.

Maverick met me in the reception area of his office. Seeing him leaning against the doorjamb, checking his watch like he was waiting for his first appointment, sent my hormones into overdrive. *Damn it, I can't be mad when he's looking sexy like that.* No one should look as good as Maverick did. He was almost inhuman! Since he'd shown up, I'd pleasured myself almost nightly to avoid doing something stupid! Looking up from his watch, Maverick's eyes grew larger under his glasses when he noticed me, a hot smile curving over his perfectly white teeth.

"Good morning," he said in that mind-melting English accent. "I was just wondering where you were. You're never late."

My jaw ticked, nostrils flaring as I told myself to be strong against the sexual aura circling this man like a planet. "Mind telling me why *Dudley* is in *my* office, moving his things to *my* desk?"

Maverick remained silent, still smiling. It pissed me off royally.

"Did you really decide to fire me?" I asked, arms outstretched beside me.

"Aaron," Maverick interrupted.

I ignored him and kept ranting. "Why? Is it because of the coffee date thing?"

"Aaron," Maverick repeated slightly louder. He crossed his arms and feet, still propped against the doorway. Again, I ignored him. This went on a few more times, like a scene from a reality show. Maverick ended it, saying, "I didn't fire you."

That shut me up, and if I were honest, I appreciated it. The ruckus likely looked ridiculous, but I couldn't keep myself from laying into the guy. He frustrated the fuck out of me!

My body slowly eased into a less tight mess. I felt more confused than reassured. "Then why give Dudley my desk?"

Maverick straightened, placing his hands in his pockets. "Come into my office. There's something we need to discuss."

A throat lump threatened to choke me. *Is this where I learn the truth? Where he tells me if he remembers me as the moron from the bar? Or tell me he's only been nice because he wanted us to work together?* My shoulders slumped like a dejected teenager. I wasn't sure I could take another rejection. *What else can I do but get ready to have my heart crushed... Then again, it's not like I'd said anything to Maverick about ... what exactly? The way my cock stands at attention when I see him? How weird a conversation would that be? The way I nearly texted him when Cole showed up, or how I think about him when I...* Definitely a weird conversation and none of them sharable with my boss.

I followed Maverick into his office like a man walking toward the hangman's noose. *What's the worst thing I'll have to do? Look for another job?*

Maverick waited by his office door for me to enter. The delicious smell of his cologne punched me in the face, sending porno movie fantasies flickering through my mind. He closed the door and stepped around where I stood paralyzed.

"You needn't stand there," he said, leaning his fine ass against the oak desk.

I took in the familiar gunmetal grey suit, tie, white shirt, and black Italian shoes. The only thing I could think about was what kind of body he hid under all that. *Fuck. Could I please get a grip?*

As though he knew what I thought, Maverick grinned. "Have a seat, Aaron."

"I ... uh." I cleared my throat. "I'd like to stand if that's okay."

Maverick nodded. "Very well." He closed his eyes and removed his glasses, setting them on his desk. His attention returned to me, all business. But that subtle deviousness lingered somewhere in his darkened eyes. "Mr. Crosley is in your former office because I offered him a new position."

Yeah, I got that. "What does that have to do with me? If I'm not fired, then where am I supposed to put my things or work?"

Maverick's grin widened. I swallowed again, knees threatening to drop my full weight to the floor.

"Simple. I have promoted you," he said. "Congratulations. You're my new paralegal. That desk," he gestured to the empty desk, "is now yours."

My eyes widened until they burned. "Wait, what!" That was not what I expected in any scenario. Especially after how I'd acted in the hall and when Maverick first arrived. Like a babbling brook, I rambled, "Why? I don't have any experience with that kind of work. Leslie does! She worked for Travis for years. Why not ask her?"

Maverick waggled his finger and stood. "I have observed you these past weeks. You have the eye for detail and organization that I need to make my office run smoothly. Perhaps you noticed I'm very particular about how I want things to work. I don't doubt Miss Abernathy's efficiency. That isn't the issue." He shook his head. "No, it must be you. I will work you hard, but I know you can do this."

Words stuck on my dried tongue. I *did* like order, and Maverick had cleaned up Travis's mess, including getting new computers and cleaner files. The firm ran so well the papers had renewed their buzz about it since Mr. Kimball's death.

Silence lingered between us as I searched for anything to say—any excuse for why I didn't want to take the position. It wasn't because I'd get a promotion. The slight pay increase would help pay my tuition. And I didn't mind extra work.

What bothered me was the proximity! I'd be at Maverick's beck and call, forced to see him way more often than I did delivering files or in the breakroom. On the other hand, being close would offer me more opportunity to follow Elliot's advice and give Maverick a chance. But that didn't make this decision any easier.

"What do you say?" Maverick asked.

I exhaled, dropping my head. "Not like I have a choice, do I?"

"Sadly, no." A large hand landed on my shoulder. I snapped back to meet down-turned eyes. The corners of Maverick's mouth mimicked his eyes. He looked sad, like the thought I might walk instead of accepting his offer hurt him. "Is being my assistant such a horrible thing?"

I shook my head, hands waving rapidly. "No, no. It's not that. I ... it's just..." I couldn't breathe, sweat beaded on my brow ridge, and my mouth dried. Racing blood from my head dizzied me. *I really like you.*

The air became heavier the longer Maverick searched my eyes the same way he did when I thought he saw into my mind, heart, and soul. It was like he knew how he made me feel. How my body reacted to his touch.

"It's just what?" Maverick asked without a hint of emotion. His hand drifted from my shoulder to my forearm, the touch so gentle, I fought a shudder.

Gnawing on my bottom lip bought me time to flip through my mental excuse book—none of which sounded like something Maverick would buy. Telling the truth definitely wasn't an option. Everything I mulled over sounded sad and overused—namely things involving my busy schedule, my lack of training, or how I didn't want to. The latter flew into the "No" column of a checklist faster than a week-old sandwich.

"Fine. I'll go get my stuff," I said.

The frown fell from Maverick's face, his smile radiant yet reserved. "Thank you."

"You don't need to—" I stopped, realizing the closeness of Maverick's body. The heat radiating from him threatened to overwhelm me. My eyes sank to his lips. *Man, I really want to kiss those.*

"Yes, I do." Maverick smiled and leaned closer to murmur in my ear, causing my skin to break into gooseflesh. "I want to *know* you, Aaron. I want you to trust *me* as I trust you."

I backstepped, hitting the chair with my calf. Sweat formed around my collar and dripped down my back. "Um, I'm going to go..." my finger pointed to the door, "get my stuff now."

"Aaron," Maverick said. I glanced over my shoulder. Maverick had his arms crossed, crumpling the already tight fabric of his jacket and shirt. His eyes' examination hadn't gone unnoticed. "I look forward to working with you."

To keep my blush hidden, I rushed from the room.

CHAPTER 14

"Aaron, I'm so sorry!" I heard Leslie shout, the sound of her high heels clacking on the floor. I'd packed another box of desk decor from my previous station and was headed toward Maverick's office when she reached me. Leslie bent over at the waist, holding up a finger. "Sorry. It's hard to run in these."

"It's ... okay, Les. What's up?" I asked, sorry she felt she needed to sprint. "Everything okay with Frankie?" If things between them weren't working out, I'd have a word with the guy.

"What? No, no. Everything's fine! Frankie's a wonderful guy." She straightened, readjusting her dress. "You know how I get everyone coffee in the morning once a week?" I nodded. "Well, I totally forgot about yours! They made it, and I forgot it!" Tiny hands closed around my forearm. "Aaron, I'm so sorry! You must think I'm a horrible friend!"

Another side of Leslie that made her so cute: her worry and need to apologize over everything. Her choice to get coffee for everyone came about before Mr. Kimball died. He'd asked us all to choose a day we'd like him to pay for coffee, and we all decided Tuesday would be great. The tradition stuck after Mr. Kimball's passing.

I looked into my friend's misty doll-eyes, smiled, and shook my head. "It's fine. You don't have to apologize." To make her squirm, I closed my eyes and cocked my head like a smug bastard, nose in the air and all. "I think I can forgive you if you make breakroom coffee. Judith already made it but I do not want to subject my stomach to that torture again."

Leslie's lips pursed, her cheeks slightly puffed. "Fine, slave driver." She cocked her hip, arms folded. "Anything else I can get his majesty before I return to my peasant duties?"

We both laughed. *This is the Leslie I know and love.* "Nah, I think that is all, fair lady," I replied.

I turned to leave, again stopping when Leslie asked, "Is it true?"

Oh no. How far have the office rumor boats drifted? "Is what true?"

"That Mr. Waylan promoted you to his personal desk jockey without asking." Leslie's face had changed from pouty, cocky, and now—*is she mad?*—in five minutes. "It is true, isn't it?"

I knew better than to test Leslie when she got like this. All joking—or willingness to joke—was a mask for her big sister persona. Despite my being older, Leslie always found a need to watch over me. Hell, she did it to all of us she considered friends, but I'd known her as long as I'd known Elliot. We used to work in the same bar and vouched for one another when the firm jobs came up. Leslie wanted to be a lawyer until her mother fell ill, and Leslie had to drop out of school to take care of her.

"Yeah," I said. "It's true. But it's not that bad. The pay raise will help with tuition, and the location will get me out of that stuffy file room." I chuckled. "Honestly, have you ever tried sitting in those chairs? They're made for hobbits. I'm a big guy! I need my space."

My attempt at light humor didn't work. Leslie lowered her arms, stepped forward, and gently touched my hand. "I only want to make sure it's what you want. You know how much I want you to be happy. Doesn't seem fair he up and demanded you move like that."

Don't I know it. "I'll be fine. Thanks for worrying." The heavy box in my arms made my muscles tremble. "If it's okay with you, I'd really like to set this down. I'll get some coffee in a few."

Leslie nodded, and we parted ways.

The walk to my desk felt more like walking to the gallows. Tension mounted; my heartbeat skyrocketed. Maverick's decision to promote me had come as a surprise, though not a fully unwelcome one. I wanted to find out if he was attracted to me or was just being nice. I wouldn't learn either stuck in the filing room or only seeing Maverick in passing. Texting sounded like a good idea, but what if he only wanted to make a better work environment? How awkward would reading the guy's signals wrong be?

He said he wanted to know me. To make me trust him. Why would he want that? I couldn't figure it out. Theories about our office relationship went out the window with compact discs. *Does someone who wants to make a peaceful office space care about trust or wanting to know someone?*

The deep thoughts distracted me. The box in my arms filled with various kitchen-based knickknacks stared back at me. Everything I thought I wanted danced opposite the fantasies about Maverick. *Stay focused. Think about what you want for yourself, Aaron.*

The next thing I knew, I hit a wall—namely Maverick's body walking toward the lobby door—sending me backstepping, almost falling on my ass.

"Easy," Maverick said. He took the box from my arms and set it on the desk. "I thought you might want some help."

I readjusted my vest, shirt, and collar. "Thanks. That box got heavy quickly. Think it's the last one, though."

Maverick half-chuckled. "Good to know." His hand extended. In it, a piece of yellow paper.

Muscles in my lip and eye twitched. "What is that?"

My boss drifted closer, our foreheads almost touching. A mischievous smile drew his lips upward. "It's my coffee order."

You have to be fucking kidding me! The urge to slam my fist into his perfect face replaced any emotion brought on by the sexy-as-sin lawyer.

Maverick threw his head back, laughing, though not loud enough to alert the entire department. "I'm kidding. It's what I'd like you to get done today. I know you like lists."

I wanted to kill the guy. "Oh yeah, and how do you know I like lists?"

"You covered your old computer monitor with them. I assumed that's how you liked to organize things, which is why I made one for you." Maverick reached into his pocket, producing another note. This time a pink sticky. "*This* is how I like my coffee."

I'm going to fucking kill this man!

"I heard Miss Abernathy say she was making some." Maverick angled his head to the ceiling, raising his hand to rub his temple. "Heaven knows I'll never drink Judy's again. I thought it would burn a hole in my stomach."

Angry or not, I loved how karma kicked this guy in the balls pay-it-forward style. *Serves him right for not asking before "promoting"* me. *And for telling me how he likes his coffee like I was some tart he could order around.*

To give Maverick some salt to lick, I propped a hand on my desk. "Maybe next time you'll think before you drink." I shoved his "coffee" order back at his chest. Doing so was a huge mistake. *His chest is ... it's so hard. God, what is he hiding under there?*

Like a shark to blood, Maverick jumped at whatever physical signs betrayed me. "Something bothering you, Aaron?" He pinned me between the desk and his body, hands on either side of my hips. *Yes. Please. Touch me. What am I thinking? No!* "Aren't you going to finish that brief stab of yours? Or do you feel something you like?"

I shifted my thoughts from horny teenager to baffled holdout. *Did he just say what I think he said? Right here? In his office?* As if my thoughts about him touching me weren't weird and out-of-place enough!

"I can see this is going to be great fun. You like to play games. So do I." Maverick's eyes bulged from his skull the moment he ended his sentence. He reminded me of a deer blinded by the headlights of a truck. The poor animal had no idea death drew closer until it was too late.

That was how I felt thinking about what this man said. I didn't know what passed between us. But I knew he felt it too. This moment—this smartass exchange I started to get Maverick back for wanting me to get his coffee—something neither of us had seen coming.

I couldn't help it; my cheeks heated, eyes dropping. Anything to break the connection. "I should probably ... get started on this list."

Maverick closed his eyes and backed away, letting me go without a fight. The withdrawal stung worse than I thought.

"You probably should. Go get your coffee first. I want you alert for the day ahead."

"Okay," I said, unsure why I sounded like a dejected lover. My heart hammered my ribs. Pinching at the zipper of my work pants led me to adjust myself. *What just happened? Games? What did he mean by games? Am I playing a game?* If I was, I didn't know. Though the jab I made had meant to tease him a little. And the cocky way I leaned against my desk appeared more sexy "yes, invite me to bed" than I intended. *Oh God, did I just start something?*

I looked back at Maverick, who appeared put together. He stared at my desk, brows crinkled like he was angry. I saw— or rather felt—a hint of confusion emanating from him. *He feels it too. How much trouble have I gotten myself into?*

Maverick limited his interaction with me for the rest of the day. *He's probably thinking the same thing I am. Weighing his options on how bad—not to mention potentially dangerous— teasing one another might be.*

Around 6:30, a nasty strand of storms moved in, rattling the windows. A perk of the office living on a higher floor, we often left work early if a cell called for a tornado or a risk of one. I'd always appreciated that policy.

A groan escaped my throat as I lifted my arms above my head. Bones popped in my neck as I moved from side to side. My back did the same after I stood. *Ow.* I rubbed my head against the dizziness. Despite the ergonomic chair, I experienced some discomfort in the lumbar region.

"Aaron," Maverick called from his office. "Would you come in here for a moment?"

I didn't like the stern tone. Anytime someone used that voice with me, it meant I'd done something wrong and likely had a punishment coming my way.

After turning off my computer, I collected my jacket, phone, and backpack with my college books in it. I took the books to the office in case spare time opened up and I could study.

"Yes?" I asked, peaking through his door. The rest of me followed when he glared at me. *This is it. I'm so fired. And all because I couldn't keep my mouth shut or control my over-eager cock.*

Maverick closed his laptop, leaned back in his chair, and propped an ankle on his thigh. "You did well today as I knew you would." Off came the hipster frames, folded and put on his desk. He rubbed his nose bridge with a thumb and fore-finger. "That isn't why I called you in. I won't be long since I know you have Roxxie to feed."

Our eyes met. I couldn't get a read on what Maverick was thinking. He appeared to be studying and weighing his options. Without a word, he stood, crossed around his desk, and drew closer to me. Each calculated step made him appear more like a model.

I debated on bolting, buying myself more time to think. I'd met this man a few weeks ago, wound up in his bed drunk, and resigned myself never to see him again, only to have him become my boss. The whole scenario had played out like a sick joke written by a twisted mind!

What happened after sent my heart into drumline speed. I thought I'd have a heart attack.

Maverick closed the distance between us, crowding into me until my back landed against the wall. The hungry eyes from the cocktail bar had returned. *That's it. It is him. I'd never mistake those eyes, no matter how drunk I was.* There was no doubt left in my mind. *Maverick Waylan is the man from the bar.*

CHAPTER 15

Maverick's nearness gave me the perfect chance to reach out and touch him. *Or do something stupider, like steal a kiss and risking getting thrown out on my ass.*

"Forgive me," Maverick said, his voice husky, head dropping. A brief silence—save for the heartbeats in my ears and Maverick's heavier breathing—lingered between us. When Maverick finally raised his head, his eyes had turned from their usual hypnotizing jade to a smoldering deep green. Keeping my mouth shut took my willpower to the end of its rope.

"Aaron, I am a very patient man. I can wait out the most stubborn people, but you ... you have surpassed many before you." Hastened breaths pushed the smell of fresh hazelnuts and a hint of something I couldn't place into my face. The scent intoxicated me, making my mind journey to the forbidden thoughts of what being with this man right now in his office would feel like. "There's something I want to ask you."

I swallowed, my head a storm of dizziness, anticipation, and terror at what Maverick might say. Sweat dripped down my spine and clammed up my hands. I'd dreamed of him doing something like this, had fantasies that would make a porn director blush. But now that he'd actually followed through with the pent up tension I knew we both felt, I got scared. Every memory of every rejection played out in my mind. The last time I'd dared fall for someone, they'd hurt me in the worst ways.

"I..." I tried saying anything while avoiding the man's eyes. "I should probably..." I attempted to duck his arm to get more space, but he moved it farther down to keep me from leaving.

"Not yet. I've let you run, given you time, but not anymore." He moved in closer. I wanted to stop playing these games, go home with him, and release the frustration I'd dealt with on my own for weeks. Strong fingers took my jaw, leading me to look into the eyes I'd fought to avoid. "I'm tired of this. You are too. I can see it. You're incredibly observant, Aaron. I know you can sense what I feel."

Subtle trembling began at my fingertips as I fought raising my hands, wanting to throw all caution and worry about what anyone would think or say through the window and embrace Maverick's mouth in a boxer-brief-melting kiss. But I hesitated. If I kept these fantasies to myself, I wouldn't risk getting hurt.

My eyes drifted to Maverick's lips. The smile across them showed me he noticed. He moved closer until only inches remained between our mouths.

Please ... please kiss me. I battled shutting my eyes and closing the distance to take Maverick Waylan in our first kiss.

"There's something you need to know," Maverick said, his heated breath teasing my lips. "Something I want you to know if this goes any further."

If? Did I read this wrong? "You ... um ... have a boyfriend?" I asked, trying to alleviate the sexual tension.

Maverick blinked a couple times, then laughed that glorious laugh capable of tearing every ounce of will from me. "No, Aaron, I'm not seeing anyone." His eyes narrowed.

"Though I hope to change that soon. Come to dinner with me. Tomorrow after work."

Tomorrow? Isn't that sudden? What does he think I need to know? Is he finally going to tell me he is the guy from the bar? Are there going to be conditions I have to follow to be with him? Does he expect me to be his dirty little office secret? I wouldn't do that again. Couldn't do that again.

"I don't know," I said. *Why not, you idiot? This is your chance to find out!* Was I scared to learn the truth? Terrified what Maverick might have to say? Or would I get angry at him? Angry he'd let this twisted game between us play out for weeks. I'd spent days tormenting myself, wracking my brain trying to find out if Maverick was the guy from the bar.

Elliot's words ghosted in my head. *Let this play out. See where this goes.* I would be taking a risk, breaking from what I knew was safe, but as I stared into Maverick's hungry, longing eyes, I found I didn't care.

"I'll need to go home, get cleaned up and change," I replied, my cheeks a tanning bed of heat by now. "Would that be okay?"

The crinkled brows slowly relaxed. Maverick's demeanor softened and changed into one a relieved man might have after working up the guts to ask his crush out. His mouth turned up into a smile, and his eyes relaxed at the corners. The muscular arms caging me against the wall fell to their owner's sides.

A single strand of his hair broke free from the rest. I almost melted, watching Maverick push it from his glistening forehead. "You've no idea how glad I am to hear those words. Yes. That's fine. I'll pick you up around 8:00. There's a restaurant I think you might enjoy, considering your current interests."

"How...?"

Maverick waggled his finger, tsking through his teeth. "Not now. I promise I'll reveal more tomorrow."

I grabbed my leather jacket, turned, and left, my heart racehorse kicking at my ribs all the way to the elevator. On the ride down, my eyes stared at my feet. *There's so many things wrong with this. So many ways this could go wrong. He's my boss.* My hand hit my eye socket. *No, this is so stupid! He's my boss! What will everyone say?*

I'd just gotten a damn promotion. If I slept with Maverick, rumors might circulate that I'd spread my legs to get where I was. I also had my college dreams to think about.

Let this play out. Elliot's words sounded mocking. I lowered my hand, took a deep breath, and repeated my friend's words out loud.

The following day, New York's sky opened in a fury. Lightning reflected off the building windows. Thunder bounced and echoed loudly. And the weather wasn't the only thing out of sorts.

My day started with a trip over Roxxie and an unpleasant meeting with the kitchen floor. After making sure I hadn't severely injured myself, I rushed through my morning routine, running past all the checklists on the refrigerator in a frenzy on my way out the door. My hands shook so badly from the other day's encounter with Maverick I nearly dropped my morning coffee after running into a guy on his phone. I apologized, backed away, and ran out to the street for a taxi.

In the state I was, I forgot my umbrella, relying on my jacket pulled over my head to keep me dry. The makeshift "umbrella" did little, and I wound up damp from my boots to my knees. I lost both my coffee and muffin in my rush to get out of the taxi and into the warm, dry building. All the way up the elevator, I cursed internally, wanting to know if life was finished using me as its personal punching bag.

Once through the glass door and into the breakroom, my mind broke from the physical realm, blocking all external noise. I didn't hear Josh calling my name until he came up behind me while I clocked in.

"Hey!" he shouted next to my ear. I jumped, squeaking like a teenage girl whose parents caught her in bed with her secret boyfriend. Josh leaned against the wall. "Okay, talk," he ordered, a hand on his hip. "I've known you to space out, man, but nothing like this. You're actually late. Do you know how much that makes me feel like I'm in an alternate dimension?"

Tell me about it. I felt the same. Especially now that I entertained the idea of going on a—*what was this exactly? A date? Or something more* casual, *like the diner?*

"Sorry. Lot on my mind. What was it you needed again?" I asked, locking my things in a locker and taking the key.

"Marks wants you to take the guest list for the renaming of the firm. I swear, the guy has become a kiss ass since Waylan showed up."

"Yeah, I'll ...I'll take it," I said. Thinking about going back into that office after last night brought a heated flush. *Maybe he'll actually kiss me this time.*

"Good," Josh replied. He started leaving. "By the way, between you and me, don't."

The sudden comment hit like a dodgeball. When he didn't continue, I said, "Okay, I'll bite. Don't what?"

Josh's smile widened to reveal his perfect teeth. "Don't worry about what we think." I opened my mouth to protest his insinuation, stopping when he held up a hand. "Please. We all know. It's not like your super weirdness these past few weeks hasn't told on you. Go for it. He's hot as hell and perfect for someone as Type A as you."

"I am not—" I hushed when Josh lowered his head and raised his brow. My lips pursed.

"Yep, that's what I thought. Anyway, I'm glad for you, man. Tell me how it goes," Josh said, then left me alone to ponder my Type A-ness.

Josh's words haunted me all the way to Maverick's office. The door remained ajar, and Maverick's voice flowed out, a siren song leading the unsuspecting—and overly horny—to their doom. Like a curious child on Christmas Eve, I tiptoed closer to listen.

"I don't care what she wants. This is my life to live as I see fit."

She? Did Maverick have an ex-wife or something? Someone he left behind overseas, or maybe from his time in the States? *Stop. Don't make any stupid assumptions. Maybe it's his sister or something.*

Squeaking of the chair wheels and the sound of whining leather accompanied Maverick's quickened rise from his seat. I peaked in to see him leaning over his desk, a death glare on his face. A thick knot blocked my throat. I'd never seen him so angry.

"I've said what needs to be said. Know this, Connor. If she, or you, or anyone in that family does something foolish, I don't care who she thinks I am to her. I'll disappear, and she'll never hear from me again." Maverick didn't give "Connor" a chance to reply, slamming his phone into its holder.

Afraid of what he might think of my eavesdropping, I tiptoed back toward my desk. My heel thunked against the desk corner, making me grit my teeth and wince. I glanced at Maverick's door. There was a sound, but he didn't come through right away, leaving me enough time to slide my chair back and sit.

Damn, remind me not to piss him off. I don't know who that is, but I feel sorry for poor Connor.

Whoever Connor was, he gave me a glimpse into Maverick's personal life. Their one-sided talk didn't sound like it happened between strangers. My heart became lead at the thought Connor might be an ex. Like my mind usually did, it formed thoughts of Maverick being married to the guy or divorcing him. *And who was this unnamed woman? Does Maverick go for guys and girls? Maybe whoever tickles his interest? Does that mean ... I'm just a temporary thing?* That thought pissed me off. The last thing I wanted to be was some "piece of ass" for a silver-spoon Brit. I'd done that before, and dammit, I wouldn't do it again.

My thoughts bubbled like a cauldron when Maverick finally came out, sighing loudly and stretching his arms above his head. He looked a mess—his sexy hair undone on the left side, allowing a few sprigs to flop over his black-circled eyes—and tired.

When he saw me, a smile replaced his frown. "Good morning." Both of his shoulders relaxed as he sauntered over and leaned on his forearms on the desk's left cubby. I guessed he saw the scowl—or heard my grumbling—because his head tilted like Roxxie's when she thought I was mad. "Something wrong? You aren't canceling on me tonight, are you?"

Canceling on him? God, what an asshole. I let my eyes drift to look at him. He'd shed the blue suit jacket, his tie dangling over the desk's edge. The white button-up shirt offered a teasing hint at the chest I'd dreamed of seeing multiple times. *A very sexy asshole.*

"No, I'm not canceling," I said, averting my eyes when he noticed my ogling. "Just got a lot to do today for a certain bossy Brit."

Maverick chuckled. "Good thing you're getting comfortable enough to make such comments. I wondered if you might fear me."

Damn, he's arrogant. Hot and arrogant. Not a good combo. "Don't flatter yourself." I opened my email and prepared to start the day's assignments.

Maverick straightened and leaned his back against the desk, arms and ankles crossed. The jovial smile reverted to a flat lined mouth. Both eyes seemed to stare off into another world. I couldn't help myself; I had to ask. But doing so bluntly could land me in the "creeper" zone.

"Doing okay?" I asked between checking his calendar and scrolling through emails.

Maverick shrugged. "I'd be lying if I said yes. Today didn't start out ... nicely." I kept quiet, letting him talk. "But that's not important." His smile returned. "I'm looking forward to meeting you tonight. You won't believe how long I've wanted to tell you what I'm going to."

I remained quiet. Again, he'd dodged telling me about himself. In the weeks he'd been at the firm, I knew he'd been keeping secrets about his family. I wasn't sure why those secrets hurt as badly as they did. *Maybe it's because I want him to trust me. Or...*

The last thought didn't get finished.

116

CHAPTER 16

"**N**o coffee or muffin this morning?" Maverick asked, the last two words rising an octave.

I didn't appreciate the sudden change in conversation yet entertained him since he seemed to need it. The way his eyebrow tilted high reminded me of my little sister when she thought I stole her hairbrush and hid it. My older sister was almost always the culprit, claiming since she had "seniority," she had the right to the fancy hairbrush and pins.

"Lost them," I replied, deadpan, my attention on the calendar. "You have a court date coming up next week. Oh, and a subpoena needs delivering."

Maverick ignored the work banter. The guy likely knew I was trying to distract him. He read me like an open book. "How could you lose them?" When I didn't answer, my boss pulled rank, walked behind me, and turned my monitor off. "Ever heard of an umbrella? You're soaked."

Thank you, Captain Obvious. Like I already am not in a horrible mood. "I hadn't noticed." Thanks to the erection I fought to hide, my groin already chafed. "Can I please get back to work? I'd like to forget how bad my morning's been."

Maverick pulled my chair back and spun it. The guy's "Dr. Jekyll and Mr. Hot" routine—as Elliot liked to call it—both infuriated me and turned me on. Blazing jade eyes analyzed me. "Let me help you with that. Soaked polyester can be such a hassle and leave the most wretched chafes in," Maverick paused, lowering his gaze, "unfortunate places."

My breathing hastened. Blood blistered in my veins. Whatever restraints Maverick kept on himself the few short weeks he'd been here had disappeared, and I was the one in his crosshairs.

This must be the real Maverick. The one behind all the efficiency, secrecy, and cordial gentlemanliness. "I..." I tore my eyes from him. If I didn't, I'd probably do something stupid, like beg him to finish the kiss he started the night before. *Think of something. Anything. Anything to throw him off.* "I'll be okay. There's actually a spare set I keep in my locker."

Maverick straightened, his eyes lighter after I doused the heat. "That's good," he said, voice deflated like I'd refused him a chance to see me take my pants off. "Get changed then. You're correct. I have a subpoena and a few other files to be delivered and picked up from the courthouse." A devious, I'm-getting-you-back smirk crossed his face. "And guess who's going to do the deliveries?"

Son of a bitch! "Are you kidding me?" I shouted.

Maverick shook his head, took a sticky note and a pen, and started writing. "Not at all. You are my assistant; therefore, it is your job." He handed me the note and a credit card. I couldn't believe what I read. "Get yourself one, too. And a muffin if you like. I'll cover it today."

I reiterate: SON. OF. A. BITCH! Is he seriously sending me out in this downpour to get him some damn coffee?

Maverick's smirk made me want to hit and kiss him. Or maybe hit him, then kiss him to help ease the pain. Not telling him he'd have to rely on his hand to stroke his overgrown ego tonight took every ounce of stubbornness I had.

Instead, I threw his attitude back at him. "Anyone ever tell you how much of a frustrating dick you can be?"

Maverick burst out laughing, drawing near enough to kiss me. Warm breath passed over my lips, the potent smell of cinnamon blew into my face. *Did he chew some gum?* My cock strained against my polyester pants, making me painfully aware of how badly I wanted to sample him. Keeping my eyes from rolling to the back of my head in sheer ecstasy became a losing battle. I opened my mouth, if only to taste his breath.

"You've no idea." In a move rivaling a Russian ballet dancer, Maverick pulled my chair away and spun it to face the door. "Now, get that pretty little ass of yours out of that chair. I'm aching to finish the workday so we can meet tonight."

Did he really just say that to me? Here? Where ANYONE can hear him? I admitted inwardly how hot the timbre of his voice made me. *I guess he's really through dancing around.* My uncertainty jostled me momentarily until Josh's words that I shouldn't care what anyone in the office thought swept my hesitation away.

I stood, careful to keep the chair between Maverick and me. *If he wants to be like this, he's in for a surprise. I can play, too.* I raised my nose at my boss, smiling a coy smile and teasing my tongue over my teeth. Maverick's eyes followed the gesture.

In that moment, I knew I had to get out of there, or we'd both wind up in his office doing something I wasn't ready to do at work.

The rest of the workday passed by with little upset aside from a few colleagues at the courthouse—of the female variety—who wanted to know if I'd give Maverick their phone numbers. Hearing their swooning, near orgasmic tones brought a slight puff to my chest. I'd had no idea how well-known Maverick was in his world of law. Knowing he wanted me was elating and terrifying.

Maverick remained in his office, all flirtatious and jovial moods sucked from him. I wanted to ask why the sudden change yet kept it to myself, guessing Maverick's mind had drifted back to the phone call.

I suffered too, thinking about the night and how the dinner would go. *Would he want to go back to his place?* Damn, I sure did. What gay man could look at a guy like Maverick Waylan and not want him to fuck their brains out?

A quick glance at the clock: 5:30. Time to call the day and enjoy the weekend. I thought of nudging Maverick's door open to see if he knew. *Bad idea. We might not make it to dinner if I do.* My feet took me to the breakroom, finding Leslie, who beamed when she saw me. Had I not noticed her, she might've knocked me to my ass with the force of her hug.

"I'm so happy for you!" she said, keeping her voice down. *Wow, word travels fast. Had Maverick told her? God, does Travis know?* "What took you so damn long? Geez, Aaron, I thought you'd never say yes."

"Wait, what?" My eyes bulged. *How obvious was I?* "You knew?"

Leslie put both hands on my shoulders and pushed, her eyes rolling. "Hello? The running, the hiding, the avoidance. You didn't exactly hide it well. "The only thing you didn't do is jerk off in the office bathroom while thinking of him." My cheeks heated. "Oh my gosh, you're so bad. You did!" Leslie chuckled. "You so did."

I confessed to nothing. "Keep it down. Please tell me Travis doesn't know."

Leslie punched out, handed me my timecard, and moved so I could do the same. "You're kidding, right? Travis is oblivious to anyone not sucking his cock under his desk. And I highly doubt he's thinking while Brianna's mouth fucking him."

Brianna Wagner worked in the copy room. She had the hots for Travis for as long as Dudley had them for me. I had secretly hoped they'd end up together since they both shared the same geeky hobbies. I didn't want to believe she'd lowered herself to be Travis's new cock sleeve since Leslie told him to go fuck himself.

"Wow, that's harsh. Must be pretty desperate to get laid," I replied. I put my timecard back in its slot, wondering if Maverick planned on fixing the archaic form of timekeeping. "Seriously though, everyone knows?"

Leslie rolled her head toward me. Her shoulders went up, hands palm up in a "duh" pose. "Speaking of getting laid." She elbowed my ribs. "You and Maverick?"

Had this been the cartoon where the cat drank wine only to spew it out when asked a shocking question, I'd be the cat. Sleep with Maverick? On our first date or whatever it was? Sure, I'd thought about it. Fantasized about it. Secretly hoped for it. But now that Leslie had dropped the "L" bomb, I didn't know what to expect.

"I ... I don't know," I said, rubbing my nape. "It's only our first ... you know..."

"So?" Frankie chimed in, joining Leslie and me on our walk to the elevator. "Hey, babe," he said and kissed Leslie like I wasn't there. *Guess I know what those two are doing tonight.* "C'mon, man. You totally want to fuck him. Nothing wrong with that. He clearly wants you. I mean, badly. Been asking everyone questions about you."

He's been what? "He asked about me?"

Leslie and Frankie nodded.

"Like, what kinds of questions?" They glanced at each other like fellow convicts in a hidden conspiracy. "Really?" I asked, huffing and crossing my arms. "Traitors."

They both laughed.

"Seriously though," Frankie said. "Good luck tonight. I'll admit I was the last one who figured out the big secret."

My toe tapped the floor. I leaned a hip against the railing while the lovebirds went at each other for the rest of the ride. *What exactly do I want to happen tonight? Anything? What is this? A date? A get to know you?* Each question sounded like a reworded repeat of a previous one. Maverick hadn't made his intentions clear, and I wanted to make sure I didn't ride my dick into another poor decision. *Would Maverick want to do anything or even be interested?* My head rested against the elevator wall. *I know what I want. I ... want him.*

Loud pinging and the doors sliding open signaled the end of our ride. The lobby's dark marble floor reflected my face back at me when I stepped out.

With one last glance at Leslie and Frankie, I slumped my shoulders and marched to the parking garage.

I arrived home to find Roxxie waiting patiently by the door. *I swear my dog knows how to read a clock. She always knows when I'm supposed to get home.* Bending at my waist, I ran my fingers through her soft fur. Her tail smacked the floor with a loud "thud."

"Sorry, Rox, no walk tonight. Got a ... date. I think." I said, setting my keys on the door-side table. I hung my jacket on the mounted hooks. Roxxie followed me into the kitchen, where I refilled her food and water bowl. *I'll have to let her out before I go.*

I left Roxxie to eat while I walked down the short hallway to my bedroom. The small apartment wasn't ideal for a six-foot, broader-shouldered guy like me. Some of the narrower doors—namely closets—were a pain to get into. My laptop waited on the small corner desk. *I should check my email before leaving. Maybe the prof sent something about that position.*

Curiosity prompted me to turn on the local food network to see if Dad's show was on. Lucky me, it was, and I watched the man both congratulate and condemn the contestants. *Poor bastards. Wouldn't want to be them right now.*

My chest muscles tightened. Fists formed at my sides. My heart felt heavier than an Acme anvil. Seeing my father act like the next Ramsey or Cowell pissed me off. I grabbed the remote, turned off the television, and threw the damn thing across the room. If the remote broke, I didn't care. I'd bought the stupid television.

I need a shower. Reminding myself of how much I hated the sperm-donor always made me feel filthy. I turned on the shower in time to hear my phone ring from the kitchen. When I reached it, I saw my sister, Rebecca, calling. *This can't be good.* I swallowed and answered.

"Hey, little brother," Rebecca said, her voice betraying her fatigue.

Who knows how long she's stayed in her office this time? "Hey, Bex, how are things going?" I asked.

Rebecca's sigh caused her voice to turn robotic. "Not great. Especially with this new headline about you and some rich boyfriend."

Great, I'm in for the nagging of a lifetime. "Not my fault. The camera vultures need fresh stories now that our dear old dad's show is gaining momentum. Besides, he's not my boyfriend."

"I'm happy for you. You know that. You deserve to be happy. Be careful for a while, though. For all I know, our dear old dad is the one riling up the press." Rebecca took a breath. "You know how he is. All the better to screw you with, my dear."

We shared a genuine laugh. It felt good to tease one another, even during a dark situation.

"I promise I'll be as careful as I can, Bex. You should probably get onto Polly more than me. Remember, she likes the press. Good or bad, doesn't matter as long as she's in it." I checked my watch. "Listen, I'd love to chat more, but I have—" I didn't get to finish the thought.

"Say no more." Rebecca sounded like a teasing girl I used to chase in our front yard. "You can deny it all you want. But you and I both know this is a date."

Uuuuugh. "It's not a date, Bex. I don't know what it is, but I'm not meeting someone tonight smelling like sweat and desperation. Not sure he's into that." We both laughed again. "I'll be careful. Promise. Love you."

"Love you too, baby brother. I'll text when I can. Hopefully, it won't all be dad drama." She paused, then added, "Wear that cologne I got you for Christmas. It smells super sexy. It drove Tammy Ryan insane!"

I rolled my eyes. "I'll do that." *Hopefully, that woodsy, musky smell is something Maverick likes.* "Hey, Bex?"

"Yes?"

I'm fixing to sound really, REALLY desperate. "I'm really into this guy." My cheeks heated. Here I was asking my big sister how to tempt Maverick to fuck me. "Any ... you know ... tips?" *Wow, like you've never tempted a guy back to your bed before?*

Awkward silence filled my ears, along with the occasional static. I walked the hall to my bedroom and took my shirt off.

"Umm, might want to ask Elliot about that. I'm not exactly entertaining a thriving social life nowadays. Just be yourself. Let him know you're available. Not by throwing yourself at him, but you know, be sexy. I have to go. Paperwork needs finishing before I can leave here."

I nodded like she could see me. "Thanks. Talk soon." We hung up. I put the phone on the bed. Steam leaked from the bathroom. *Let him know I'm available. He already knows. What am I so worried about?* Post-its containing all the chores and tasks I wanted to do in my bedroom flapped in the ceiling fan's breeze. My biggest concern—in blaring neon colors—stared me down.

Can he accept all of me?

CHAPTER 17

Picking the perfect blend of sexy-but-not-slutty clothing turned out to be harder than I thought. As I stood in the confines of my closet, rubbing my chin for what seemed like fifty days, I couldn't decide on how far I'd go to get Maverick's attention.

Harnessing my inner Elliot seemed like the best bet. My best friend oozed style and likely would choose something cute and sexy. Or he might go all out and have me wear something Maverick couldn't resist. I debated for what felt like hours.

"Screw it," I said through a sigh. My fingers drifted over the silk of a vest. "Don't want to wear the same shit I wear to work." Another drifting took me to a tight-fitting club number Elliot got me for my last birthday. The shirt shone in the light, and its fabric felt silken between my thumb and finger. Each button reflected the closet light with the fabric's motions. "Guess this works. Sexy, easily removed, yet not enough to make me look like a total gutter-slut."

Along with the shirt, I pulled out a pair of black skinny jeans and biker boots. I'd only worn the boots once, hoping they'd help me keep my ex's attention. *We know how that worked out, don't we?*

Roxxie whimpered from the doorway.

"What do you think?" I held the shirt over my bare chest. "Think he'll like it?" My dog's tail went ballistic, pulling a half-chuckle from me. "Hope he feels the same way you do."

Knocking at my door made me check my watch. *Hmm, it's still early. He said he'd pick me up around 8:00. It's only 7:30.* The knocking grew heavier and more frequent. My guts twisted at the fear bubbling within them. I knew that knock. How I wished I didn't.

My legs shook as I left the room, went down the hall, and stepped up to the door. Peeking through the peephole confirmed my worst fears. I clenched my teeth, holding the doorknob as if to keep out the one man I never wanted to see again. *Dammit! This is so like him!*

"Open the door, babe. I know you're in there," Declan's muffled voice called out. "Listen, I'm not here to cause any trouble. I just want to talk."

Like hell he does. He probably saw that fucking news story. Possessive bastard wants to make sure I know who I belong to. I motioned for Roxxie to stay quiet. She growled, so I shushed her.

"Aaron, I know you're there. Open the door, baby." He paused, his forehead thudding against the door. "Please."

I didn't care how he knew I was here. He probably charmed it out of my landlady like he always did when he deigned me important enough to visit.

It'll be okay. Maverick will be here soon. Just have to stay quiet.

I felt like a coward. I'd told Declan off before, yet this time felt different. That old fear of his temper flared up. He hated feeling replaced and always suspected I'd cheated on him. *Those nights were the worst.* I still remembered the bruises on my ribs, arms, and back and the burning pain left in my ass the following morning.

"No," I said to Roxxie. "This has to end. I can't keep doing this. I've told him off before. I can do it again." Before opening the door, I latched the chain, a comfortable barrier between us. "What do you want, Declan?" I kept my eyes and voice devoid of emotion despite the raging storm going on inside. *Damn, why does facing him never get easier?*

Declan held his hands up. "It's Cole, remember?" Roxxie growl and barked at him. "Christ, never really did like that thing."

"That thing is my dog. Now what do you want?" My frustration blossomed into anger, helping me to push away my lingering fear. Cole started this conversation amicably, but it wouldn't end that way. *They never did.*

"Easy, big boy. I'm only here to apologize. I've been a real jerk to you—"

I cut him off. "So, what you're saying is you're either once again having a hard time finding an easy fuck, or you saw that news story and came to mark your territory." *Screw it.* I unlatched the chain and opened the door. Roxxie stayed close, growling and occasionally snapping at Declan.

The corner of Declan's lip ticked. That meant he was struggling to keep control. His eyes explored me from head to toe. "Wow, babe. You look ... hot. How long have you had those boots?"

There was a time I would have given anything to hear him say those words. Thinking about my date with Maverick—a man ten times hotter than Declan—urged me on.

"For a while. Worn them around you before, but did you give a shit to notice? Not really. If you came to gawk, congrats, you've done that." I leaned against the door, crossing a foot over the other. "Why not quit the eye stripping and tell me why you're here? I have a date in fifteen minutes."

Declan's eyes turned to dinner plates. "Date? You? Since when are you dating anyone?"

"That so surprising?" My mouth turned up the higher my confidence grew. He wouldn't do anything. Not with Roxxie here, ready to tear his high-priced clothes apart. "He'll be here soon. Might not want to hang around. Hate to see you embarrassed by a real man."

I'd pushed too far. Declan's mask cracked, a scowl forming over his once-handsome face. Both nostrils flared. His lips became tight lines.

"That's it. I'm done being nice. Yeah, I saw your newest headline, you little slut. A rich daddy picked your worthless ass up." The words stung less than I thought. Maybe it was because Maverick assured me he adored everything about me. "It won't last long. Soon he'll wake up, and see how bad a mistake he's made—"

The elevator at the end of the hall chimed. I hoped Maverick was the one getting off so Declan would see him and leave me the hell alone. I had enough, but obviously Declan didn't get the hint. I needed Maverick's help.

Maverick walked around the corner, pausing when he noticed us. *Oh, thank God.* That dream-inducing face dawned its stern "lawyer" look. Hard eyes under creased brows homed in on Declan and me. Fists balled at Maverick's sides, his shoulders drawn to his square jaw. Each step Maverick took pushed the tense situation to the back of my mind. I couldn't stop admiring the change in my boss's wardrobe. The clothing he wore mimicked those the night we met at the park. A black turtleneck sweater hugged his broad chest like a second skin, and his slacks did nothing to hide the powerful legs I longed to see, touch, and caress.

God, I want him. I swallowed a shallow knot to keep Declan from knowing what I was up to.

When he reached us, Maverick glared at Declan. Invisible sparks flew between them, leaving me feeling like Switzerland in the middle of two raging bulls. Maverick's gaze shifted to me. My heart stalled at the storm clouds hazing his eyes.

Declan ended our moment by belting out a laugh. "Are you fucking kidding me?"

Maverick looked at me. I shrugged a shoulder. As long as I'd known Declan, he'd always been a drama queen. Whatever got him the most attention, Declan did as loudly and obnoxiously as he could. I felt sorry for Maverick; the only encounter he had with Declan was the night I kissed him to make Declan jealous.

"This is your sugar daddy? Maverick fucking Waylan? Wow, you really are a whore," Declan said, wiping a fake tear from his eye.

I stared at the floor. Heat flushed my face. Tears stung the corners of my eyes. Dammit, how bad would it be if Maverick saw me crying from what a bastard like Declan said?

For the first time, Maverick's fingers brushed against my cheek, pulling my attention from the floor. I gasped, letting his thumb and fingers guide my jaw to look up at him. *He's ... so tall.* I liked tall.

Declan's laughter ended, his eyes bulging and jaw ticking like he couldn't believe Maverick dared ignore him.

"Why don't you close the door, Aaron?" He glanced down at Roxxie. "It appears she's quite upset. Take care of her. I'll handle things out here."

I didn't know what to think. By the looks of him, Declan didn't know either. Through his smile, Maverick kept the professional coolness. I understood and did what Maverick said.

He'd given me an out and I took it. But curiosity had me plastering my ear against the door.

They spoke low, surprising considering Declan's flamboyancy. I expected him to make an ass of himself, but no, Maverick somehow wrangled him like a scared cow.

Time seemed to go on forever when the whispering stopped. Then a knock came at the door. My hand shook as I reached for the knob and opened it to see Maverick's smile. Declan lowered his head, refusing to look at me.

"He has something he wants to say to you, sweetheart," Maverick said.

I shouldn't ask. I'm not going to. Whatever happened in front of my door could stay as secret as Atilla's conversation with the pope. I didn't care.

"Well," Maverick prompted.

Declan's nostrils flared. "I'm ... sorry, Aaron."

A punch to the face wouldn't have stunned me as badly. Declan had never apologized for anything he did to me. He did the opposite, lording it over me every chance he got. *What did Maverick say?*

Ignoring Declan, Maverick held a hand out to me, the other arm behind him. "Shall we? I would hate to delay our first date any longer than needed."

I nodded, easing out and turning to lock the door. Declan, saying nothing, watched me take Maverick's hand. Maverick led us down the hall to the elevator.

We stood close, giving me a chance to smell Maverick's famous cologne. The scent mixed perfectly with his aftershave and shampoo, making my mouth water. He always smelled wonderful. Even when we bickered at the office, Maverick's scent drove me wild. I knew little about him, but damn, did I want to know more.

My hands fiddled with the jacket I cradled. "Um, what did you say to him?" I angled my head to see that panty-melting smile. "I mean, if you ... want to tell me."

Maverick bent to whisper, his breath tickling my ear. "I warned him I don't approve of cowards." I didn't hear what else he said through the throbbing in my groin. He said something about his family, but my brain had drifted elsewhere. The guy had the "what was I saying, doing, or asking" effect every time he turned his sex aura up to infinity.

The elevator dinged, ending my fantasies.

Maverick placed a splayed hand on my lower back, urging me forward. My shirt rode high, giving his pinky and ring finger contact with bare flesh. The intimate touch sent my nerves on alert. "We have so much to talk about, Aaron. I can't wait to get you to the restaurant."

Fuck the restaurant. Who wants to eat when they're horny as hell? Can we just go to your apartment? Or hell, back to mine? I don't give a shit!

We walked through the lobby to the parking garage. The valet—*I have a valet?*—took Maverick's key and left.

"Believe it or not, I never knew this place had one of those," I said.

Maverick chuckled. "I assume it's on a volunteer basis. Perhaps some extra money when the building needs the added help?"

Makes sense in this neighborhood. We had your friendly street-wandering window washers and shoe shiners. I'd used the latter frequently to help them earn some extra cash. Sometimes a saxophone player stood on the corner playing the Pink Panther theme song repeatedly. I gave him some change when I had it.

The valet returned with Maverick's car. Its shiny silver exterior shone like it just received a new wax job.

Maverick opened my door. "Your chariot awaits, my handsome prince."

Really turning on the charm tonight. That's ... good? Maybe I'll end up getting laid after all.

Thinking about getting laid excited me, yet I couldn't suppress a nagging concern. Maverick Waylan was my boss. Not only that, he kept secrets. Secrets usually fell in the "no" category on my checklist for the perfect guy. I had a feeling Maverick Waylan's secrets, if discovered, could get me into huge trouble.

CHAPTER 18

I watched the night sky speed by, its stars blocked by the bright city lights and blazing screens advertising the newest clothing, jewelry, and diets. Advertisers left nothing out. One advertisement featuring a gorgeous, shirtless man staring at the sea, his hair billowing with the breeze, made me glance at the silent driver beside me.

Maverick hadn't said a word since we left my apartment. His stare never once left the road. Lights danced in his focused eyes, drawing out the gorgeous green hues. Instead of slicking his hair back, Maverick let some of it flop into his face.

I can't believe how beautiful he is. I thought of the man on the billboard, replacing him with Maverick. Longing to dig my fingers into Maverick's hair plagued my mind. *Damn, how mad would he be if we forgot dinner and went straight to his place?*

Maverick's glance toward me brought heat to my cheeks. I quickly turned my head away to focus outside, hoping he hadn't spotted me. Not looking at him didn't help. I knew that stare. He gave it to me often in the office.

"Mind telling me what's going on in that head of yours?"

Oh, boy. Busted. I turned back to see Maverick half-smiling. "Nothing really. Just enjoying the night." I tried staying cool, but I felt he didn't buy it. "You?"

We stopped at a red light. Maverick's eyes met mine. The red from the headlights illuminated his eyes beneath heavy lashes. "I have many things going through my head presently. Many of them you will have to wait for. One, I've waited a long time to tell you."

Maverick's tone and the way the tip of his tongue teased his lower lip caused my cock to take notice. That potent sexual aura I first experienced when we met in the bar caressed me like a physical touch. My entire body hummed, sending blood south. Not asking him to give up dinner and take me somewhere, anywhere, to fuck my brains out became a ball-ravaging battle.

Honking behind us severed Maverick's spell. I wanted to give the jerk the finger for ruining such an amazing moment.

Sometime later, we headed toward Manhattan, near the bay area. I loved coming here with Roxxie when I needed to get away from college, work, and life pressures. The spotlights on the Statue of Liberty, the sounds of the ferry and other boats gliding over the water, and the gorgeous city lights in the distance eased my mind-tearing stresses.

On a nearby pier sat a restaurant dedicated to various types of seafood dishes. I had done some research on it for my college essay. Its owner came from New Orleans and designed the place to resemble a boat floating in the Louisiana bayou. From what I found, the owner was a top chef of Creole dishes.

My face plastered against the car window like a kid seeing Six Flags for the first time, hands splayed on the glass. "Wait, really? You're taking me here?"

"Surprise," Maverick said, his mouth drawn up. "I thought you might like this place."

How does he know all of this? In the weeks we'd worked together, I never told Maverick anything personal. Anytime we spoke was business related, our exchanges curt and to the point. That or I ran from him like my ass was on fire.

Maverick pulled into a parking space facing the bay. After shutting the engine off, he opened his door, walked around the front of the car, and opened mine. He held out a hand, bending at his waist. "Shall we?"

My heart fluttered. No one had ever been as nice or respectful of me. Maverick had every right to give me every four-letter word in the book. Yet here he was, holding a hand out like a prince.

Playing coy, I reached a hand to my chest. "Why thank you." Corny as hell, but why not enjoy it? This man told off my ex without screaming at him right outside my door. *He's definitely a prince.* But man, did I hate feeling like a damsel needing a prince to save me. Or I would have, if the prince wasn't Maverick Waylan.

Maverick took my hand. Using his strength, he pulled me until our bodies were flush together. His free hand touched my lower back, sending gooseflesh over my body. "I want to get to know you tonight. No more hiding. No more running. You are free to ask me what you want. All I ask is for you to open yourself to me. Can you promise me that, Aaron?"

Thankfully, we were alone in the parking lot. Sounds of lapping ocean waves joined the ferry bells and the distant roar of honking cars.

His fingers brushed my knuckles as though he wanted to ensure he hadn't hurt me. Storms of passion raged in the sexy lawyer's eyes. Within the storms, I saw the same tinge of pain I sometimes glimpsed after I ran from him. It was as if now that he had me, Maverick wanted me to know that he wouldn't release me easily this time. The thought of that should've sent me running, but it excited me to know how badly someone like Maverick wanted me.

My eyes widened as I studied the thin line of his lips. *He's serious. He ... really wants to know me.* Being the moron I was, I silently hoped he wanted to know *all* of me.

"I ... I promise," I said.

"Thank you." Maverick's face visibly relaxed, his age lines and jaw softening. Slowly, he released me, gesturing at the restaurant. We started walking. Then Maverick added, "This is, of course, my treat."

I almost stumbled over an invisible rock. "What? You can't be serious!"

"Oh, I am. You have worked hard these past few weeks. Consider this a personal thank you."

Personal thank you? "Mav, this place costs a small fortune." My hands went to my mouth. *Did I really just call him...?*

Maverick halted, turning on his heel, a wide grin on his face. He reached for my hands and eased them down. "Don't. I'm glad you're comfortable enough to call me that. While we're alone, I'm not your boss." He drew close, backing me against a car, his hand beside my head. "I'm only someone going after who he wants."

Could he be any more gorgeous? Once again, Maverick backed away. But not before I felt a rather impressive erection gently touch my thigh. *Oh, yeah. There's going to be some hot sex tonight. No doubt about it.*

Maverick put his hands in his pockets and walked away. Only after I broke out of swooning-horny-teenager jail did I realize I hadn't voiced an alternative plan to him paying for everything.

"Evening, Mr. Waylan," the hostess greeted, her eyes and mouth agape. Before we walked in, she'd looked bored, toying with her phone and feigning organization of the menus. Perky boobs strained behind a tight blue button-up. She wore her platinum blonde hair pulled back in a tight ponytail.

I rolled my eyes. *Easy there, tits. He's not gonna shag you right here in the doorway.* Frustration and a twinge of jealousy at the woman's familiarity niggled at me. *How long has he really been in New York? Has to be longer than I thought if he knows this chick.* Thinking about more, I wondered if Maverick liked both men and women. Sexuality—like hordes of other things I probably should've asked before following my aching dick into this dumpster fire—never came up. *Maybe I can find an excuse to leave. Like ... nausea.*

"How many do you have joining you tonight?" Blondie shared a quick look my way. Her red lips pouted briefly before she returned her attention to Maverick.

Maverick ignored her attempts at flirting. "Only two tonight."

"Two more?" She asked, likely hoping he didn't mean only us.

Chuckling, Maverick said, "No." He looked over his shoulder at me. Warm eyes, full of admiration—and dare I say boyfriend-like attraction—delved deeply into mine. "Just me and my handsome companion."

If swooning like a fanboy wouldn't get me odd looks, I'd do it.

Blondie didn't like Maverick's answer. Her lips pursed. *You can die now*, her eyes glared. "Yes, sir." She took two menus, faced the main dining room, and said, "This way."

Amazed, I took in all the nautical paraphernalia adorning the walls. Looking at this place from the outside, I never imagined such a vast interior. Ship wheels, paintings, framed photos of boats, and various pieces of netting, buoys, and life rings hung from the wood-planked wall. The servers were also nautically themed and wore vests over white-button shirts, black pants, and red bow ties. Delicious smells wafted from the open kitchen.

Blondie took us through the main room to an area behind two glass-paned doors. When they closed, the room would make for a perfect meeting area. An ideal place for someone like Maverick to hold interviews with clients, other lawyers, and legal assistants.

"Will you have your usual drink and appetizers?" Blondie asked Maverick, all flirting gone beneath the scowl distorting her face. She set the menus on the wooden table.

My curiosity about how often Maverick visited New York blossomed. He must have been a regular here.

"Not this time," Maverick replied. He gestured a hand at me, pulling me from the hurricane of questions I wanted to ask him. I opened the menu, staggering at the prices. "It's alright. Choose what you like. This fine establishment has some wonderful Creole and Cajun dishes. I assume those will be more appealing to you."

Yep, so many questions. "Okay," I said, my voice more squeak than speech. Roaring in my stomach led me to start with an appetizer and a tea to drink. The vastness of the menu made choosing a single dish difficult. "Can I have more time for the main course?"

"Of course," Maverick said and turned to Blondie. "He'll need a moment."

Blondie nodded. "Very good. Bryan will be your server tonight, Mr. Waylan. Get a hold of me should you need anything else."

The way she said those last words sounded like she already envisioned them naked and fucking each other in bed. I watched her sashay her ass through the doors, closing them behind her.

Overwhelmed with jealousy and confusion, the entrée dishes became nothing more than blurs. I slammed the menu down harder than I meant, capturing Maverick's attention.

He gently placed his menu down, locked his fingers, and leaned his mouth against them. "Is something wrong?"

Hell yes, something's wrong! "Did you hire a private investigator to stalk me or something?" I crossed my arms, leaning against the maroon leather of the booth. "Because you seem to know more about me than you should."

Like he'd done many times, Maverick baffled me. Instead of yelling or chiding me for acting so immature, he laughed. "Is that what's bothering you? No, Aaron, I didn't hire a private investigator. I watch people, analyze them. It's a skill that differentiates great lawyers from good ones."

"And that means?"

Maverick resumed his previous posture. "It means I take in every blink, every turn of the head, every breath, and every subtle movement the body makes. I learn habits and pay attention to the smallest details. For example, I can tell you want to know how Sandra knew me. Why she spoke with such familiarity."

I'm creeped out now. Not in a bad way, but still creeped out. "And why would I care if you know her?"

"Because you're jealous," Maverick said. Under the table, his leg rubbed against my calf, easing closer to my inner thigh. Half-lidded eyes met mine in a blistering gaze capable of shattering every human inhibition. "I think it's fetching. Your jealousy. It reveals something about you I'm eager to explore."

He leaned back, resting an arm over the booth, eyeing me from across the table. "I think there's something else you've wanted to know. I saw it the first time we met at the office. You recognized me, didn't you?"

He said it so bluntly, yet the curtains draped over the thoughts that tortured me for weeks ripped away like a spent band-aid in five words.

Maverick sighed. He turned his head away. "I'm exactly who you think I am, Aaron. Who you've wondered I am. The man you kissed at the cocktail bar and went home with."

Dizziness slammed into my head. I had to focus on the salt and pepper shakers to keep from falling over. Awkwardness overtook the sexed-up teenager inside me. I wanted to be angry. Should've been furious that Maverick let me torment myself for weeks while he studied me like a caged animal.

But I wasn't. Happiness that the secrecy, uncertainty, and doubt had finally ended swept away any anger.

"Why didn't you tell me?" was all I thought to ask. "Why keep it a secret?"

Maverick lowered his head. All the pride, confidence, sexual prowess, and cold efficiency seemed sucked from him. His left shoulder dropped. I couldn't tell if his eyes closed.

A deep breath escaped through his nostrils. "I didn't want you to think my desire for you was only to finish what we started that night."

CHAPTER 19

When he lifted his head, the same concern he displayed in his office laced his eyes. "Aaron, I don't think you understand. That night. At the bar, I thought of a million ways to approach you. But nothing I came up with sounded right."

"Why would you care?" I asked, more snappily than I meant to. "It's not like a guy like you couldn't get an easy lay. What made me so special?"

Maverick's hand snatched my wrist. As he pulled me toward him, he rose, our noses nearly touching. "I don't think you realize how sexy you are. Especially when you let that sassy side come out to play. You're correct. I probably *could* get anyone I wanted, yet I allowed you to kiss me to make your ex jealous."

Blood pumped furiously through my veins, heating my body and bringing attention to my needy cock. The closeness of our mouths gave either of us ample time to close the gap and enjoy our first kiss. Chills ran down my spine when Maverick's thumb rotated softly over my pulse point. I imagined him kissing the spot he caressed.

"Knowing what you know about me now, do you believe I let just anyone use me like you did?" Maverick asked in that sultry tone I adored. "Do you think someone with my reputation would devise the proper way to pursue the man I want instead of simply asking him to come to bed with me?"

142

Hearing him talk this way, I recalled the first time I looked into his eyes. *I couldn't remember his face, but those eyes. Hunger.* That's how I remembered them. Maverick's eyes had devoured every step I made toward him after Elliot pointed him out. *Elliot.*

Our server returned with our drinks. Maverick released me quickly. I lounged back, taking the opportunity to mull over what Maverick said. *I didn't even notice. Elliot was the one who told me Maverick was watching me that night.* Guilt churned my stomach like a rat clawing at my guts. My plan at the bar was to get revenge on Declan while liquid courage flowed through me.

"Thank you, Brian," Maverick said, his eyes never leaving me.

"Are you ready to order your meals?" Brian asked.

I observed Maverick as he ordered. The more I learned about him, the clearer my two-sides theory became. Talking to Brian, Maverick remained polite and to the point, like he did with clients, court dates, and work in general. It was only when he talked to me, caressed me, closed the gap between us, or other beyond sexy things that Maverick let his sexual side out. *He's like a gorgeous plant. One side is innocent, existing in its natural habitat. The other is wild, driven by primal hunger.*

Comparing Maverick to a predatory plant—or anything predatory, for that matter—sounded sinister in my head. But dammit how it turned me on. I'd never had anyone want me so badly. Having someone as hot and powerful as Maverick wanting me sent me to cloud nine.

"Sir?" Brian asked.

"Huh? Sorry. What?" I replied.

"I asked what you'd like tonight."

Panicked, I fumbled with and a dropped my menu. "Um, I'm not really sure." My eyes shot to Maverick's, and I mouthed, *Help*.

Maverick took the menu, opened it, and pointed. "I believe this will suffice."

"Very good, sir," Brian said, taking both menus. "I'll return with some butter biscuits and your appetizers, Mr. Waylan."

"Thank you," Maverick said, smiling.

Brian left us alone in the stifling cloud of intensity invading our airspace.

To avoid looking too stupid, I took a pink packet, tore it, and emptied its contents into my waiting tea. The lemon spun with the spoon as I blindly over-stirred the drink.

Maverick picked his drink up and took a sip, licking his lips. "The perfect blend for a night like this," he said. The storms in his eyes danced with the candle flames.

Setting the cup down, silence resumed. Maverick rested his chin against his fingers, watching me. Studying me. I tried recalling as much about the cocktail bar as possible. Emotions battled in my head about how I should feel now that Maverick revealed a card in his hand. I knew how I should react. Pissed. Anyone else in my position would tell the guy off and get the hell away from him for treating them like a cat does a mouse before pouncing.

I relaxed back, teasing the edge of my glass with a finger. Maverick was everything I wanted. Hot, successful, protective, obviously interested in mind-numbing sex, and somehow crazily aware of what I wanted in a partner.

The last thing I want to do is screw this up. "You must think I'm such a jerk." I swallowed the nerves seizing my throat. This whole situation had disaster written all over it to start.

Maverick was my boss. *God only knows what Travis would do if he found out.*

Maverick's ears perked, eyes blinking. "For?"

Frustration bubbled to a head. His acting like he was fine getting used by a drunk, desperate moron didn't sit right. No one acted that coolly.

"Cut the crap," I snapped. "How can you sit there and think what I did was okay? I felt horrible for it, and here you are dropping this bomb, pretending like you aren't the least bit pissed." *I'm so getting my ass fired for this, but fuck, I can't stop my feelings.*

Maverick's face remained deadpan.

Feeling like an emotional basket case, I reminded myself not to screw this up before we even tried ... whatever this was. "I'm sorry. I... I didn't..."

Strong fingers took the hand I rested on the table. They turned it over. And like we'd dated for months, Maverick pressed my palm to his lips. All the words on the tip of my tongue froze as I watched this beautiful man savor my wrist and palm. His tongue teased my fingers. Eventually, he sucked a digit into his mouth, following the length until it popped from his mouth.

"Mmm, sweet," Maverick purred.

Guess I had some sugar left on my finger. Not complaining, though. That was hot as fuck.

"I understand your frustration, Aaron. Believe me, the emotions I experienced after I found out you left troubled me as well." Maverick let my hand go and dug through his pockets. "I didn't make my decision until I found this." He opened his hand. In his palm, the band my sister gave me lay neatly tied with a bread tie. "That is when I decided I didn't care how long it took me, I'd find you. Find you and make you mine, no matter what it cost me."

Talk about a hit to the gut. How was I supposed to digest food after having all these powerful emotions thrown at me? *Make me his? He doesn't even know me.* I needed time to get my wits straight before messing things up.

Scooting from the booth, I stood above Maverick. "Need to head to the restroom. Nature calls and all that shit." *Nature calls? How lame an excuse is that?* Maverick raised a brow. "Be back soon."

Cold water burst in a powerful stream from the silver faucet. My neighbor gawked at me like I was a crazy person when I splashed my face multiple times. I stared at the mirror, water dripping from my face and free-hanging hair strands.

Calm down. Don't ruin this. He's being honest. Why are you so scared of someone actually caring for you? I knew the answer. But voicing it made it real, and no way in hell would I do that. *He's different. Give him a chance.* With the thought that Maverick might be worrying just as bad as I was, I dried my face and stepped out of the bathroom.

Smells of butter-soaked seafood slammed into my nose. My stomach roared with anticipation. As I walked, I made a mental note of the dishes.

I arrived back at the booth to find Brian had already delivered the appetizers and biscuits. They reminded me of those cheese and butter biscuits my father used to make before he lost his mind. Mom took over making them after he left—*Bless you mom, how I love those.*

"Welcome back," Maverick said. "Feeling a bit better?"

146

I nodded, blushing at the heavy English tone I dreamed whispered in my ear while we were in bed. "Yeah. Sorry about that."

Maverick shook his head. "No apologies necessary. I realize I've been mistaken in giving so much away at once. This is new to me as well."

I slid into the booth and took a biscuit, tearing it apart and savoring the delicious mix of herb encrusted butter and cheese. "So good."

"Indeed. Shall we continue where we left off?" Maverick said.

Rocks niggled in the pit of my stomach. Taking a deep breath, I reminded myself what I said in the bathroom. "Sounds good." I popped a piece of biscuit into my mouth and swallowed. "Listen, I don't know why you think I'm so different from everyone else." Maverick tilted his head curiously. "But I want to know you too. Why don't we start small? Who's Connor?"

Maverick choked on the biscuit he bit off, and I realized I might have stepped on the wrong stone. I backtracked. "I mean, I didn't mean to hear, but your office door ... and well..." *This is it. This is where you get fired. Nice job, asshole. All because you couldn't respect his privacy.*

That gorgeous laugh filled the small room. "Of all the things you could ask!" Half-lidded eyes honed on me. "One must wonder if you make eavesdropping a habit, my dear Aaron."

My spin stiffened, hands plunging into my lap. "I didn't eavesdrop! You practically yelled at the guy!" Another wrong move. "But it's none of my business. It's not like we're dating. Sorry I said anything."

Maverick rubbed my calf with his under the table, the knee easing into my groin. "You don't need to worry about Connor. He's not who you think—if you are indeed thinking what I believe you are." I swallowed, readjusting the aching cock between my legs.

If we don't get out of this place soon, I'm going to need to go back to the bathroom.

Brian saved my life when he returned with our food. Eating provided the perfect excuse to keep quiet. But Maverick re-engaged by asking various types of questions between bites. A few personal questions—mostly to do with family issues—rubbed me wrong, so I asked him to give me leeway not to answer. I promised to tell him more once we got to know each other better.

In exchange, Maverick told me about his family.

"I know your mom's heavy into the fashion scene," I said. "Why come here and do the whole lawyer thing?"

Maverick's face grew solemn. He placed his fork and knife down. "If you can imagine, my mother is quite controlling. Should anyone go against her wishes, she makes their lives difficult. She chased my father away and disapproved of any choice my brother and I made that didn't align with her vision for us."

I swallowed a shrimp and whistled. "Wait, you have a brother?"

Maverick nodded. "Yes. Connor."

"Damn." A nervous laugh. "You think she'd approve of me? I'm not exactly Hollywood material. More like celebrity by proxy."

The silence following felt like someone stretching a rubber band until it screamed. Maverick ignored his food, staring off into the bay. I watched the lights glimmer in his eyes—tiny orange and white flickers like fairies twirling around a mid-summer fire. Maverick kept his spine straight. His chiseled features were like a hero in *The Odyssey* or *Beowulf*. I let myself imagine what he was like in the courtroom. After the initial shock of my somewhat unwanted promotion, I became intimately connected with how organized and methodical Maverick ran his cases.

Anytime I sat in a client interview with him, Maverick listened to each client intently, focusing on their face and glancing at the notes only when he stopped to think about his next words. He did the same with me in our previous short talks and knew me better in a few weeks better than anyone did for months, all without me saying a word.

He was a powerful man. *And he's interested in me? How can I fix this? Please tell me I didn't ruin this.* "Sorry. That was out of line. What I meant to say—"

Maverick sighed and held up a hand. "Aaron, if I may be frank. Let's just say my mother doesn't approve of my choice in partners."

My brow raised. "I'm assuming she knows you prefer men, right?"

Maverick aimed a "you're not serious" look at me. Picking up his fork, he speared a shrimp and pointed it at me. "In my family, career, having male heirs, and looking good for the press are all that matter. I happen to be the woman's favorite, so she expects more of me. To hear I'm not interested in whatever woman my mother sees as the perfect mate creates friction between us."

I lowered my head, pushing a green bean around with my fork. "Oh. You mean—"

He nodded. "Unfortunately. Let's just say we have fought many times over my lifestyle."

"What about Connor?"

"The family disappointment, I'm afraid. In dear mother's eyes, at least. I've always found Connor a well-respected but somewhat brutal businessman. The kind Mother usually adores. Sadly, I believe her disappointment in Connor is because he resembles our father. Petty as that seems." Maverick popped the shrimp in his mouth, resuming after swallowing. "I believe her sternness with me is because I'm the eldest. The one expected to handle the burdens of all family expectations."

"Then, why isn't your mom disappointed with you and not Connor?" I asked. The woman's logic made no sense.

"Because I'm the more successful between the two of us. Connor's strong in business, but his strength when dealing with people lacks. His short temper and inflated ego sees to that."

"Damn, and I thought things were hard for me."

Maverick smiled, slowly extending his fingers to brush my knuckles. "That's why I understand when you talk about the pressures your family deals with. I have no doubt Mother would disapprove of you, but I certainly do not."

Fuck her then. "Hey," I said. Maverick glanced up. "It doesn't matter. I think you're amazing, sexy, successful, and—" My mouth turned to ash. *Did I just say that?* We'd talked so much about multiple things, mainly our crazy families, I hadn't noticed how quickly the food disappeared. My wet dreams were about to become reality. That realization along with what I said brought blistering heat to my cheeks.

Maverick didn't miss it. A subtle tick in his jaw pulsed, and the beginnings of a grin pulled at the corners of his mouth. Maverick looked over my shoulder, and in seconds, Brian stood beside our table.

"Can I get you something, sir?"

"Yes," Maverick replied. "The check. We'll be leaving shortly."

Brian dipped his chin, turned, and left. Getting our check didn't take long and soon he handed the leather book to Maverick, thanking us for coming.

Maverick paid for the meal in cash. To see that much money on the table blew me away. *I rarely even keep five dollars in my wallet.*

Pushing his plate aside, he slid from the booth to stand above me. "Sexy, am I?" Bending at his waist, he held out a hand. "Come home with me? I'll happily show you how sexy I can be."

I looked at the food, back at him, then the food. I still had some food left. "Yes," I breathed out. "If I can take my leftovers with me."

"I do believe that can be arranged, sweetheart," Maverick said, a coy grin on his face.

CHAPTER 20

Maverick walked into the parking lot first. I kept a safe distance behind—*not to admire his amazing ass, nope*—thinking about the events about to unfold. Blood rushed to my ears. The erection straining behind my tight pants ached with need. I hadn't gotten laid since my last pathetic crawl back to Declan. I didn't know what to expect from a man who actually gave a damn about me.

My hands clenched, I kept my mouth shut until we made it to Maverick's Audi. He waited for me to get closer before opening my door.

"You know you don't have to do that for me," I said with a laugh. "I'm not some chick who—" I didn't get the last words out. Maverick's mouth crushed against mine, his body pinning me against the icy body of the car. My ass hit the doorframe, but I ignored the sting of discomfort in light of the hottest kiss I'd ever had.

Maverick held my face with one hand, the other on my hip. He ran his thumb pad over my cheekbone multiple times as his tongue poked through my lips and teased my teeth. *Let me in*, he seemed to say. I didn't hesitate, opening my mouth to allow his exploration. The delicious taste of wine and buttery seafood washed over my tastebuds and down my throat. He sucked my tongue, and I moaned, tilting my head and allowing him more access. Maverick's height and his thigh pressed against my cock caged me into the most amazing experience. *Please don't let this ... don't let him be a dream.*

I couldn't help myself, slowly dry humping his leg for some reprieve against the agonizing hardness between my legs.

After he pulled away, Maverick laid his head against my neck. Hot breaths made my skin clammy, yet I didn't give a shit. "I should get you home before we do something that will require my legal skills."

I cursed. The last thing I wanted was to give him a chance to escape. *Talk about irony.* "Fine," I said with a sharp exhale. "But you better drive like a fucking stampede of demon bulls is chasing us."

Maverick's wide eyes blinked once and he laughed. "I must admit, that's one I haven't heard before. You're very interesting. I'll go as fast as I can. But we don't want to be pulled over, do we?"

I shook my head. The last thing I wanted was something else to delay what was about to be the most amazing night of my life.

"What kinds of music do you like?" I asked once both doors closed, and Maverick started the car.

He turned on the radio, and soothing sounds of smooth jazz swooned into my ears. While I loved listening to things like this while studying, hearing it now threatened to lull me to sleep. Listening to this stuff probably helped him unwind after a full day of that professional composure he always kept.

As if he knew what I thought, Maverick chuckled. "I know. This music makes me sound boring."

I waved both hands. "No. No. I like jazz when I'm studying and doing college work. It helps me stay focused."

Maverick turned the radio down, leaving the music as background noise. He sighed again, lowering his eyes. "It reminds me of my favorite cafe back home. I guess that's why I still like to listen to it. I still have moments of homesickness. Much like any man."

"Why not go home, then?" I asked, though that is the last thing in this world I hoped he'd do. "Does facing your mom really scare you that badly?" Not that I had any right to say anything. Facing my father scared the hell out of me. I was always too afraid we'd wind up fighting.

For the first time, when Maverick directed his gaze at me, he scared me. "You don't know what she's capable of. If she doesn't know where I am, like I hope she doesn't, it's better for both of us. She would do anything to get rid of you, Aaron. That's how vindictive and conniving she is."

I swallowed the knot in my throat. The action didn't go unnoticed. Maverick licked his lips as he stared at my neck. Heat hit my cheeks. I broke his gaze and watched the lights of the harbor disappear in the rearview mirror.

The harbor soon faded into the shadows of the glass buildings making up Park Avenue. I remembered the morning I ran from Maverick's condo into the bustling sidewalk, got splashed by a taxi, and kicked myself, trying to recall who I went home with. Reliving that moment, I kicked myself again. Had I not darted from the place, I would have gotten to know Maverick sooner.

We said nothing for the rest of the ride to Maverick's apartment. I spent too much time thinking about what he said about his mother hurting me to get rid of me. Suddenly, everything I thought sucked in my life didn't sound so horrible. Sure, Dad abandoned his family to go play with Hollywood's

Playboy Bunnies and pat the backs of kids he'd never have to see again, but what Maverick went through was manipulation Hell.

It wasn't until Maverick pulled into the half-circle space where the valets catered to the rich and well-off in front of his building that I realized how different our lives were. Maverick came from prestige and tons of cash. Despite my father's standing, Mom barely scraped enough from the barrel's bottom to take care of me and my sisters. Growing up, I dreamed of what living the celebrity life might be like. In the eyes of a star-struck twelve-year-old, I deserved it because of who my dad was.

I wonder if I'd run from my dad if he did what Mav's mom did. Say to hell with all the cash and live like my mom did.

Maverick pulled his Audi up to the valet podium. We got out, and Maverick handed his keys to the young man, instructing him to take the car to Maverick's personal parking spot. I imagined what would happen once we passed the lobby and got into the elevator. Would he make out with me? Maybe let me rub my ass against his cock?

I purred softly to myself. *That sounds perfect.* A scheme to seduce Maverick formed in my mind. Until now, we'd teased one another with sharp jabs and the occasional soft touch— not including the mind-blowing kiss I relived the entire drive back. Maverick did most of the open flirting, slamming me repeatedly with waves of sexual hunger. *My turn now. Prepare to have your mind blown for once, Mr. Waylan.*

Maverick's hand rested on my lower back, urging me forward. My heart thumped louder in my ears as we passed through the revolving doors and across the lobby. The elaborate blacks and golds of the columns and floors became familiar with each returning memory. Golden-doored

155

elevators lined a short, elaborate hallway. On the opposite side of the lobby, a busy bar with boisterous patrons added to the cacophony. I didn't remember the bar, but I wanted to visit it.

A loud ding announced the elevator's arrival.

Maverick held the door, letting me walk in first. I prayed silently that no one would follow us. Someone up there finally answered my prayers in the best *deus ex machina* moment ever. As the doors shut, I pressed my ass against Maverick's groin, his hardened cock cradled between my cheeks perfectly.

Like a stripper, I eased my ass up and down his shaft. A soft moan reached my ears. *He likes that. So damn perfect.* I continued my movements, savoring the feeling of the hard length against me, and imagined what it would feel like inside me.

The elevator jerked to a stop, its doors whooshing open to reveal a hallway decorated much like the lobby. I moved to step onto the black carpet, but Maverick gripped my wrist, pulling my body flush against his. His free hand cradled my throat, gently directing my eyes toward him.

"You played a dangerous game just now, sweetheart," he said in the dark tone that sent shivers down my spine every time he used it. The hand holding my wrist drifted over my belly then lightly roamed over an impressive erection. I gasped lightly when his pointer finger teased the corner of my mouth. "I'm very interested in how your adorable ass will handle me once I've gotten us both naked."

My blood became blistering flames. Hypnotized, I closed my eyes as Maverick's lips tasted my jaw. *God, he talks filthy. I fucking love it.*

Just as I believed we were about to make out, Maverick released me. "We need to hurry," he rasped. "I'm not sure how much longer I can contain myself."

Don't have to tell me twice. Gripping his hand, I pulled him from the elevator. Somewhere inside, I knew exactly where to go, walking the length of the hall to his condo until I stood in front of his door, gawking at the golden numbers that had—until now—terrified me.

Leaning over my shoulder, Maverick put his key into the lock, turned the knob, and shoved the door open.

We barely made it inside before I whirled, grabbed Maverick's collar, and pulled him forward. Our mouths met with a furious barrage of kisses. Maverick sucked my tongue into his mouth then exhaled hot air into my face when he came up for a breath. Hands drifted over bodies like wild creatures with their own minds. Mine gripped Maverick's ass cheeks, exploring the firm muscle I'd fantasized about every time I pleasured myself.

Feeling emboldened when Maverick pulled my thigh up to his hip, I reached for Maverick's erection, cupping it and rubbing through his pants.

"Mmm," he groaned deeply. "Yes. That's wonderful." Darkened eyes held mine as I continued rubbing him. "You are wonderful, Aaron. So beautiful I fear the dream will end and I'll open my eyes to find you gone again."

I took his face in both hands. "I'm not going anywhere." Our lips met. This time, I sucked Maverick's lower lip into my mouth, pulling another groan from him.

"Fuck," Maverick said. It was the first time I'd ever heard him cuss. With his British accent, I didn't think I wanted to hear any other word. He could say "fuck" all he wanted if it kept sounding like that.

Maverick pulled away, his head directed at the floor, shoulders rising and falling with each heavy breath. Then he raised his head, both hands moving like lightning while working on my shirt. "I want to see you. All of you." He tore my shirt off, tossing it to the floor. Our mouths got close enough to kiss but lingered in limbo. "Show me every delicious inch of you, Aaron. I'm afraid I can't wait any longer."

He wasn't the only one. Feeling Maverick remove my clothes, smelling the potent aroma of his arousal and the pure masculine musk that hit me every time I entered his office, drove me wild. Nothing else mattered except answering the carnal call we'd both ignored for so long.

Once all my clothes lay strewn on the floor, Maverick backed away, his gaze taking me in from head to toe, then back again. "Beautiful. So. Fucking. Beautiful."

My cheeks burned under the scrutiny of his eyes. Instinct drove me to cover myself, but Maverick caught my hands, leading them down.

"No, don't do that. Your body is flawless. Absolutely nothing to be ashamed of," he reassured me. "Now, let me get you to bed. I think it's time we both got what we want, don't you?"

Hell yes. Fuck yes.

I let Maverick haul my legs over his hips. His strength amazed me. If he strained holding my weight, he never showed it. I always thought myself heavy; I didn't work out much save for running.

"Mav, you don't have to hold me like this. I know I'm not exactly—"

"Shh. You aren't heavy. For a man your size, you're actually very light," Maverick replied. "Would you call me that more? When we're together? I love it."

158

I didn't know what to say, responding with a nod.

He took us to the stairs.

I looked over my shoulder, panic setting in at the idea of him walking up those stairs with me on his hips. "Are you sure I'm not too heavy?" I asked, slightly pleading.

"As long as you remain still and trust me, I believe I can get us up these stairs."

A knot choked my throat. What panic already possessed me became fully fledged. In a desperate—albeit unintentional—attempt not to fall, I lurched my legs. Maverick lost his footing, and we fell.

My back collided with the ledge of the last stair. "Ow!"

Maverick rolled to sit on the step below me, rubbing his knee.

"I'm so sorry. That wouldn't have happened if—" I silently begged whoever was listening that I hadn't screwed the night up.

Instead of calling me every insulting name in the book, Maverick kissed the corner of my mouth. "Hush. I understand why you panicked. Worst case, I have a bruise on my knee. How is your back?"

"It hurts, but I don't think it'll ruin any extracurricular activities." Truth was, my back hurt like flaming hell, but no way would I tell Maverick that. He'd refuse to touch me again until he made sure I didn't hurt at all. "Can we ... have sex now?"

Maverick guffawed. "Yes. I believe we can."

Thank you, whoever you are. I'm still getting laid.

"Do you remember the way?" Maverick asked, standing, and offering me a hand.

"Surprisingly, yeah. I do." I took his hand, letting him haul me up. "But you are eventually going to get naked, right? Because you ... kinda have to be naked to have sex."

A playful swat on my ass sent me scuttling up the stairs. He didn't need to answer verbally. The smile he wore told me all I needed to know.

What made this moment even more amazing was how everything we did felt natural. Maverick loved my teasing, and I adored how filthy he spoke. And damn, was I looking forward to the slutty, hot sex I knew I was about to have.

CHAPTER 21

I waited impatiently on Maverick's bed, my legs tucked under me. The softness of his sheets cradled my cock. To ease the strain, I rubbed my engorged length against the cream silk. Maverick had asked me to wait while he went to his bathroom to retrieve condoms and lube. Subtle pulsing in my hole excited me. I hadn't gotten properly laid in years. Any sex with Declan had been out of sheer need. He never focused on what I wanted. Rather, Declan went with every degrading activity he thought of to remind me of how pathetic I was.

"I apologize for keeping you waiting." Maverick's gorgeous voice pulled me from the Declan-fueled rage gurgling inside.

I raised my eyes, barely keeping my jaw from plunging to the bed. Maverick stood gloriously naked, leaning an arm against the bathroom doorframe. An impressively long and plump cock pointed up at its owner.

H'oh shit. He's bigger than I could've imagined. Will he fit? God, I hope he fits.

Maverick beamed broadly. "Like something you see, sweetheart?"

"Yeah. Hell, yeah," I said, licking my lips. My sexy lawyer—*fuck* yes, *he is*—strolled forward until he towered over me. Maverick's body surpassed every wet dream I'd had. All I could think about was exploring every delicious muscle of the abs on the same level with my face.

The bed caved as Maverick placed a knee on the edge and crawled over the sheets. He didn't stop, eventually bumping his forehead against mine. "Do you prefer lying on your back or stomach, beautiful?"

My palm pressed against his chest, the thumb over his nipple. "I have something I want to tell you." Maverick sat back, his head tilted. "I haven't really … um … been with anyone for a while. Weird as it sounds, I'm … well—"

Maverick's fingers traced my face down the jaw to my Adam's apple. They lingered there, stroking and tracing along the dips and rises of my throat. My body broke into gooseflesh. "It's okay. I'll take this slow. Get you nice and stretched. If being on top makes you more comfortable, I'm fine with that." He closed his eyes, craning his neck and humming. "I like that image."

I think my heart just exploded. I want to know what those images are. Not to mention the droolicious thought of his fingers inside me, stretching me. *Yeah, my heart definitely just exploded.*

Maverick lowered his body over mine, his elbows propping up his weight. "I'll find out how sexy you look on top of me soon. For now, let me pleasure you, Aaron. I want to explore every gorgeous inch of you."

I couldn't have stopped what happened next if I wanted to. The smoldering eyes roaming over my face weren't those of a patient man. Like mine, Maverick's restraints disappeared. We were both naked and vulnerable to the sexual cloud engulfing the room.

Maverick's lips took mine. As he did, our bare cocks pressed against one another. I thought I'd come from the sheer pleasure that alone sent through me.

"I think they're happy to meet finally, don't you?" Maverick murmured.

A firm hand gripped both of us, dragging and pushing the shafts. The friction tore a gasp from me.

God, he's going to destroy me before we even have sex.

My body lurched, pressing us closer together while Maverick crooked his head and dragged his tongue over my Adam's apple. "I've wanted to do this since I saw you in the office," he muttered against my neck then sucked the flesh, lightly nipping. "Your skin tastes like the sun. Warm and comforting, yet the sun's rays have nothing on the pleasure your skin is giving me."

Shit, shit, shit, don't cum yet. How embarrassing would that be? Here was a man who knew exactly what he did to me. His entire body caged me with a heat hotter than a furnace. Muscles harder than stone held me in place as their owner ravaged my throat, kissed up my jaw, and blew hot air in my ear.

"You are more than I ever dreamed, sweetheart," Maverick purred, sucking my earlobe, then releasing it with a pop.

"You've dreamed of me often?" I asked, chuckling.

Maverick held my face like I might vanish if he didn't. "More than you know. Something about seeing you asleep in this bed felt ... right to me. I'd never experienced that with another, and I want to explore those feelings."

Each word tickled the tiny hairs in my ear. Combined with the hold Maverick on me and the smooth glide of his body over my chest and abdomen, I could no longer think. I'd drowned in euphoria, my heart a rampaging bull behind my ribs. Heated blood brought rivulets of sweat that trickled down my sides, cheeks, and arms. Without thinking, I raised my leg, running my thigh down Maverick's side. My foot followed the hard curve of his ass down his hamstring to his calf.

Maverick released our cocks and caught my leg behind the knee, raising it. With eyes devilish and full of filthy promises capturing mine, he licked and sucked the skin of my inner thigh.

Holy hell. Am I sure this is the same calm guy from work?

The torment continued when Maverick lowered my leg, following it to plant a kiss on the deep V of my hip. There, he took a deep inhale through the nose. "The smell of your sex is intoxicating."

"Ah!" I grunted when Maverick's mouth found one of my balls, sucking it inside. Panting, I opened an eye. Maverick watched me, still terrorizing my ball sack. "Fuck, you're filthy."

Maverick's dark laugh rumbled against my flesh. He crawled up my body and kissed me, thrusting his tongue deep into my mouth. "I have only just begun driving you mad," he said with a rasping breath.

I waited, helplessly pinned beneath him, as he crawled over me to take something from above my head. It wasn't until he sat on his knees that I noticed the small, plastic bottle. Maverick popped the lid and filled his hand with the contents.

"Raise those gorgeous legs for me, Aaron. I want to see the beautiful hole I've fantasized about filling since I first saw you." Maverick gripped his dick and began masturbating.

I hesitated doing what he asked. As badly as I wanted the same, something inside me seized up. I jumped when Maverick took my leg and guided it up. He stopped and stared at me with concern.

"I'm ... I'm sorry. It's—" I looked away, the sting of tears threatening to unleash themselves.

Instead of chiding me, Maverick kissed my inner thigh again. His hand glided down my hamstring to my ass cheek. "There's nothing to be sorry for. I imagine much of this pain and hesitation has to do with that bloody idiot from your apartment."

A finger following the path under my balls to my hole brought another jump. The soft pad rotated over the entrance. Maverick's face rubbed against mine, his stubble tickling me. "It's so soft and hot. Just like the rest of you." He kissed me behind the ear. "Trust me, sweetheart. I won't hurt you. Remember, you can be on top since it's been so long. I only want to prepare you to take me inside you."

Blood rushing from my head dizzied me. I raised my other leg, flattening my lower back against the smooth sheets and feeling completely exposed.

Maverick backed away, kneeling above me. His eyes examined my lower body. More fingers probed my entrance but never penetrated. "Bloody hell," Maverick said, breathless. "It's even more glorious than I thought. So fucking pretty."

I could listen to him cuss all day. Seeing this side of Maverick filled me with pride. I felt like I had a piece of him all to myself—a side of him he rarely showed to anyone. *And the most amazing thing? He wants me so badly he was willing to chase me down until he found me.*

I gasped, pulled from my musing when a single digit finally pushed past my ring of muscle. The sting of the invasion only lasted seconds, replaced by a subtle pressure. My first instinct was to push Maverick off and bolt from this place, but I fought to remember he wasn't Declan. I didn't have to do drugs or entertain fantasies anymore. Maverick wanted me as I was, not as he wanted me to be.

"You're tight, Aaron," Maverick said. "I'm going to need to relax you before I even think about taking you." His free hand took my face, holding it still. Not once did he quit finger-fucking me out of my damn mind. "Stop thinking. Whatever dark place your mind is taking you to, don't follow." Another finger entered me, spreading me, and reigniting the bite of pain. "Feel. Your body is hungry. It fights my entry but refuses to release me when I pull away."

He's right. I can feel it too. Every time his fingers push in, I feel sick, but when they leave, I want them back.

"Aaron," Maverick said, tightening his hold on my jaw. "Stop. If you aren't ready for this, I won't force you."

No. Please don't stop. I want you so badly. "N-no," I finally said through my sex-addled brain. "I want … you."

Maverick kissed me, tender and reassuring. "Then don't think. Feel. Relax in this moment and know how much I'm enjoying pleasing you."

I took a deep breath, closing my eyes, then released the tension with each inhale and exhale. The pressure from Maverick's invasion lessened every time I released a breath.

"Good," Maverick mused beside my ear. "I can feel you opening for me." When he withdrew his fingers, I almost whimpered. Standing on the edge of the perfect orgasm, only to have it torn away, was the worst.

Maverick squirted more lube into his palm and rubbed his shaft. The enormous length glistened in the faint light of the room. "Let me get you ready." He positioned the bottle over my crack and squeezed. Cool liquid seeped down and over my hole.

I rolled over so I could crawl up Maverick's body, watching him unpackage a condom put it on. He laid on his back, propped against the pillows and headboard. As I prepared to straddle him, I wondered if he would even fit or if he would split me in half.

Maverick's mind-reading powers reared their head again. He smiled a half-grin, eyes mimicking it. "I know what you're thinking. And, yes, I will fit."

Dunno if I love or hate that he can do that.

Swallowing, I crawled up Maverick's legs, once again admiring how tall he was. The finality of what we were about to do set in the longer I let myself think about it. Here was my boss. *My hot-as-fucking-hell, mind-reading, brain melting boss.* And I was about to have sex with him.

"Aaron." Maverick took my wrist, gently tugging. I expected him to order me not to think again. Instead, he said, "You look so bloody beautiful there."

His reassurance emboldened me. I stared down between my legs, where my throbbing length dripped pre-cum onto Maverick's stomach. Seeing that refueled my sense of pride. My position gave the perfect vantage point for me to watch myself mark him, spread my cum all over those gorgeous abs and chest, claiming him as mine.

With another breath, I rose to reach between my legs. My fist closed around Maverick's waiting penis. *This is it. If I do this, there's no going back.* I let go of the thoughts telling me I was wrong. Warning me if I did this, I'd be what Declan always told me I was. *Here goes nothing.*

Moving slowly, I rotated Maverick's tip against my slicked hole. Every few turns, I put some pressure against the rim. Like I feared, the muscle held tight. If I wanted to get anywhere, I'd have to add some force.

Okay, you can do this. Sure, it'll burn like fucking hell at first. Your eyes might even tear up, but it's been what? Five fucking years?

Maverick waited patiently, stroking my dick when it softened. "You can do it," he said. "Take it slow."

Teeth clenched, I exerted the right amount of pressure to force the rim muscle open. Maverick's tip pushed into my body. The pain of his entry sent shocks through my hips and lower back. Nausea gripped my stomach. Had Maverick not held my arms, I would've jumped off and run.

"Shh," Maverick said. "You feel amazing. Hot and so goddamn comfortable."

Tears stung my eyes. My teeth clenched harder, hurting my jaw. I didn't remember my first time aching this horribly. *Then again, Declan wasn't as big as Maverick.*

"Let me help you." Maverick adjusted himself so he could thrust inside me if he wanted. His motives became apparent when both hands held my thighs. "Open your hips. You can lie against me and push down when you're ready." I did as he said, letting his tip linger inside me as my body became used to his width. "You feel so wonderful, Aaron. Breathe."

The bed dipped with our weight. Maverick's heels pushed against the sheets, causing his cock to slide deeper inside me.

"Ah!" I gasped. Pleasure and pain slammed into one another the more of Maverick I took in my body. *Fuck, God! Fuck!* It felt like I was being torn apart. Only when Maverick angled himself to rub against my prostate did overwhelming ecstasy replace the pressure.

"Oh, God," I said with a moan, arching my neck. "Yes. Right there." Each word came on rushed breaths.

Maverick chuckled beside my ear. "I'm glad I found your pleasure spot. Ready to straighten up and take me all the way in?"

Was I ready? Fuck no. My ass was on fucking fire. But damn, did it feel good to have sex again. I pushed back to my knees and lowered my body. Inch by inch, Maverick's girth pushed the tight walls of my ass apart, intensifying the burn. Tears welled in the corners of my eyes. My nails gripped the flesh of Maverick's chest, leaving red marks.

"Hah," Maverick gasped, ignoring my digging nails. "Oh, Aaron. Sweet, sweet, Aaron. Yes. Breathe. I'm almost there. For fuck's sake, please breathe. I must take you as I want."

I needed no more encouragement after that. Through the pain I'd likely feel tenfold in the morning, I fucked Maverick like I'd dreamed of.

The bed bounced. Springs whined. Think of every corny sex scene in a movie and we said or did it. With each withdrawal, I thought my insides would follow Maverick's dick. But none of that mattered as my body grew used to the penetration. Once the immense pleasure of Maverick's cock hitting that perfect spot overtook the ache, I threw my head back. Loud moans and groans, light screams, and hissing through teeth emitted from me. *I hope he doesn't mind that I'm a screamer.*

"Fuck!" I shouted, shooting hot jets of cum on Maverick's stomach. That good old slutty side Declan liked to mock came out, and I smeared the sticky liquid all over the gorgeous man under me.

"I'm elated you got your pleasure. Now, I'm taking mine." Maverick grasped my hips. Using his heels, he thrust deep as he could. Each withdrawal nearly took him out, only to slam back inside with enough force to send me forward. "Fuck, Aaron, your ass feels amazing!"

I smiled, too winded to speak and too tired to do anything but let him take me. He finally came inside me with a roar.

CHAPTER 22

My finger traced the contours of Maverick's chest down his stomach to the light shadow of hair ending at the sheet. The rest of him hid beneath silken waves that did nothing to stop my imagination from reliving what we did.

Worn out, my ass on fire from the pounding he gave it, I rested my head on the bend of Maverick's shoulder. He had both arms raised above his head, eyes closed, and a smile on his face. Every once in a while, Maverick hummed. Mainly when my nails ran over his lower abdomen. *He likes that. I wonder if he might like this.*

I shifted my weight to my elbow, using my forearm to push me closer to the gorgeous nipple begging me to suck it. Before teasing the hardened nub, I looked up. Maverick had one eye open, watching intently. Behind the drooping eyelid was a hint of curiosity. Maverick made me feel daring. Like I could do anything I wanted to him and he'd be okay with it. Nothing we did felt forced. Even when I thought about running after the initial onset of pain, I didn't feel awkward or insignificant.

Maverick saw me. Really saw me. Not only for sex, but as someone he wanted. Someone he would chase down to have.

Elation filled me, and I lowered, never taking my eyes from the man above me. My tongue circled Maverick's nipple. I waited until it glistened with saliva before sucking it into my mouth. The musky smell of his cologne married perfectly with the scents of arousal and sex. Salty sweat and heated skin filled my mouth. *God, I can't get enough of him. He's like a fucking drug.*

"Keep doing that, sweetheart," he framed my face with his hands, "and I might push this gorgeous face into the pillows while taking you," Maverick said, his voice brain-meltingly sexy with its English rasping. "I doubt your poor little hole can handle the fucking I want to give it."

Part of me wanted to ignore the agonizing flame in my ass if it meant experiencing what Maverick had in mind. Thankfully, my more responsible half halted any further nipple teasing. I glanced at the digital clock: 2:30 am.

"I should go," I said, pushing the sheets aside and throwing my legs over the edge. None of my clothes were nearby. *Great. Where'd we leave them?* I stood. Pain in my rear end sent me back down. "Ow."

Springs whined as Maverick shifted his weight. A warm palm pressed against my shoulder. I looked back to see Maverick's version of puppy dog eyes.

"Stay," he said. "Please."

I wanted to. Fuck, if he only knew how much I wanted to. This was the first time we'd been together. I didn't want to move too fast or make any stupid, emotionally driven mistakes. *But there's Roxxie. She'll need to go out and get fed a second time.*

At least, that's the excuse I went with.

I found my jeans in a pile near the bedside table. The rest of my clothes had somehow migrated closer to Maverick's closet. Sometime between my grabbing my jeans and crossing to the closet, Maverick got out of bed and put on a pair of workout pants. They rode low on his hips.

Did he seriously not put any underwear on? Ignoring that seemed the smarter choice. Thinking about Maverick naked under those pants did nothing to help my resolve to leave.

I almost had my shirt on when Maverick wrapped his arms around me, his face buried in my hair. "Don't go. Please, Aaron."

This vulnerable side would take some getting used to. At work, Maverick commanded respect. Nothing appeared to shake him until I came around.

His hands held me flush against him. The hardness and heat of his body created an enclosing furnace.

Does he think I'll just disappear? That if he lets me go, we'll never— Realization struck. I opened my mouth to speak, but Maverick beat me to it.

"I want to see you again," Maverick said against my hair.

"You do. Every day I at work." I knew what he meant. Didn't keep me from wanting to hear him say it, though. Somewhere inside, I wanted—needed—to hear him say it.

Maverick shook his head, tousling my hair. "No. Not like that. Like this. I want to—"

"You mean you want to see each other? Like to *see* see each other?" I thought my heart might do a 180 or go into cardiac arrest. Whichever came first. "Mav, you're my boss. Don't you think ... well, you know."

"I don't care," Maverick said sternly. "When you left that morning, I vowed to myself I'd never stop searching until I found you. Being your boss doesn't change that." He held my jaw, angling it so he could kiss along the bone. "I want to see you, Aaron. Here, your home, my office—"

His ... office? Really?

A dark chuckle blew hot air into my ear. "I know what you must be thinking. That little gasp betrayed you." *Shit.* "Yes,

Aaron. I do plan on fucking you in my office. In fact, I already know when and how."

Cocky, egotistical bastard.

"However, that part of my plan has to wait. Feel free to mull it over. I love seeing you stew when I don't give you all the answers you want." Maverick kissed my neck and traveled down to my shoulder. "Tonight, I beg of you, stay. I want to feel your warmth beside me."

My resolve slowly shattered under the sadness and desperation in his voice. Elliot had a friend in the same building as me. She lived a few doors down and had come over a few times when Elliot and I spent all night gossiping or making fun of our bosses. I didn't talk to her much, but she walked and dog-sat Roxxie when I attended class or worked all night on a case for Mr. Kimball.

"Let me make a call," I said. *I am such a pussy.*

Maverick let me go. I turned to see a smile plastered on his perfect face as I reached for my phone. My thumb shook over the keypad. *Elliot is not going to like me mucking up his evening.*

I knew exactly what my best friend did on the Fridays we didn't go to the bar. Odds were his boyfriend was balls deep in Elliot's ass, and knowing El, he'd murder the soul daring enough to bother him during such a pounding. I scrolled through my contacts to see if I'd get lucky by having my neighbor's phone number. When I didn't find it, I cursed internally. *How can I not have the damned number?* I mentally kicked myself more, scrolling back to El's number and dialing. *Not like I want to, but I don't have a choice.*

The phone rang a few times, making me wonder if El would answer at all. *I know if someone interrupted me during the erotic euphoria I experienced earlier, I'd definitely kill them. Can't blame him if he doesn't—*

"Bitch, you better have a fucking good reason for calling," Elliot answered, his breath heavy. I swallowed a gulp, nearly speaking, when El said, "Hey, knock it off, or I'll get the paddle again."

"Okay, I didn't need to hear that."

"You called me, remember? What's up? And make it quick, please. I'm having to fight off a horny bear." Shuffling occurred in the background, followed by repeated "quit its" and a "don't make me get the leash!"

Didn't even know El was into that stuff. "I promise I won't take up too much of your time." Maverick nuzzled into my neck, kissing and sucking at the skin. I muted the phone and said, "No hickies. The last thing I want to explain is where those came from."

"You wear a high collared vest," Maverick replied. "I highly doubt anyone would notice."

Clearly, he didn't know Elliot. I'd see my friend on my off day at his salon for lunch, knowing I'd get hounded with all kinds of questions regarding how good Maverick was in bed.

"Just hang on, okay?" I unmuted the phone. "El, I need you to call Ricky. I can't find her number and—"

"You lucky slut!" Elliot burst out in his "praise and celebration" tone. That high-pitched congratulations voice friends give you at parties. "You know you're going to give all the details. Especially if you're staying the night."

I nodded and rolled my eyes, knowing he couldn't see me. "Yes, El, I already know. Would you call her? I'll try to be home—"

Elliot cut me off. "Don't even worry about it. You focus on getting that hot cock in your needy ass. I'll take care of Miss Roxxie for you. That's why you're concerned, right?"

"Yeah."

"Cool. No worries. I'll call Ricky. If she can't go, I'll just head over myself. Mind if I bring my boyfriend? Promise we won't do anything in your bed. Hell, I promise not to do anything but make out on your sofa."

"So didn't need to hear that. That's fine. Thanks for doing this."

"Sure, now let me go before I'm forced to throw this damn phone. You get your sexy self back in that man's arms. See you Monday!" Elliot made a kissing noise, and we hung up.

"Well?" Maverick purred in my ear. "Stay?"

Chuckling, I reached to pet his face. He took my hand, entwined our fingers, and kissed from my palm to my wrist.

"Stay," I replied, and we went back to his bed.

I woke the next morning with a moan followed by a stretch. During the night, I'd rolled onto my stomach. The sheets hung over my hips. One butt-cheek peeked from beneath the cream silkiness. I purred and shivered like a satisfied cat.

Maverick's fingers ran up the length of my spine. They repeated their path a few more times before their owner drew close and kissed my shoulder.

"Good morning," he said. "I trust you slept well."

"Well" was an understatement. I didn't think I'd slept that good since Declan kicked my sore ass out of his apartment years ago.

"Yeah," I murmured into the pillow. "How long have you been up?"

"Since about six. I enjoyed watching you sleep." Maverick's lips replaced his fingers, following the same path his fingers had.

I moaned. Maverick's fingers ran over my side to the divot between my hip and lower abdomen. Every nerve in my body skyrocketed to attention, including the rod I fought humping the bed with.

Maverick hummed against my back. Positioning his body under the sheet, he pressed his cock against my ass crack. "If only you weren't hurting from last night's activities, I'd happily take you again."

Wanting to experience that pleasure again nearly had me telling my aching ass to shut the fuck up, but I needed to leave. Elliot agreed to check on Roxxie if his friend couldn't do it. That didn't mean I had the time to screw around and keep Maverick in bed all day, much as I wished I could.

"I need to go anyway," I said. "Roxxie needs to get taken for a run. And I've got some college work to do and chores to get done before work Tuesday."

Maverick's dejected sigh tugged at my heartstrings. Neither one of us wanted to say goodbye. I learned more about Maverick Waylan in one night than the few weeks I worked with him. We had tons in common, yet I suspected Maverick kept something from me. I couldn't say anything. I was keeping something from him, too. Something made me find any way I could to keep him from coming to my apartment.

"I have to go into court later today," Maverick said. I turned to see he'd put on the same pants from last night. "You're welcome to get cleaned up before leaving if you like. Feel free to eat something as well. We have leftovers from last night. But if you'd like breakfast, I'm afraid I don't have anything resembling vegetable juice."

I rolled my eyes. "My diet isn't that bad."

"Says the man who had trouble eating pancakes at the diner we went to on our first outing together," Maverick teased back. "I mean it, though. Make yourself at home. Perhaps bring Miss Roxxie next time so I don't have to suffer the premature departure of her handsome owner."

Again, I rolled my eyes, head shaking. *Smart ass.*

Laughing, Maverick went to his bathroom, leaving me alone in the room I fled from the first night we met. Uncertainty and embarrassment had plagued my first visit to this place. Seconds passed, and I heard the hissing of the shower. The sound brought back another memory. A memory of my being terrified the no-longer-mystery-man would see me as a man-whore.

Boy, was I wrong. Now, I didn't feel out of place. Everything was ... right. Like I belonged here. Like I was welcome here.

I wonder if he'd mind if I saw him in the shower. Curiosity took over, and I soon felt my legs leading me toward the door. *He wouldn't, right? I mean, he fucked my brains out last night. Surely he wouldn't get upset if I saw him in the shower.*

My hand reached for the door. Questions howled in my head like angry banshees. The previous night showed me how sexual Maverick could be. How demanding and hot he was under all the professionalism. He tortured me with the most erotic pleasure I'd ever experienced and swore to have sex with me in his office. I wanted to know if he did things other guys did in the shower. *Oh, come on, of course he masturbates in there. Don't all guys?*

As a kid, I once saw my older sister making out—or fucking—her boyfriend in the bathroom. *Would Maverick want to do something like that? Have sex under the showerhead?*

Before I knew what was happening, Maverick opened the bathroom door with nothing but a towel on. Water dripped from his gorgeous hair, down his face. Rivulets tempting me to lick them up fell over the dips and rises of his shoulders, chest, and lower stomach.

Holy hell, I should've left when I had the chance.

Smiling, Maverick said, "I didn't think you would still be here."

Diffuse the sex, diffuse the sex, diffuse the sex. "I was about to leave. Not my fault you take such quick showers."

"Is that so? Then, I assume there's something you needed to get from my bathroom." Hell, he had me. Maverick cupped my face, his other hand grabbing my hip and pulling me forward. "Did you want to watch, Aaron? Perhaps join me? You could have. I wouldn't have minded the pleasurable company."

Shit. Shit. Shit. "No thanks. I like my ass inside my body. Anyway, I'll be going now." I tried pushing away, but Maverick held me close.

"When can I see you again? And don't give me an 'at work' response. I mean, see you. Like this." He kissed me, the tip of his tongue exploring my gums and teeth.

I came up for air, hands splayed on his naked chest. "I'll text you. Promise." My cheeks heated. "I ... actually had something I wanted to ask you."

Maverick waited silently, his eyes searching my face.

None of the words came out. Shame and embarrassment surrounded what I wanted to request of him. In some ways, I didn't think I deserved to ask. I looked everywhere except at Maverick. The throbbing between my legs didn't help, either. All I could think about was...

Another smile, more devious than the one he'd used in his office, tugged at Maverick's lips. "You want me to suck your cock next we meet, is that it?"

How the hell does he do that? My eyes roamed over Maverick's shoulder to the bathroom. Heavy thudding and rushing blood made me lightheaded. I'd always wanted to know what getting a blow job was like. The one time I asked Declan had ended horribly. I learned never to ask again.

Maverick kissed my lips and forehead. "You can ask me for anything, Aaron. I want your trust and will do anything to get it. If that is what you want, then believe me, it would be my greatest honor."

The love shining in Maverick's eyes caused my eyes to mist. *Damn it, how embarrassing is this? Am I really about to cry?*

Maverick tilted my head so my eyes met his. "Come home with me Friday after work. We will pick up Roxxie and get you packed for the weekend. I want to see you longer than a single night. Is that alright with you?"

Staying the weekend with Maverick sounded better than "alright." It sounded like a dream. Especially when he agreed and understood how much Roxxie meant to me. The only thing I could think of that might hinder our weekend together was the upcoming renaming party Travis wanted to throw for Maverick.

"I don't know. We still have a lot to do for the law firm's renaming thing. Might have some late nights at the office," I said. "Maybe take a rain check until after the damn thing?"

Maverick shook his head. "I already have plans for that night. Even if we have to work, I'd love for you to come home with me. If you don't want to, I won't force the issue. Think about it?"

I nodded. For all Maverick did for me, the least I could do was think on his offer. But I definitely couldn't let him come to my place. Not with all the checklists hanging everywhere. He might think I'm some overly controlling freak.

How soul crushing would that be?

"Thank you," Maverick said, kissing me again. He released me and backed away, hands out to his sides, palms up. "I'm not worried. After all, you will say yes. It's only a matter of time."

I reiterate. Smug bastard.

And fuck was I falling for him fast.

CHAPTER 23

My apartment door squeaked open as I nudged it. I hadn't eaten anything at Maverick's, so I'd asked my cab driver to stop by Early Bird. Neither my muffin nor most of my coffee lasted long. *Guess I didn't realize how hungry I was. Go figure after the pounding I took last night.*

Roxxie didn't run to me, which worried me considering she never waited long to bombard me.

"Rox?" I called.

Footsteps coming down the short hall scared the hell out of me. I readied to defend myself with an umbrella, of all things, only to see Elliot saunter around the corner in nothing but an oversized shirt.

Elliot rubbed his eyes, stopped, and looked at me and my weapon. "You're kidding me with this, right? Did you forget what I said?"

Rolling my eyes, I put the umbrella down. "No, El, I didn't forget. Just didn't expect to see you walking half-naked out of my living room. What are you doing here? I thought you were just checking on—"

Josh Bianchi joined us in the kitchen. His eyes bulged when he saw me. "Um ... I can explain."

I wasn't sure I wanted him to. Josh and Elliot stood together in my kitchen both half-clothed. Everything made sense now.

"This is Brandon?" I asked, thrusting a finger at Josh. Joshua Brandon Bianchi was his full name. Brandon keeping his boyfriend a secret made more sense now. "Are you fucking kidding me?"

Elliot shrugged a shoulder. "What? We talked one day while I waited for you to stop crying over Declan in the bathroom, hit it off, and hooked up. Josh asked me out a few weeks after. This," Elliot rotated his finger at me, "is why I didn't want to tell you yet."

That explanation did little to help me. I shouldn't have gotten as wound up as I did. The taxi ride gave me time to think about some things, like why in the world someone like Maverick wanted to be with someone like me. Leaving him didn't ease the situation. I wanted to stay longer. Maybe the entire day. If not for Roxxie, I would've taken Maverick up on his offer to wait for him.

Add in his request to see me again regularly, and my mind became a torrent of pent-up agony. Maverick Waylan had me twisted into a ball of emotional checklists. Pros and cons battered each other on a mental battlefield that a mind without caffeine shouldn't have to comprehend this early in the morning.

I propped my ass against the counter. Josh and Elliot stood silent, their eyes scrutinizing every move I made. Josh moved closer to Elliot as though my best friend needed protection against me. Couldn't blame the guy. I reacted irrationally.

"Sorry, El, I'm still mulling over last night. Thanks for watching out for Roxxie." To make peace, I half-smiled, crossed the small space, and reached a hand to Josh. "Congrats, man. Careful though, this one's a handful." Elliot smacked my arm, earning a laugh.

Josh took my hand, his face relaxing, a sigh emitting from his nostrils. "Thanks. Sorry we kept it a secret. Elliot didn't know how to tell you. I wanted to so many times. I know this one's a handful. But he's worth all of it." He walked back into the living room.

Elliot followed his boyfriend. The two soon returned with Elliot helping Josh pull his shirt back over his head. "I'll get out of here so you two can chat," Josh said. The two casually kissed.

"Hey, Josh," I said, following him to the door.

Josh halted, looking back at me. "Yeah?"

I folded and unfolded a fist, gnawing on my lower lip, trying to come up with the words I wanted to say. "Do you really care what goes on between me and Maverick? Even if it's at work?"

The guy burst out laughing. "Are you kidding me? Dude, not at all. The two of you can fuck in the janitor's closet. I don't give a shit. No one cares, man. Might be careful around Dudley and that old crone at the secretary's desk, though. You know Duds has the hots for you."

Shit, I hadn't thought about Dudley. If he found out, it'd devastate him. It wasn't like I owed Dudley anything, but the guy was more sensitive than I was.

And that was saying something.

"Hey, don't worry too much about it. Dudley's chased your ass since you started there. Might be time for him to get let down easily," Josh said. "Gotta go. I'm already running late for my other job."

"You have another job?" I asked. Secretive Josh had another job?

Josh nodded. "Yep. I'm a bartender at Rouge. And sometimes bouncer. Not all of us have the pleasure of working with one of the senior partners." He paused, probably noticing the guilt-ridden scowl on my face. Throwing up his hands, Josh added, "It's fine, man. I can barely stand the few hours I'm at the firm. I'm thinking about going to the bar full time." An arm went around Elliot's waist, pulling him close. "At least then I can have my man there to look at if I get bored. Then when I'm on break—"

"Okaaay." Elliot patted his boyfriend's chest. "Don't think Aaron wants to know that detail. I agree though." He tossed a glance my way. "If your new boyfriend wasn't the boss, Aaron, I'd suggest you quit too."

"Hey! He's not—" I protested.

"Yep, you better go, babe," Elliot said to Josh, cutting me off. He and Josh kissed again, and Josh left. "Now, you and I have some chatting to do." The beaming smile I used to crush on Elliot for shone my way. "How hot was he? Please tell me all the juicy details."

Elliot made coffee while I took Roxxie outside to do her business. I promised her we'd go on a late park run as an apology for being gone all night. She hated when I did that and got antsy. One time I had to stay at the firm late. The neighbor called me complaining Roxxie was barking and scratching at the door.

After getting coffee, Elliot, Roxxie and I retired to the living room. Roxxie jumped on the couch beside me. Elliot took a spot on the floor nearby. I'd always invited him to sit in the chair or beside Roxxie, but he refused, telling me the floor was his favorite spot.

"Spill it," Elliot demanded, jabbing a finger at me. "All of it. Don't you dare try to leave anything out."

I relayed all the information, starting with dinner, keeping most of the saucy bits to myself at first. But we knew each other too well, and Elliot rose to his knees and thumped my head anytime he sensed I left out any juicier details. My story ended with this morning and how hard it was for me to leave.

Elliot's smile got wider—if that was possible. "You are falling hard, fast, babe. I can't tell you how happy I am. You hadn't swooned over anyone since ... the other guy." He dismissed "the other guy" with a hand wave and eye-roll. "So, how was Mr. Hot Lawyer? Long? Thick? Veiny? Cut? Your ass hurt?" Elliot probed.

I waved my hands. "I, uh, don't think Maverick would approve of me talking about his dick to my best friend. Besides, how is the condition of my asshole any business of yours?"

Elliot's finger moved down to the awkward way I sat. "Maybe because you keep shifting and wincing when you hit the wrong spot. Your ass is on fire. Admit it."

Damn his observation skills! Between Elliot and Maverick, I can't keep any secrets!

Crossing my arms, I huffed, averting my eyes. "Okay, so it hurts. Not like it hasn't been ... what, five years since I last got laid? Give a guy a fucking break." My cheeks felt as hot as my asshole.

Elliot guffawed. "Fine, I'll ease up. Seriously, though, I'm thrilled for you. Are you seeing him again?"

My finger tapped my bicep. Mav and I would see each other again. There was no doubt about that. I wanted to, no, *needed*, to see Maverick again. *Elliot's right. I'm falling hard and fast. Is that stupid, though? I barely know the guy.*

"You're doing the overthinking thing, again," Elliot said. "Don't. Remember what I said? Let this thing play out. Maverick makes you happy. That's all that matters."

"Declan showed up at my apartment," I interjected.

Dinner plates replaced Elliot's eyes. "You're shitting me. Really? Dicklan showed up?"

I nodded.

"Of all the shit-faced, ball-sucking motherfuckers!" Elliot shouted. "What the fuck did he want?"

"The usual. Started out all apologetic. Shifted to how much of a whore I was and called Maverick my sugar daddy. Insulted how I had sex. Blah, blah, blah..." I had to stop talking about it or risk getting pissed off. "Maverick told Declan off, El. In the hallway in front of my damn door."

Elliot applauded. "Love the man even more. What'd he say?"

I shook my head. "I don't know. The whole thing was weird as fuck. I've never seen Declan's face turn that red. He actually apologized to me."

"Holy shit! Talk about the pope and the Huns. Has Declan bothered you since?"

Another headshake. Declan probably did what he usually does when facing a real man—run. He'll go home and lick his wounds, scheming on how to hurt me in some twisted sense of discipline. Somehow, though, I doubted he'd do the same thing this time. Not since Maverick had an enormous influence and the power to smash Declan into the ground.

"I'm scared, El," I said. "Maverick doesn't know about..." My eyes drifted over the checklists and whiteboards I kept in my kitchen and living room. "What if he thinks I'm ... you know? A freak."

"He's a lawyer, Aaron. I highly doubt he cares how organized you are. It's creepy, no arguing that, but if Maverick wants you as much as it sounds like, he won't care. I've heard rumors about his mother. Believe me, if he's willing to charge horns with that bull, he *really* wants you."

Another thing I didn't think about before diving in. Go figure. Maverick's mother finding out about Mav and me terrified me more than Travis finding out.

"I should get going," Elliot said. "My shift starts at one today. Drop by if you like. Babe, when was the last time I did those colors?"

"My hair is black, Elliot," I said, rolling my eyes.

"Yeah, but I could give you some nice lowlights. Get that raven feather thing going on. Just something to think about." Elliot picked his clothes from the floor. "Let me get dressed. Be back soon."

Elliot left shortly before 10:30. I took Roxxie on a quick park run. My dog wasn't happy since the local place didn't have Central Park's vast running trails. Though getting out placated her enough to let me open my laptop and check on the week's college assignments without her nagging.

Two test grades came through—lower than the previous. *I did what I could. At least they're high Bs.* I clicked over to my email to see a subject line capable of stalling my heart for a moment. *The internship. I ... I got it!*

A weight fell on my heart. Instead of the elation I expected, I felt—*what? Sad? Disappointed? What the hell? This is what I wanted. A way out of this place. A chance to finally live up to the life I imagined for myself?*

I clenched my teeth and squeezed my eyes closed as war waged inside me over a beautiful face with a smile I adored. *I will have to leave him.* The realization slammed into my gut like the hardest punch. *Will I ever see him again?*

My previous life plans didn't include falling in love with someone, let alone someone I met in a chance encounter. The more I thought about it, the more my life was shaping out like a cheesy kid's movie where the protagonist had plans to run away from a shitty life to follow their dreams. *Okay, that's just bad. Don't think of it like that. But hell, is there any other way to describe what's going on right now?*

I didn't reply to the email.

I couldn't.

Not yet.

I had an urge to talk to Maverick about this. But if I did, it would crush him. *Maybe not. I mean, it's not like we're boyfriends. And there's always texting and phone calls, right?*

I smacked myself the moment that thought came to mind. Long-distance relationships—especially for a horny, sex-loving guy—were torture. *Besides, Maverick might have an idea about how I could both stay with him and follow my dreams.*

Resourcefulness, which was not one of my strengths, poured from Maverick like water over a cliff. If anyone could help me sort this out, Maverick could.

I can't worry about this now. There's a ton of work to do.

And I still had to decide how and when I could see Maverick again.

Roxxie whimpered beside me.

I glanced at her, a lazy smile curling my lips. "Hey, how about that Central Park run?"

Claws tore across the floor faster than a cat on too much catnip. Scratching at the door, high-pitched whines, and not-so-subtle barks gave me my answer.

Laughing, I changed from my sweats and old t-shirt into running clothes. Running always helped me clear my head. It gave me a chance to break away from stress.

A text message beeped through my phone. I looked at the screen, my eyes widening.

CHAPTER 24

The rest of the weekend passed with little upset. I took most of Monday cleaning my apartment, slowly checking things off the multiple checklists hanging on the refrigerator, cabinets, pantry, and wherever else I hung the damn things.

Many of the boxes on the kitchen white board had checks in them by the day's end, including those involving the essay I finished early, yet forgot to turn in.

Mom called Sunday, asking me how I was, if I knew how things went with Rebecca's battle with paparazzi, and if I'd asked the new man in my life to be my boyfriend. I always rolled my eyes at that one since Mom made it her mission to be the saving grace of my love life. Some of those conversations got awkward. Mostly regarding gay male hygiene and health. I shuddered.

During the call, I felt guilty because I spent more time thinking about the text message I got before my run with Roxxie. What I read made me gasp so hard, I went over the words multiple times.

As I stood in line at Early Bird, I read the words again. The rampaging throb in my ribcage kicked up.

[Maverick: I can't stop thinking about you.]

That was all it took for me to become a melting mess. Six paltry words held more power than anything anyone had ever said to me in my adult life.

"Morning, Aaron. Your usual?" The adorable red head who never held back hints he wanted to "do" me, said. I must not have responded fast because he waved a hand in front of my face. "Hello?"

"Oh, sorry. Yeah, the usual. Thanks."

"You okay? Seem a bit loopy this morning."

I offered a small smile to appease him, paid, and took a seat next to the large glass window overlooking the clothing stores across the street. Running had given me a chance to do a lot of thinking. And what little down time I had on Monday evening allowed me to mull things over on a deeper level. I concluded I didn't care what I had to do. I wanted Maverick, and I'd do anything I needed to have him. He completed me, filling a hole my dumpster fire of a life had plunged into when I met Declan.

The redhead brought my coffee and muffin to the table, standing there with a hand on his hip. "You didn't answer me. Are you okay, Aaron? I'm here to talk if you want."

I smiled again, rose, and put a hand on his shoulder. I didn't say anything, only taking my coffee and muffin before walking out of the door.

Am I okay? I think so. Finally, I think so.

At least, I thought I was okay.

I walked into the law firm, meeting a frantic Leslie, who grabbed me by my free arm and pulled me into an empty office.

"Shh, don't let him find you!"

"What the hell, Les? Let who find me? You can't be that fucking cryptic and not expect a guy to freak out," I said, tugging my arm free.

Leslie shushed me again. "Dudley. He found out you're seeing Maverick. I swear I didn't say a thing! Maybe he overheard someone talking." She held up two fingers. "I swear I didn't tell him."

Fucking fantastic. Nothing like drama to greet a new workweek. "Doesn't matter, Les. I'll be too busy to explain. I still have to complete Mr. Wayland's—"

Arms crossed, Leslie cocked her hip, raising a brow.

"What?"

"Mr. Waylan? Really? Please, Aaron, what did we tell you? No one cares about you banging the boss, okay? We all worked our asses off helping him get your stubborn self to go out with him." Leslie jabbed a perfectly manicured—and fucking sharp—nail into my chest. "Knock off the 'Mr. Waylan' shit."

Fuck, it's a conspiracy. I fucking knew it. They are all in on it. I wrapped my arms around her and pulled her close. She patted my back. "Thanks, Les."

"You have no idea how relieved I am to hear you say that. I thought you'd kill us!" she replied, pulling away. "Seriously though, be careful. Dudley—"

"Yeah, I know. I've known for a long time. Just never knew what to say to the guy. Don't want to hurt him, you know?"

She nodded. "You're so sweet. Better get to work. Your honey will wonder where his squeeze is."

I shouted at her, only to hear her giggling, heels clanking as she darted away.

Squeeze. Good grief. You fuck a guy once, and your co-workers think you've married him. How bad would it be for me to shatter their dreams as a joke?

Huffing, I walked to the break room to clock in.

Coffee smelling more like toxic waste than anything drinkable permeated the small room. The scent hit me so hard I backstepped, tripping over one of the two chairs. My back hit something firm. A familiar, musky—*and so fucking sexy*—scent replaced the burning coal smell.

"Bloody hell, can't leave you alone for a second, can I?" Maverick teased. His height made me crane my head to see those gorgeous eyes I dreamed of all weekend.

Maverick wore a dark grey suit and matching trousers, complemented by a white shirt and black tie. The sexy ensemble went perfectly with his hipster glasses and black leather work shoes.

Christ, I love to see him all professional. Well, I liked him better naked, but this wasn't bad. Finding my words took me more time than I should've needed.

"Hi," in a swooning voice was all I managed.

"And a good morning to you too," Maverick replied. "How was your weekend?"

Come on, tongue. Work for me. Stop gawking. It did worse. It started rambling. "Not bad. Spent most of it doing college work, spoke with Mom on Sunday, and cleaned the apartment yesterday." Pausing, I ran a hand over the back of my neck. Heat flushed my cheeks. "Got a ... really nice message from a guy I think I like."

Maverick's brow hooked, that cocky grin playing at the corner of his mouth. "Oh? What did he say?"

Unfortunately, being in the breakroom exposed us to too many prying eyes. The scene played out like some high school hallway. Josh and Frankie chuckled from their spots at the main desk. Leslie and Edith, another clerk, pretended to go back to talking.

Right, like I'm that stupid, guys.

Then there was Dudley. If I wanted to avoid him, leaving the break room sounded like the smartest idea.

I cleared my throat. "You, uh, think we should head back to your office? If my calendar's right, you have an early appointment, and I have to work on finalizing your guest list for the renaming next week."

Maverick snuffed a laugh through his nostrils. "I applaud that one. It's actually a good ploy to get away."

My lips pursed. I didn't tell him it wasn't a ploy as much as an attempt to get out of the spotlight. Then I did what I typically did when Maverick threw my attempt to one up him—turned into a total ass. "Fine, if you want your list unfinished and to be late with your client, that's your problem. Doesn't really matter to me."

The comeback didn't work this time.

Instead of taking the hit like he usually did, Maverick used his body to shove me backward, closing the door behind us. His torso pushed me until my ass hit the counter near the coffeepot.

Nothing but the hum of the slowly dying refrigerator made a sound. The silence left nothing but the rhythm of my thudding heart and heavy breathing in my ears. I tried to think of any reason we should stop what was happening. Inside, I wanted to continue. To see how far Maverick wanted this to go.

Blood rushed south, my cock painfully aware of Maverick's thigh pressed between my legs. I grunted, fighting the urge to rub against the soft material of his pants. The beads attached to the leather bands I always wore on my wrist tinkled against the marble counter.

One of Maverick's hands caged me. The other ran from my hip to my ass, back to my side, and under my shirt. His soft touch sent shivers down my spine.

"Clever and sharp tongued as always." Maverick breathed in my ear, making me shiver. "Keep throwing that sassy mouth my way, and I'll show you what you can do with it."

Shit, he's talking filthy again. I closed my eyes, relishing the heat of Maverick's body.

Images of the firm muscles of his chest and abdomen formed in my brain. My tongue teased my teeth, remembering how it rolled over Maverick's hardened nipple.

God, I want to do that again.

I let one hand travel up Maverick's bicep to his shoulder. Something about the taboo nature, the danger of getting caught, heightened my arousal. The breakroom had no locks. At any moment, someone could come in wanting coffee or day-old donuts.

Maverick took my lips with his, thrusting his tongue into my mouth and exploring its depths. "Mmm, you've had your muffin this morning." He sucked my tongue into his mouth. "Chocolate goes so well with your natural taste. I wonder if it's the same," he mused, rubbing between my legs, "down here."

Oh fuck. Oh fuck. Oh fuck. I clenched my teeth. *Don't cum. Please don't cum. I'd be so embarrassed.*

Like he read my mind, Maverick backed away. "I should let you go, yes? If I held you any longer, I'd have to take a chair and block the bloody door until I finished sampling you."

I admitted to being disappointed at the sudden withdrawal yet was thankful considering how terrified I was of discovery. If Travis ever found out, it'd be the end of me.

I followed Maverick out the door, watching the repeated high school scene and rolling my eyes at each of the gigglers.

Maverick continued to his office while I walked around my desk to turn the computer on. The monitor no longer screamed at me, and the massive desk helped keep all my planners organized in one place.

I sat down and started a list of everything I needed to get done that day.

"Aaron," Maverick called from his office. "Would you come here, please?"

Sighing, I stood, made my way to Maverick's door, and leaned against it. "Yeah?"

Maverick stopped messing with his open laptop and came around to rest against his desk. "I wanted to ask you something." He looked away, lips tight. The crow's feet around his eyes became more pronounced. He almost looked nervous. Same as he did the morning he begged me to stay with him. "I'm not sure how you will take it."

"Mav?" I asked, fear he might have changed his mind about us rearing its ugly head. *Did someone call him over the weekend? Threaten him?* I drew closer. "Hey, you okay?"

Maverick raised his head. The smile he wore did little to hide the uncertainty hiding in his eyes. "I'm fine, sweetheart. I was wondering if you might come with me to this ridiculous party Travis wants to host."

I barked a laugh. "I'll already be there. You made me your assistant. Be kinda odd if I didn't, right?" My joke had no effect.

Maverick's eyes became stern, his business side taking over. "I don't mean as my assistant."

A gasp escaped me. "Oh, you mean ... oh." I lowered my head. "I don't know, Mav. We've barely started seeing each other."

"I plan on changing that. You know I won't force you to do something you don't want to, but I want to see you much more than at work." Maverick reached out and pulled me against him. My hips nestled against his lower stomach and forced my back to arch. The position put my back into a rather painful posture, but the way he held me told me he needed this.

We stood there in a moment more powerful than our romp in the sheets. I let my hand stroke his hair, the other rub his back. Intuition led me to think he had spoken to someone over the weekend. He held me, not saying anything.

He's so gorgeous when he's vulnerable. "Mav, did someone say something to you? Like your mom or brother?"

"Why do you ask?" Maverick asked with a muffled voice, his head against my chest.

I swallowed. *Hope I'm not over-stepping here.* "It just seems ... I don't know. Like you're sad or afraid."

Maverick huffed. "You know me so well already. Yes, Connor called, but that isn't the reason." He pulled away, both arms around my waist, chin against my sternum. "You didn't reply."

"Huh?"

"My text. You didn't reply." Maverick burst out laughing, letting me go to run a hand through his hair. "Look at me. You must see me as a desperate, overly clingy fool."

I waved my hands defensively. "No, I ... I don't think that." I sat on the chair in front of him. "Truth is, I think it's sweet. I've never really had anyone who cared enough to pursue me like this. I guess I'm wondering why more than anything."

"I'll tell you what I told you before. Being with you feels right to me. Whatever stress or pain I might go through, seeing you or hearing your voice takes that away."

Silence—only interrupted by the muffled honking cars, or occasional airplane outside Maverick's window—took over for a moment.

"Will you come with me?" Maverick asked. "We don't have to announce it. I'm perfectly fine keeping you to myself." He laughed a curtly. "I suppose what I'm asking is..."

"Yes," I said.

Maverick jerked his head back toward me. "What did you say?"

Leaping from the chair, I threw my arms around his neck. "Yes. I'll go with you. Yes, I'll go out with you." This time, I crushed my mouth against his. I liked all the dancing around, the hinting, and the flirting, but I wanted more. "I'll come to your place, overnight bags in hand. Plenty of condoms and lube."

Maverick blinked a few times like I'd slapped him.

"I want you, Mav. Whatever that means." Another, more tender, kiss. "Because you make me feel the same. I don't feel lonely when I'm around you. You make me feel like I'm worth something that's not only sex." *Insert irony in 3 ... 2 ... 1.* "Maverick, I guess what I'm asking is ... will you ... that is—"

The phone ringing ended our moment.

"That's your nine o'clock," I said ruefully. "I'll go see if they're here."

I walked back to the door.

Maverick's stream of four-letter words didn't go unnoticed.

CHAPTER 25

I spent the remainder of the day working on the list I made for myself. Maverick had appointments and calls for the rest of the afternoon. I think we wanted some time apart. Or I did. As much as I loved being with Maverick, things between us sped at an alarming rate. The last thing I wanted was to screw up by not taking the time to know one another outside of having sex or because of random passings like in the park.

Which is why you're dating him, moron. Remember?

"Cambrian!" Travis's shrill voice could make wolves howl miles away.

"Why not shout louder, Marks? I don't think I hear the neighborhood dogs barking yet," I snapped, never looking away from my keyboard.

Sure, the guy was my boss, and the old me never hesitated to kiss his ass, but I didn't really care right now. Lately, my confidence bloomed. I found I no longer worried over the things I used to.

Guess Mav's kinda rubbing off on me. Not that I'm upset about it. I grew tired of being everyone's bitch.

Travis smacked his hands on my desk. "Watch it, Aaron. You think I don't know what's going on? Please. If I didn't have to suck up to Mr. Waylan's precious toy, your ass would be out of a job."

My eyes widened, fingers freezing mid-type. *How did he find out so fast?* Travis stayed more aloof than the crone of a secretary he employed. I hid a nervous swallow.

Marks smirked. "That's better." He slapped a paper on my desk. "I want this catering list completed by Wednesday evening. Every pass goes through me, got it? I don't care who you're fucking, whether you like it or not, I'm your boss. Screw with me, and I'll get rid of you myself."

"Is there a problem, Travis?" Maverick had returned early from his lunch. *Thank you, deus ex machina.* He eyed me, then Travis. "Is there something *my* assistant can do for you?"

Travis glared at me, the message clear: *keep your mouth shut or else.* A false, make-me-vomit-in-my-mouth grin replaced the smirk. "I was having the catering list looked at. Nothing too extensive. I'm in court all week, so my assistant will be too busy."

Taking the list, Maverick scanned over it. "I can handle this. It looks like you already have most of it where it needs to be. Aaron already has the guest list. He doesn't need to take on anymore."

I blew a relieved breath.

Travis's scowled. "Right. Well, I have a court appointment after lunch. Is my taking off tomorrow still doable?"

Maverick nodded. "Yes. Shouldn't be a problem. Have a good court day."

The other partner left us alone. I was more nervous, despite the overwhelming gratitude of Maverick walking in. He folded the paper and stuck it into his pocket.

"What did he say to you?" Maverick asked.

"Nothing really," I replied, trying to play it off.

Maverick strode around the desk, took my chair, and wheeled me to face him. "Don't do that. Don't lie to me. What did he say?"

I frowned. Every part of me stiffened as my frustration grew. Fists balled on the arms of my chair. "You know I can take care of myself, right, Mav? I handled Travis Marks way before you ever showed up in my life. I don't need you to come to my rescue. Not with fucking Declan, and sure as hell not with Marks!"

Where these emotions came from, I didn't know. The moment I said those words, I became a total ungrateful asshole. If I were honest with myself, I'd think what Travis said hit harder than I expected. I couldn't wrap my head around the idea he planned to use my relationship with Maverick for blackmail material.

Pushing the chair away, I stood, forcing a stunned silent Maverick to back away. "I need some fucking space. See you after lunch."

Maverick stayed quiet, but I knew I'd angered and hurt him. I'd have to make it up later.

I'm just so tired of everyone thinking they have to look out for me! I stopped outside the law firm's glass doors. *Maybe it's not that. Sure, it's annoying. But—*

"Aaron!"

I turned my head to see Dudley running down the hallway, waving a chubby hand. *Oh no, not what or who I need right now. Keep a smile on and let him down easy.* "Hey Duds," I greeted. "What's up?"

The short, pudgy man bent over, placing his hands on his knees. Heavy breaths permeated the silence. He raised his head, beads of sweat glistening on his worry lines. "Maverick? Really?"

I rolled my eyes, trying to rein in the lingering emotions. Dudley didn't have anything to do with the hurricane my life was slowly becoming. Not letting him down sooner was my fault, not his.

"How could you choose *him*? Are you insane? He's our boss!" Dudley snorted after the last word. He lowered his head. "Do you not know ... how I *feel* about you?"

I tried not to feel gob-smacked at the courage the little man displayed. "Look, Duds, you're a nice guy. I'm flattered you like me—"

Dudley grabbed my hand, holding it close. "I don't like you, Aaron." He squeezed his eyes closed, teeth clenching. "I'm ... I'm in love with you."

Oh, boy. Okay, how to deal with this...

"It's because I'm not as good looking as he is, isn't it? Because he's thin, muscular, has a nice accent. Is that why you chose him?"

Say something. This is going to get weirder if I don't. "Duds, I—"

Dudley got closer, making me arch my back. It hurt like hell. "Because if that's what you want, I can work out! I can't get an accent, but I'll work out, get contacts. Whatever it takes!"

And it got weirder. "Duds, that's not it. Yes, Maverick's hot, but that's not the only reason." *Can't tell him, "Oh, by the way, I met Maverick at a bar, kissed him to make my ex jealous, then met him again at work." Nope.*

Dudley let my hand go and backed away, fists balled at his sides. "Is it because he promoted you? Is that why?"

"Hey," I said, jabbing a finger at him. "That's uncalled for. No, he's not using me." *Why did I choose him? Why am I so attracted to Mav? He's hot as hell, has a sexual magnetism stronger than the largest super magnet, and, yes, his accent is drool-inducing. But ... why?* "He's done everything but use me, that's why. He sees me, Duds. Sees me as more than a pretty face. Maverick wants to be with me for who I am. That's more than anyone else in my life has ever done."

"I saw you," Dudley said. "Sure, you're pretty, but that's not why I want to be with you. You're smart, observant, self-sacrificing, and you're always looking out for the under-dogs. That's why I adore you. Can Maverick say the same? Does he even know you, Aaron? I mean, like I do. Like Josh, Frankie, or your best friend does?"

Dudley made some fair points. Maverick didn't really know me past the basic information. I couldn't place the blame on him since I'd done my best to dodge him. Our rela-tionship had spurred from pent up lust for each other.

"I'm dating him, Duds," I said. "That's how we're getting to know each other."

"Are you sleeping with him?"

Of all the ballsy... "That's really none of your business," I snapped. "I have to go. It's my lunch hour, and I'm starving. I'm sorry I can't give you what you want, Duds, but my heart wants who it wants."

Dudley said nothing else as I walked off.

Lunch dragged on. When it finally ended, I bought Maverick a coffee and a muffin as a peace offering. I'd reacted stupidly for something he didn't even do. My insecu-rities weren't his fault. God bless him. The guy took so much emotional backlash that I wouldn't blame him if he ended things with me on the spot.

I took a deep breath then blew it out from puffed cheeks. *Here goes nothing.* Shouldering his door, I pushed into his office. Maverick stood next to the wide window overlooking the New York cityscape. Between the light bouncing off his gorgeous dirty-blonde hair and how regal he looked, my knees weakened.

Please don't let me have screwed this up. Fuck, please don't let me have screwed this up.

"Mav?" I asked, my voice more like a meek schoolboy than a grown man. Maverick remained as he was. "I ... I'm sorry for snapping at you. It was immature."

The looming silence ripped at my guts. I'd do anything to make him say something. Both hands stayed in his pockets, his body turned away from me. Completely closed off.

Sighing, I set the coffee and muffin on his desk and turned to leave. "I'll shut up. There's a coffee and muffin on your desk. When you're ready to talk—"

"Aaron," Maverick said.

I spun. Rushing blood and the pounding of my heart heated my body. Sweat dripped down my back. Both hands grew clammy.

Maverick faced me, toying with his glasses. "Will you close the door, please?" There was no jovial tone. Hell, there wasn't a tone at all.

I'm so fired. Potential boyfriend or not, he's still my boss. Without a word, I did what Maverick asked, staying with my back against the door. *Can't blame him. I was out of line. Way out of line.* I kicked myself for entertaining the idea of being with a co-worker. Especially my damn boss.

Maverick joined me near the door. His height made me feel like a mouse towered over by a cat. For what seemed like hours, he stood there, staring at me.

I kept my eyes on the floor, horribly aware of the throbbing shaft getting pinched by my zipper. Make up sex was always hot. Only this time, I didn't think I had that to look forward to.

The subtle touch of fingertips on my stubble made me jump. I expected to get yelled at or sternly reprimanded, not caressed.

Maverick led my face to stare at him. Using his thumb, he teased my lips. "Are you feeling better?"

What the...? "Um, yeah. Aren't you mad at me? I was a real dick to you."

"I was upset, yes. Then I made Travis tell me what he said to you." Maverick kissed my lips softly. "Knowing that, I understand why you acted the way you did. However," he paused, glaring at me, "never speak to me like that again at work. I am still—"

"I know. And I'm sorry. I'm really sorry."

Maverick nodded, a tiny smile tugging his lips. "Still, seeing you like that is one of the sexiest things I've ever experienced. The things I wanted to do to you after witnessing the intensity in those hypnotizing blue eyes..." He hissed through his teeth. "We might have to explore them once we get to know each other better. Why not come over tonight? Let me enjoy this sassy mood of yours."

"Tonight?"

"Yes. I know you completed the guest list. You checked it off in your planner. I don't mind getting dinner—"

Dinner. That's it.

Since we started seeing each other, I dreaded having Maverick at my place. Letting him in terrified me, yet I didn't want to keep secrets anymore.

"Why not ... come to my place? Tomorrow," I said. "I'd like to cook for you."

Maverick cocked his head like he couldn't believe what he'd heard.

Feeling sexy, I pulled on his tie, forcing him to step closer. Our proximity allowed me to place a hand on his ass. I squeezed, earning a hiss. "What do you say? Will you let me cook for you? There's something I need to tell you, too."

"Of course," Maverick replied. "Is eight o'clock good for you?"

I nodded. "Perfect."

That gave me enough time to take Roxxie on our run and stop by the store. For what I had planned, the ingredients had to be fresh.

I wonder if he'd let me feed him.

Another thing to explore when our relationship grew stronger.

"Good. You better let me go, or I might not be able to wait for my chance to taste you," Maverick said, his raspy tone betraying a growing lust. "Promise me something."

It was my turn to cock my head like a curious cat.

Maverick stroked down my face to my neck. "Let me help you. If something stresses you, I want to be there to help you carry the burden."

My eyes stung. The sincerity and concern combined with the natural light gave Maverick's eyes a brightness rivaling an angel. Each gentle stroke and kiss to my neck reminded me of how much he adored me.

"I promise," I replied. "Will you do the same?"

Maverick moved away, locking his eyes with mine. He kept secrets; I knew that. I didn't expect him to tell me everything starting out.

"You have my word," he said.

With a curt nod, I opened the door and departed.

CHAPTER 26

The rest of the day went by without a hitch. I finished up the work for the renaming event. Around 5:00, I checked my list. Some things hadn't gotten finished, but they were small, so I let the disappointment slide off.

Before clocking out, I peeked into Maverick's office. He was still typing furiously on his laptop. *I shouldn't disturb him.* I thought for a moment then stuck my head in and told him good night. He stopped what he was doing and beckoned me over.

Walking to him didn't take a second thought. I had to keep myself from strutting and showing off to entice him. He looked busy and likely wanted to get out of here as badly as I did.

I reached his desk, planning on sitting in the chair.

"No," Maverick said in his sexy lawyer voice, accent thicker in fatigue. "Come here."

Confused yet curious, I walked around his desk and stood above him.

Maverick's arms embraced my waist, a hand freeing my shirt from the confines of my pants.

Once my skin showed, he placed a kiss on the divot of my hip, lightly sucking the skin before kissing it again. "Good night, sweetheart. I'll count the hours until we can be together again."

A shudder started at my tailbone and shot up my spine. How I wanted to take him home. Every night felt lonely, the bed cold.

I didn't make a move to leave. Being close to him took away the emptiness.

"Come home with me tonight," Maverick said, nuzzling into my hip. Strong hands cradled and kneaded my ass.

"I can't. I don't have any spare clothes, and there's Roxxie to consider. I'll see you tomorrow after work, and again on Friday."

Another soft suck and kiss graced my hip. "May I taste you, Aaron?"

My eyes bulged. A gasp escaped my throat. *Here? Is he serious?* Everyone had gone home. Even Travis clocked out earlier than usual.

"I ... Mav..." I couldn't deny him. Getting sucked off in his office was an erotic dream. One of many I had since he asked to see more of me. Not one night went by without me masturbating over the idea of getting dirty at work. I'd imagined Maverick laying me out on his desk and fucking me since he told me he planned on it. "Are you sure?"

No words came as an answer.

Maverick eased his chair away, stood, marched to his door, and locked it. He returned to his chair and sat. With his hands on my hips, he guided me to lean against his desk.

"You've no idea how many times I've thought of this moment. How I've plotted ways to remove that bloody vest and pleasure you with these fucking trousers around your ankles." A dirty Maverick was the hottest sin. He only talked like this after reaching the end of his restraint.

My mouth became a desert from heavy breathing as Maverick went to work on the button and zipper of my pants.

Once my briefs came into view, Maverick placed his lips over my hardened shaft, teasing it through the fabric.

"I love the scent of your arousal, Aaron." Lust-filled, half-lidded eyes stared up at me. "It makes me want to do so many things to you." He nipped and tugged at the cotton with his teeth. "Shall I free your amazing cock? It seems to need it."

Fuck yes. I craned my neck. "Yes," I breathed. "Please do."

I winced as Maverick bit my hip bone. The earlier sucking grew in intensity.

Maverick bit the flesh he sucked into his mouth then pulled away with a pop. "I want everyone to know you're mine. All mine."

His. I closed my eyes, relishing how much Maverick wanted me as he pushed my pants and briefs down. Cool air hit my heated sex, making me shiver.

"So fucking perfect," Maverick said and kissed my leaking tip. He wasted no time dragging his tongue from the root and back, swirling it around, tasting the pre-cum. "You taste so good. I can't wait to swallow all you have to give me."

"Damn, you're dirty. Has anyone ever told you that? Or maybe that you seem like you have twin personalities?" I asked, laughing.

My words ended when Maverick took my tip into his mouth, swapping between sucking and twirling his tongue. When he pulled away, the plump head glistened in the dim lamplight.

"I've let no one close enough to say such things," Maverick replied. A glisten flashed across his pupils. "Not until you."

I didn't know how to take the high praise. Every time I thought I figured Maverick out, the crafty lawyer threw another curve ball. Though I didn't think it possible, my cheeks heated more. I took my eyes from him, not knowing what to say. This mouth-watering man had the strange power to turn me into a slush pile with the slightest bat of an eyelash. And man, did he have some heavy lashes.

Maverick blew on my tip. The cool air hitting moist skin made me shiver. "Hold still, beautiful. Let me savor you." His mouth engulfed me to the hilt, and he breathed through his nostrils with each slide up and down my shaft.

Holy shit, it's like he's taking me down his damn throat.

I couldn't take anymore. My hand went into his hair, fingers twisting in the silken layers. The other hand cradled Maverick's face. Using both, I began thrusting.

"Fuck," I said, dragging out the word. *His mouth is so soft. Warm and so fucking soft.*

Declan never gave me head. If he did, I doubted it would be this good. Maverick hummed against my flesh. The vibrations heightened my need to cum. To take his mouth and make him mine.

Mine. I opened my eyes to stare at the ceiling. *That's right. He's mine.* This powerful, alluring man who demanded respect from everyone had his lips wrapped around my dick, not anyone else's. Maverick had surrendered his pride to chase me. Of all the people he could have had, he swore to never stop searching until he found me. Reminding myself of that gave me a boost in confidence.

Taking Maverick's head with both hands, I held him still, sprinting after the orgasm I teetered on with each thrust. My balls drew up, the base of my spine tingling.

Maverick delivered the final stimulation when one of his fingers found my hole.

"Fuck!" I shouted as Maverick began finger-fucking me.

One final thrust into his mouth shot hot streams down his throat. I hissed when Maverick continued sucking me. He kept his word, swallowing every drop he could get.

Exhausted, legs shaking, I propped myself up against the desk. *I can't believe I just did that. At my damn job. Am I insane?* I looked up in time to see Maverick licking his lips and teeth. *Yep. I'm definitely insane. Insane for this man.*

Maverick dropped to his knees, took my underwear and pants, and lead them up my legs and over my ass. "Take some time to steady yourself."

"That was fucking amazing," I said with one breath. "You put Dyson to shame."

"You're welcome," Maverick replied.

Dazed and possibly still hungover from the erotic explosion, I crushed our lips together, spearing my tongue into Maverick's mouth. A delicious mix of me and the remains of black coffee tickled my tastebuds. Our bodies left no room for air to get through.

Exposed skin met polyester since I didn't bother zipping up. I wanted this man close as long as I could.

Maverick bit down on my lower lip, sucked it into his mouth, then released it with a pop. "I should go. Court in the morning. No doubt you remember."

I remembered.

Like Travis did earlier, Maverick had court all day tomorrow. I dreaded being left alone to deal with Marks, but knowing Maverick would come to my apartment for the first time eased the discomfort.

"Yeah," I said, zipping up. Smiling, I bopped his nose with a fingertip. "Don't worry. What I plan on cooking for you will make all those boring hours worth it."

Maverick laughed. "I look forward to it." An arm wrapped around my waist, drawing me in. "Did you enjoy my first tasting of you?"

I looked away, knowing the burning in my cheeks turned my face a strawberry red. "I ... I liked it. Would you ... do it again? Sometime?"

"Of course," Maverick said and kissed me. "Have a good night, sweetheart."

A quick swat to my butt sent me on my way. I flinched and yelled, "Hey," receiving another laugh from the sexy man staring at my ass. The amazing feeling of Maverick's adoration left butterflies in my stomach.

I can't get enough of him.

The following workday dragged on with me constantly checking the clock like a high schooler waiting for a boring class to end. Rain created another muggy day. Add in the gusts of wind slinging rain-shaped razors, and I should have hated getting out of bed.

Maverick left for a full court day. I stayed on his heels the way Roxxie stayed on mine to the door. Every stop he made, I mirrored, including a visit to the filing room. Since my chat with Dudley, I'd avoided my old office like the bubonic plague.

Not today.

"Are you sure you don't want me to come? I'm supposed to be there since I'm your assistant, right?" I asked, practically begging for any reason to go with him.

Travis and Mr. Kimball took their paralegals to court all the time. They performed the tasks their attorneys weren't able to. Namely, picking up documents, setting up meetings with the opposite side, and grabbing lunch if the attorney couldn't leave.

Why won't Maverick take me with him? Does he think I won't be able to handle it?

Maverick rounded on me shortly after we crossed the glass doors into the hall. Gratefully, we weren't in anyone's line of sight.

Taking my chin with his thumb and fingers, Maverick gave a half-lidded stare. "There is no way I'm letting you in the same courtroom as me, Aaron."

I pouted. "Why? Don't think I can handle the asshole side of you? Oh wait, I deal with that part of you every damn time you order me to get coffee or lunch for you."

Maverick half-laughed. "No, but that's good to know." He kissed my lips in the middle of the hall, uncaring if anyone saw. "I'm not letting you into that room because I would imagine too many things with you constantly staring at my ass."

Heat spread from my cheeks to my ears. I thought my constant ogling of Maverick's ass went unnoticed. *Shoulda known better. The guy's practically psychic!*

"Hey! I do not always stare at your ass!" I crossed my arms, falling against the wall. My eyes averted downward. "It's not my fault your brain is always in the gutter. You promoted me to this, remember? Not like I wanted it!"

Our lips met again. This time, Maverick pulled me flush against him. His boldness heightened my nerves. Anyone who stepped out and rounded the corner would see us. And with my sister still battling the First Amendment regarding our family in court, I had to keep my head down.

"I will see you tonight," Maverick said, leaving me to watch him walk away, my eyes faithfully on that fine ass of his.

I returned to my desk where I sat eating lunch. A textbook lay ignored before my keyboard.

Not even the constant interruptions from Travis did much to dissuade me from not-so-subtly checking the clock. I still had to get to the store to pick up ingredients for dinner after work.

Finals were approaching quickly, and I still hadn't told Maverick about the out-of-state internship. We'd worked on the renaming party during work hours. Off the clock, I spent more time wanting to be with Maverick any chance we got.

And those weren't much. We'd only gone on one date. Two, if I counted the brief morning breakfast at the diner after Maverick and I met in Central Park. And I'd only gone to his house and gotten sexed silly once. *But what amazing sex it was.* Then Maverick blew my mind again by sucking me off in his office! *Elliot's right. I'm falling fast. I don't think I could leave him even if I wanted to.*

My phone vibrating on the desk took my attention from the jumbling thoughts rolling in my mind. Rebecca's name showed up beneath her picture.

Wide-eyed, I picked up the phone. Bex never called me at work unless something bad or important happened.

My heart thudded in my chest as a trembling thumb lingered over the green button. Scared and feeling like something horrible was about to happen, I ignored the call.

She's going to kill me.

CHAPTER 27

uck. Fuck. Fuck. Fuck. I smacked my head with the heels of my hands.

God only knew what the hell I looked like on my way to clock out. Everyone stopped me to ask how I was or if I felt sick.

Yeah, I feel sick.

In my apartment, I leaned against the kitchen cabinet, sliding down to the floor. My brain pounded against my skull as I dropped a weighted head on a knee. The other leg stuck out in front of me. I kicked the near-empty bottle of Jagermeister across the tile floor.

Along with a spinning head from Rebecca's shocking news and the alcohol, a storm capable of shaking the apartment windows rolled in. Deep booms rattled the pains, scaring Roxxie. She was waiting out the storm in her television side nook, cuddled deeply into her pillow.

The last thing I wanted was for Maverick to see me looking pathetic. I'd sent him a text on my way out of the office.

[Aaron: Hey, sorry. Gonna have to reschedule dinner. Stomach's feeling gross. Guess I should be careful about where I get sushi from now on.]

I inserted a smiley face, hoping he didn't catch on that something was wrong or that I lied. Truth was, I didn't want to see him. Not after what Rebecca told me.

Maverick replied quickly.

214

[Maverick: I'm saddened to hear that. Is there anything I can do? Bring you some soup and Ginger Ale?]

He's so fucking perfect.

I smiled.

[Aaron: No. Just need some time. Might not be at work for the next few days.]

The moment I sent it, I knew the last part of that text wouldn't work. Maverick arrived at my apartment promptly at 8 pm.

"Aaron," his gentle voice said through the door.

Fuck. Of course, he'd show up. I heaved a sigh. "Go away, Mav."

In that moment, I didn't care who Maverick was to me. Not in the official sense, anyway. I wanted time to think. Time away from the sexual aura bleeding from the handsome man at my door.

This is what you get, I told myself, propping a forearm against my door. *This is what you get for letting your guard down and thinking that being with a guy like Maverick Waylan would be okay.*

A thump sounded against the wood. "Aaron, what's going on? And don't give me any of this food poisoning bullshit."

My anger at the situation boiled. "What the fuck is wrong with you?" I shouted, careful not to get too loud. "I told you I don't need you to come to my rescue—"

"Are you drinking?" Maverick interrupted sternly. "You left early today right after sending me that message. And now I'm at your door, finding you knackered as a sailor. What. Is. Going. On?"

Standing, I clasped my hands into fists. Maverick's tone was pissing me off. I wasn't his bitch to demand an answer from. He wasn't my boyfriend or really anything to me. Giving a fuck about being nice went out the window like a stone.

"That's none of your damn business! I have a life outside of you, you know? Outside of you and that fucking firm!" Tears stung the corners of my eyes. I clenched my teeth so hard my jaw hurt. "I just want some goddamn space!"

Everything grew silent save for the occasional thunderclap.

Something sliding down the door frame beat through my alcoholic haze.

"Aaron, please open the door," Maverick said softly. His voice sounded closer. *Probably dropped his forehead against the door.* "Tell me what's happened. Has someone hurt you?"

Hurt me? Fuck yes.

I stormed to the living room, picked up the New York Times and Entertainment magazine, and stomped back to the door. Opening it, I met Maverick's beautiful, tired, and concerned face. His dark eyes had circles underneath them. The hair he worked hard to keep well-kept flopped in his face.

Ignoring how beautiful he was took all the willpower I had.

I thrust the paper and magazine into his chest. "This happened to me!" Tears broke free, streaming down my face.

Maverick analyzed the front story, his eyes widening beneath his hipster frames. "Where did they get this?"

"Fuck if I know! Check out the fucking photographer's name!" Hate burned inside me. *This is so typical. I should've just dealt with his bullshit!*

Paper folded and ripped the tighter Maverick's hold on it became. Eventually, he tore it apart, fisting it in white knuckles.

Declan had his revenge. Somehow, he'd gotten photos of Maverick and me kissing in the parking lot outside the restaurant. He'd sold the photos to the newspapers.

Star's Wayward Son Finds New Squeeze in Wealthy Heir.

The subtitle read: *What will this mean for the fashion world's most notable name?*

"You should go. Chances are your mom already knows, and I need to keep out of the limelight for the sake of my sister's case," I said, sniffling.

Maverick did the opposite. He pushed his way in, forcing me to step back. I didn't let him touch me. I was too angry at myself for being so stupid and at him for not keeping my concerns in mind.

"I'm not leaving you to deal with this alone," Maverick said, picking up the empty bottle.

I laughed. "You really are thick, you know that? I said I want some goddamn space."

Maverick tossed the bottle in the trash, turning to me. "I heard you. I'm choosing to ignore it." Moving quickly, he took my wrists and pinned me against the wall. I struggled in protest against him. "Listen to me, Aaron. You're hurting, I understand that. But do you really think pushing me away is the right answer?"

"Fuck you!"

"Soon," Maverick replied with a smirk.

"Like hell!" I bucked my hips, pissed at the erection rubbing the cotton of my pants. "All you had to do was leave me the fuck alone and stay that damn mystery guy I kissed at a bar!"

Maverick's lips crashed against mine, his tongue spearing into my mouth. A muscular thigh between my legs provided some relief, though not enough.

I couldn't help myself. My tongue tussled with his, tasting and exploring the depths of his mouth. Despite everything, I still wanted him. Desired him more than my next breath.

When he came up for air, Maverick said, "Let me help you sober up. Have you eaten?"

I shook my head. "Don't want any food." *I just want this to stop.* I squeezed my eyes closed. "Please, Mav. Please, just go."

Maverick released me and backed away. "Alright. I will." He didn't say anything else, opened the door, and left.

I'd never sobbed so hard in my life.

Two days went by with not so much as a text from Maverick.

I spent the time checking off more self-imposed tasks on my checklists, organizing my office space, and running more with Roxxie. Anything to keep me from grabbing my phone, calling Maverick, and begging him to forgive me for acting like a child.

The wounds Declan left behind remained raw. I needed Maverick to understand that. Declan meant nothing to me anymore, but he kept the power to cut deep. He knew my secrets, including the darker ones that could tear me down in seconds.

Rebecca fought hard to keep our family out of the news, but she couldn't do anything about Maverick's standing. His family had international publicity. Everyone in the fashion world knew Maverick's mom. I should've played it safe and stayed far away until Rebecca got our family's non-disclosure contract ironclad enough to withstand international scrutiny.

All I had to do was keep my fucking head down. I couldn't even do that.

When I missed our lunch meeting, Elliot called. "Oh my God! There you are!" he screamed through the speaker. I pulled the phone away. "Please tell me the rumors aren't true! You broke up with Maverick?"

"El, I didn't break up with anyone. Maverick and I weren't boyfriends," I said. *I'm not even sure what we were.* I lowered my head. *And now we'll never find out. I bet Mav hates me. Wouldn't blame him if he fired me.*

"Good grief, Aaron! Were you dating?"

"Sort of." I scratched my head. "Hell, I don't know!"

"Planning on seeing each other more regularly?"

"Yeah."

"Then, trust me, you were fixing to date." Elliot groaned in annoyance. "Please tell me this has nothing to do with Declan." He paused. "Doesn't matter. Look, you need to fix this."

I don't know how. "I can't, El. Mav probably wants nothing to do with me. I'm expecting to have a pink slip waiting on my desk after all the shit I said to him."

"What'd you say?" he asked, and I told him. "Oh fuck. Hmm. Okay, here's what you do. Suck up your pride, call him, and pray to the hot-guy gods he answers."

I was afraid he'd say that. "I'll wait. We were supposed to meet tonight. He wanted me to stay over, but as you can guess, that's not happening."

"WHAT?" Elliot's scream made me grit my teeth. "That's it then! Pack your bags. I'm coming to pick you up and take your adorable ass to Maverick's myself. Josh and I will watch Roxxie. Go get your man!"

"Wait ... El—" Elliot hung up. I wasn't sure if I wanted to kill him or kiss him. Either way, El had a point. I had to see Maverick.

Even if he tells me he wants nothing to do with me.

That scared the hell out of me.

I'd faced rejection.

Faced humiliation.

Endured abuse.

Out of all of it, the thing I dreaded facing most was Maverick never wanting to see me again.

I hurried to my room, choosing the best and sexiest clothes I could find, including the shorts and muscle shirt pajamas Elliot got me as a joke. They went into a bag along with toiletries, my favorite lube, condoms, and the cologne Maverick loved.

Mav, I'm coming. I'm so sorry.

Rocks fell into my stomach when I picked up the phone. Its empty screen battered me harder than hail against glass.

I scrolled through my contacts to find Maverick's name and hit dial. *Please. Please let him answer.* After many rings, it went to voicemail. That didn't stop me.

"Maverick, I'm on my way. I don't care if I have to sit outside your door. We need to talk." I ended the call, determined to chase the man I desperately wanted until I caught him.

All the rushing caused a dildo to tumble to the floor. Picking it up, I smiled, imagining what fucking Maverick would be like. *Would he let me? I sure would like to try.*

Something awakened within me the more I imagined pressing Maverick's face into the mattress. He'd be furious. Hesitant. And maybe reluctant at the idea of having sex after what I said.

How hot would it be to take him like that?

In all of our conversations about sex and partners, Maverick said nothing about whether he liked to receive as well as give. When we were together, Maverick was dominant. Yet each time he begged me to stay or to see me, he became vulnerable. And I'd never gotten the chance to top before.

That's what we're doing tonight, Mav. Tonight, I'm fucking you right out of that pissed off mood.

I placed the dildo in the top drawer, zipped my bag, and hustled to the living room to hear someone knocking—or rather beating—on the door.

Elliot called my name, threatening to break it down if I didn't open it. I rolled my eyes. Elliot and I threatened each other all the time. *Such is the nature of a best friend.*

I opened the door.

"About time!" Elliot said. Josh stood behind him, shaking his head. "Hurry! Josh is staying here with Roxxie!"

Don't need to tell me twice. "Let's go. I have a plan." I grabbed Elliot's arm, practically sprinting down the hall to the elevators.

Maverick hadn't returned my call or texted.

I hoped that didn't mean he wasn't home. *Come to think of it, I know nothing about what Maverick likes to do outside of seeing me or working.*

When we arrived at Elliot's car, I threw open the door and dropped into the passenger's seat. "Hurry, El. I have to see him."

Elliot buckled his seat belt and started his car.

My heart raced the entire ride to Maverick's condo. Along with it, thoughts about how I'd go about my ludicrous plot to nail him to the bed and have my way with him floated through my head. The idea was a stupid one. Maverick didn't seem like the type to let someone take him. Not without a fight.

I relished the idea of him fighting. I imagined frustration had a grip on him like it did on me for the past two days. *Or maybe he completely forgot me and moved on.* That seemed more probable.

If I'd learned anything in our short time together, it was that Maverick wasn't one to linger on past indiscretions. *His mother's ruthlessness probably had something to do with that.*

"Don't look so nervous, babe. You look adorable," Elliot said. "Whatever happened, I'm sure you two will work it out."

I wasn't so sure. Growing stomach rocks made me believe I was headed for more heartache than repair. *And what a shit-tastic time.* We'd planned to attend the renaming together as more than paralegal and attorney.

Since Elliot had an eye in fashion, I'd wanted to ask him to help me shop for a tux. Maybe ask Mav to go along so the two of them could meet officially.

The likelihood of that happening crashed through the ground to hell. *Damn me and my fricking emotions. Why can't I keep my mouth shut when I need to?*

Elliot passed the Park Avenue intersection. Legions of umbrellas passed in front of the cherry red Challenger. The people reminded me of ants marching off to fulfill their daily duties. Bright lights from the cars turned the figures into alien silhouettes.

I used to be like them. Going day to day, trying to get by until I could get out of this place. Then fate changed my life forever, throwing the perfect man in my way. *Mav, I have to have you back.* I squeezed my eyes closed. *I need to have you back.*

Elliot pulled through the intersection. I thought I'd die with how reckless Elliot navigated the bustling streets.

"El, not to complain, but getting to Mav won't matter if I wind up splattered on the rear end of a taxi. Just saying."

"Quit complaining!" Elliot bit back. "If you'd kept your emotions under control and hadn't let Dicklan get into your head again, we wouldn't be in this mess!"

Horns blared as Elliot cut in front of a taxi and hung a sharp right, hydroplaning on deepening puddles.

I couldn't argue. Elliot had a point. Dicklan took the photos and gave them to the tabloids to spite me after Maverick humiliated him. He likely knew I'd turn into an emotional mess and take it out on Maverick. *I fell for it. Fell for that stupid trap!*

My fists hit my knees. "El, hurry."

Another blaring horn scared the hell out of me. I gripped the emergency handle, praying silently. Not only that I'd get there alive, but also for Maverick to see he wasn't the one I was mad at.

CHAPTER 28

Elliot skidded in front of Maverick's building. I didn't wait, jumping from the car before it stopped and nearly stumbling over the curb. All the people witnessing the drama looked at me and mumbled to themselves or their partners.

"Good luck!" Elliot shouted.

I turned to wave, seeing the thumbs up he held out. Putting on my jacket, I took the steps two at a time. Anyone I bumped into yelled, but I ignored them. I needed to get to the tiny box that let me buzz Maverick's apartment.

When I reached it, I took a second to breathe deeply. Closing my eyes, I exhaled, steadying myself and making sure I didn't stumble over the bag I haphazardly grabbed.

I can do this. My thumb pressed the button for Mav's condo. He didn't answer right away. I pressed it again. *Please, Mav. Please, we need to talk.*

"What is it?" Maverick asked. His indifferent tone pierced my heart like an icy dagger.

"Mav, it's me. May I come up?"

Silence.

Fuck. "Mav, we need to talk."

Silence persisted. In my mind's eye, I imagined Maverick leaning against his door, lips tight, while he debated the pros and cons of letting me up.

Desperation kicked in. I didn't care what anyone around me thought. Losing Maverick meant more than anything.

"Look, you don't have to say anything. Just ... listen, okay?" I asked, letting my head thump against the wall. He didn't reply. "I'm sorry. I know I hurt you. You didn't deserve what I did and said." Tears pooled in my eyes. My lower lip trembled. I bit it to keep it still. "I don't expect anything. Really. Just ... please tell me you can hear me."

Radio noises popped on the speaker. My heart leapt in tandem with the pops.

"I hear you," Maverick replied coldly. "It's late, Aaron. I have court tomorrow."

No. Fuck. No. Please, no.

"Will I see you at work Tuesday?" Maverick asked after a pause.

My jaw ticked. Tears broke free, dripping down my cheeks with the rainwater soaking my hair. "Yes," I said.

"Good." The tone sounded more relaxed yet remained guarded. "Have a good weekend."

No other words came through.

Dejected, my heart torn apart and sent flying through the wind, I left the lobby and walked down the short hall to the bar I wanted to try the first time I saw it.

People had already started filling the tables, the Friday rush in full bloom by the time I got there.

I chose a raised table near the farthest window, placing my bag between my feet. I didn't want anyone to see how pathetic I was after my "near" boyfriend told me off—in Maverick terms.

Not wanting to be alone, I reached into my pocket, pulled out my phone, and dialed Elliot's number. My fingers went through my hair, pushing rain-soaked sprigs away from my face. No matter what I tried, Maverick's icy tone and indifference, ravaged my thoughts. That tone meant he'd set up walls between us. Walls that would take me months to break down, if I broke them down at all.

"Hey! How'd it go?" Elliot's hopeful words shattered any resolve I had to keep from breaking down.

I tried. Hard. Tried to find any words. Any way to get my mouth to move. But all I could do was keep the deep inhales and hiccups from drawing unwanted attention.

Images of Maverick's face, his smile, and his gorgeous body all went up in flames.

"I ... I fucked up," I said, choking on the words. "I fucked up, El."

"Aaron?" The hopeful tone died. "Aaron, what happened?"

I heard my friend speaking, knew he asked what happened, but my thoughts kept circling back to Maverick. I debated calling him but fought myself not to go back and try to talk to him again—anything to see him and make him realize I meant nothing I said to him. He'd been in the wrong place again.

"Aaron?" Elliot said, his voice shaky. "I'm coming to get you. Stay there, okay." He'd said the same during the moments I broke down over Declan.

I nodded, sniffling, "okay," and hung up.

A young, blonde woman came over. From the looks of her white shirt, black pants, and apron, she worked there. "Evening," she said. Her eyes rounded. "Hey, you okay?"

I offered a curt nod. "Fine. Just need a moment." I stood and walked to the bathroom.

Rushing blood and heat spells dizzied me. *Mav.* I repeated his name like a prayer. *I'm so sorry.* Distorted surroundings agitated me. After bumping into a few—*walls? These are walls, right? Doors, maybe?*—I came out the back exit door into an alleyway.

Cool breezes did little to help the heat flashes. Nausea churned my stomach.

Falling to my knees, I vomited and spent an unknown amount of time sobbing. To anyone passing by, I probably looked like a drunk or a tweaker needing his next fix.

Mav ... I ... I love you.

Eventually, I stood. Like a zombie, I walked out of the alley and into the bustling New York night.

I'm not sure when, but Elliot found me at our favorite cocktail bar after checking Maverick's building. I thought Elliot would yell at me since I didn't call or text to tell him where I'd be. Maybe thump me in the head like he did when he got pissed.

What I didn't expect was to have Elliot sitting silently next to me. Occasionally, he reached a hand out toward my forearm but withdrew it quickly and sighed.

"Want to tell me about it?" Elliot asked.

I shook my head. "Nothing really to tell." The emotions from earlier dwindled into the worst feeling of all: numbness. "I fucked up," I said with a laugh. *Like I thought I would.*

"Well, let's start with what you said. Did you try to go back and talk to him? Say anything other than what you told me over the phone? Text? Call?"

I felt the anger rising again. "No, El. I didn't. Somehow I don't think blowing up Maverick's phone with apologies will fix this." My fists white-knuckled. "He was so cold. Like I was a client or Travis."

"Easy." Elliot rubbed my back. "Give him some time to cool off. You were pretty harsh on him."

Things had moved too fast. Of that, I was certain. Had I slowed things down, we might have avoided all the bullshit. Relationships often started with lust turned crazy. And sometimes they worked.

"You don't have to stay with me, El," I said. "You've already gone through this insanity with Declan. No reason to go through this, too." I took a drink of my Gin & Tonic. "I only have a couple of weeks left, anyway. Then I can kiss this piece-of-shit city goodbye."

"Oh! You got the internship!" Elliot cheered, beaming. The smile didn't last long, vanishing into a hollow "oh" shape. "Does Maverick know?"

"Fuck would he care for? I'm not his problem." The words sounded bitter, and I felt like a total jackass. *Jackass is better than whining bitch.* "Here's to pipe dreams." I gulped the last of the alcohol.

The cool liquid burned and warmed my belly simultaneously. Given any other night, I'd enjoy getting shit faced and gone home to have some personal time.

Elliot smacked the back of my head. "Quit being a bitch. You screwed up. Get the fuck over it!" I couldn't keep my gaping mouth shut. Elliot rarely said things like that to me. "If there's anything I know, it's how much Maverick wants you. Fuck, Aaron, I think he's in love with you."

My wide eyes grew larger. *Will I see you at work Tuesday?* Mav had said. *Why would he say them if...* I hadn't thought about it; too much time went into wallowing and feeling sorry for myself.

"What do you mean, he's in love with me? Elliot, he all but told me to fuck off. I hardly think he meant 'I'm so in love with you, Aaron. Why not come up and have hot make-up sex with me?'"

Elliot's brow raised. A devious smirk curled his lips. "How do you know? Did you ever stop and think maybe he hoped you'd keep trying? Maybe he wanted to see how much you wanted him, if you wanted him as bad as he wants you."

I ... hadn't thought of that. Fuck.

I stood, took my wallet, and slammed enough money down to cover both mine and Elliot's tab.

"Speaking of which," Elliot said, pointing a perfectly painted nail.

I looked in the direction he pointed. My heart stopped, breath ripped from my lungs at the sight of the man walking through the front door. Dirty-blonde hair turned from blue, to green, to pink with the music beat. A grey suit jacket covered a tight, black shirt. Black jeans hugged muscular calves like a second skin.

Maverick.

Maverick's eyes scanned the crowd. They looked rather frustrated beneath his glasses.

"What is he doing here?" I stuttered, then glared at Elliot. "Did you call him?"

Elliot shook his head, hands upheld. "No. I swear. My hands are clean in this. Good luck though, right? You can go talk to him!"

My attention returned to Maverick. He didn't seem to notice me, aiming his eyes at the opposite end of the bar. There were private rooms for VIPs nestled in that corner. High-paying clients, musicians, and movie stars used those rooms when they wanted to commit sins out of public view.

"I don't think so," I replied. "Doesn't seem like he's here looking for me."

Curiosity tugged at me. The perfect chance to find out more about Maverick's secret life presented itself. *I shouldn't. He's already upset with me. Besides, it's not like he owes me an explanation if he meets someone here.*

Elliot hummed, placed a finger to his jaw, and tilted his head. "Do you know anyone else he'd come here to see?"

I shook my head. "I don't know much of anything about Maverick's life outside of work. He's not really one to gossip. What I know, I've already told you."

"Hmm. Well, don't let it worry you. Not like he's your boyfriend. Could be here seeing someone else," Elliot said, checking his phone. "I have to go, though. Josh is expecting me for a hot playtime."

My eyes rolled, stomach sick. "Thanks a lot for that image. I still can't get used to the idea of you using a collar and paddle on Josh of all people." Those images haunted me every time I spoke to Josh at work.

Elliot shrugged, tossing his hair. "Don't be jealous. Get your man back and see if he's into that kinda thing. Bet he is." He blew me a kiss, whirled around, and sashayed like a model out the door. Every eye in the place watched him.

Gotta love the confidence.

I glanced back at the private rooms. Whatever business Maverick had back there gnawed at me like a cow with cud. *It's not my business.* I sat back down, all thoughts of going to Mav deflated. If Mav recognized me, he hadn't made it obvious. *Because he's not here for you,* I reminded myself.

"My, you look rather downtrodden." A man's voice, carrying the same accent as Mav, pushed my self-loathing back. I looked up to see a gorgeous guy with dark brown hair, a blue button up, and black trousers standing over me. "Mind if I sit?" he asked, gesturing at the seat beside me.

Actually, I do. "No one's sitting there, so no, I guess not," I said. My shoulders drew up, posture closed. I didn't want to chat with a stranger tonight. The last time I did that, I wound up drunk in the bed of a not-even-ex-yet.

Alcohol swirled my brain.

The man sat. "Thank you. Not that it's my business, but you seem a bit out of sorts." *Great, he even talks like Maverick.* "What do you say? Let me buy you a drink?"

Good grief. What does it take for this guy to get the hint? "I'm good, thanks. Fixing to call it a night and deal with my 'out of sorts-ness' on my own." I stood to leave.

The man lowered his head and laughed. "Only one reason to act the way you are. Bit of trouble with the lover, eh?" His eyes watched my mouth then drifted down my body. I couldn't stop the heat hitting my cheeks. "Hard to fathom why someone as gorgeous as you has trouble with his mate."

"I'm sorry, and who are you?" I asked, getting flustered.

Usually I didn't mind getting hit on so hard, but this guy bugged me. Letting him flirt with me felt wrong. The guy oozed confidence like Mav, but clearly didn't bother with boundaries—something not like Maverick.

The man laughed again. "Apologies. Where are my manners? My name is Connor."

My eyes bulged from my skull. "Connor? As in—?"

Connor nodded. "Yes. Now you're catching on. I assume you know my brother."

This is who Mav came here to meet. "Um, yeah. We work together," I said, rubbing the back of my head. Connor held out his hand, which I hesitantly took.

He pulled me forward, our faces inches from each other. "I can see why he's so determined to stand against her for you.

You're quite stunning." His grip on my hand tightened. "I imagine very good in bed as well."

This is getting uncomfortable.

"Let me go."

Connor released me, smirking. "It's nice to meet you finally, Aaron. Do be careful. I would hate for you to find yourself in the wrong crosshairs. Famous father or not, I'm sure my brother has told you about our family."

Rubbing my hand, I nodded. Sweat dripped down my cheeks. Connor scared the hell out of me. Where Maverick sent out waves of sexual charisma, Connor exuded danger. Like a predator staring at wounded prey. His gaze wasn't only an action, but a force capable of pushing someone back. That was what terrified me most.

Why would Maverick's mom be ashamed of this man? If she's like Mav said, Connor is just like her. Realization dawned. *Could it be because she's threatened by him? That he could take over the family name without as much as blink?*

"Shame he got you first," Connor commented as I turned to walk away. "I would have loved a chance to show you what true sex is."

I didn't like how that sounded. Connor had obviously had more one-night stands than Maverick. By the victorious tone of Connor's voice, finding notches in his headboard for each lay wouldn't surprise me.

I stepped back. "Uh, sorry, but I gotta go." I turned to leave. As I walked away, I felt Connor's heated stare burn into my back.

Understanding of Maverick's reasons for wanting me to stay away from his family became clearer with each step I took.

CHAPTER 29

A s I walked, hands pocketed, out of the bar, I wasn't
paying attention and smashed into something hard.
The collision sent me falling to the cement.

"Fucking great," I said, rubbing my now-soaked ass and
preparing to tell off the jerk who ran into me.

"Aaron?" That deep, familiar, ball-stroking timbre froze
me. Raising my eyes, I saw Maverick towering over me. He
thrust a hand out. "What the bloody hell are you doing here?"

"Me? It's a damn public bar." I swiped his hand away,
hauling myself up and dusting off my jeans. "Do I need your
permission to be here?"

Maverick rolled his eyes, smacking his head with his hand.
"That's not what I meant."

Internal ass-holery pushed me to open my mouth yet
again. "Wait, are we talking now?" I huffed a laugh. "Because
see, an hour ago, you pretty much told me to fuck off."

Maverick's hand dropped, eyes staring skyward. "For
God's sake, must we do this now?"

"Yeah," I said. "I think we must."

"What the bloody *fuck* do you want from me, Aaron?" His
hands went out to his sides. "I don't have time for this."

I clinched my fists, biting my lower lip so hard I tasted
copper. Tears stung my eyes, but I held them back. No way

in hell was I letting Maverick see me break. Not after I dealt with his creepy ass brother.

"Why? Because Connor's in town?" I asked in a low tone.

Maverick's eyes widened. "What?"

"You heard me. I just ran into your fucking freak of a brother at the bar." I rolled my eyes, holding up a hand. "You know what? You're right. It's late. I have shit to deal with." I shouldered past, stopping when he grabbed my bicep.

"You met Connor?"

I nodded. "Yeah. Good thing we don't matter to each other anymore, right? He freaked me the fuck out."

"Aaron," Maverick said with a sigh.

I yanked my arm away. "Forget it. See you Tuesday."

Walking away from Maverick hurt worse than getting knifed in the back. The piercing pain in my heart reminded me why I didn't bother with relationships.

Did I act childish? Let's put that in the "maybe" column. Did I act childish because it was the only thing I thought of to keep the pain away? Absolutely. Did it help me get over the feeling of wanting Maverick more than my next breath? *No.*

Tuesday morning came faster than I wanted it to. After the shit show on Friday, Rebecca telling me she struggled getting a hold on the tabloids, and Mom calling to inform me Dad called her, I found sitting at my desk difficult.

To top it off, the weather reported we'd see our first winter storm this weekend. I secretly hoped it came before the party so I could get out of having to see Maverick in a tux. *Which reminds me, I still haven't gotten mine.*

Seething rage boiled inside me.

234

I gritted my teeth, fighting the urge to scream at my computer. When the phone rang, I took a few seconds to remind myself that work was work. Going to the courthouse to get whatever fucking documents Maverick needed was a chore. I hated it on a good day. Add in my current mood and the damn weather, and I was ready to explode!

Maverick only spoke to me for business reasons, and each curt sentence created a fresh cut in my heart. He interviewed more clients than usual, probably to avoid dealing with me more than necessary.

It wasn't until my lunch break that Maverick darkened my "door," leaning on his forearms on my desk. I didn't bother looking up from the salad I was wolfing down.

"Aaron, were you able to get that calendar updated?" he asked. A subtle—and I mean *subtle*—shake broke through his otherwise professional tone. "I know you've been busy."

I'd had enough. My fists hit the desktop, making Maverick jerk.

"I can't do this," I said, clenching my teeth hard. Something in my jaw popped. "It hurts too bad."

Maverick remained deadpan, but I felt him searching me like he always did.

Without looking at him, I packed up my things. "I'm cashing in the rest of my vacation time. In case you don't know, that's two weeks. Sorry if the suddenness is 'against protocol.'" I air-quoted the last two words. "Fire me if you want. It's better than feeling like a coroner is opening my chest cavity while I'm still alive."

I didn't tell him two weeks was all I had left in college. After that, I'd cash in my notice and be far away from Maverick and this hellhole.

My backpack rested against my desk. I grabbed it, turned off my computer, and started walking toward the break room.

Maverick's body blocked the exit.

I scowled. "Maverick, move." He didn't budge, so I tried stepping around him. Moving in my way, Maverick held my eyes with his. I couldn't figure out what hid behind the beautiful gaze. "I mean it. Move."

"No," Maverick said. "We have unfinished business. You don't get to run anymore. I want you tonight. At my place or yours. I don't give a fuck."

"Excuse me?" *This smug bastard! Does he really think I'm letting him fuck me after all this?* "You really are a narcissistic asshole. I'm not giving you anything."

I'd pushed too far. In seconds, Maverick had me whipped around. If I hadn't turned my face, I'd have slammed my nose against the wall. He kicked the door between the hallway and our offices closed. In the scuffle, I dropped my backpack.

"I don't know why you're angry at me when you were the one who acted like a child," Maverick breathed hot in my ear. "After our little rendezvous and drinking myself into oblivion, I realized something."

I bucked uselessly against him, frustrated at my now erect dick. "Let me go, Mav."

Slowly, Maverick unbuttoned my vest and shirt. His other hand drifted lazily down my side to my hip. "No, I don't think I will. I actually smoked over the weekend. Do you know how long it's been since I had a cigarette?"

"No, and I don't really give a flying fuck, either," I replied, straining to keep my treacherous body under control.

Maverick's hand moved from my hip, down my thigh, between my legs. "See, I think you do. Why else do you harden the moment I get near?" He kissed my hair. "Aaron,

I'm sorry if Connor frightened you. I didn't know he was there already. We were supposed to meet in private."

Trying to hold on to my rage became harder as Maverick stroked me through my pants. I let my head fall to his shoulder, hating myself for praying he'd reach inside and rub me off.

"I need you," Maverick murmured in my ear. "Beautiful Aaron, I want you in my life. Your warm body in my bed."

I hissed through my teeth with each rub of his hand over my groin. Every few strokes, Maverick lightly squeezed my balls, pulling a groan out of me.

"Not being near you or hearing from you," Maverick purred. "It tortured me." Teeth scraped over my jaw, down my neck, and to the exposed skin of my shoulder. Once there, he bit down, sucking flesh into his mouth.

"Ah, Mav." Pain mixed with pleasure as Maverick continued kissing, licking, and sucking the skin of my shoulder and lower neck. "Don't give me a damn hickey. I'm supposed to be pissed at you."

He replied with a chuckle.

Neither of us denied I lost this battle. Every stroke, kiss, and rubbing of body against body threw my resistance to the wind. The sound of my zipper lowering dragged another moan out of me.

"May I?" Maverick asked.

"Yes," I exhaled. "Hell yes."

Another dark chuckle, followed by my dick springing from my briefs. Angling it down, Maverick began his slow push and pull. His free hand held my jaw, directing me to look at him.

"You are so perfect," Maverick mused. "My beautiful Aaron." Another heated breath tickled the tiny hairs in my ear. "I have missed you. I forgive you. Please accept my deepest apologies for the horrid way I treated you."

"It wasn't ... ah ... your fault," I replied. Tingling began in my lower spine. *Ah, yes. I'm right there.* I moved my hips with Maverick's rhythm, chasing an orgasm that was bound to be explosive. *Better be. If my balls got any more blue, I'd be screwed.*

"Ah, sweetheart, you're so close," Maverick murmured. "Cum for me. Show me you are still mine."

His. That's right. I am his. I thrust my hips. Maverick covered my mouth, stifling my shout as I came. *And he ... is mine.*

Maverick held me against him. "Take some time to steady. I will get some paper towels for you to clean up."

When he released me, I fell forward against the wall. Trembling legs barely supported me after that orgasmic euphoria. I blinked against the dizziness, rotated my tongue a few times to get it wet, and took deep breaths to slow my heart.

Maverick returned and handed me the paper towels, waiting for me to clean myself up. "My place or yours?" he asked bluntly.

"Calm down, will you? I'm still trying to figure out which plane is the ceiling," I snapped. "What makes you think I'm open to a make-up fuck?"

"How about because I'm not giving you a choice? We don't have to fuck, but I want to, and will, see you tonight. Even if I have to sit outside your door until you decide to let me in."

Cocky fucker. "Fuck you." The old idea I had the night Maverick told me off came to mind. *Fine. He wants to fuck? We'll fuck.* "On second thought," I said, giving him a coy smile. "You want to come to my place?"

Maverick cocked his head, brow rising.

I finished zipping up, tossed the paper towels in the trash, and leaned against my desk. "Come to my place."

"Why the sudden change of heart?" Maverick asked.

I crossed the room to where he stood near his door. Licking my teeth, I lowered my eyelids. My hands flattened against his chest. "I want to do something different tonight." I stood on my toes and kissed his jaw. *Here goes nothing.* "Mav, tonight ... *I* want to fuck *you*."

"Is that so?" Maverick asked, his fingertips caressing my jawbone. "I'll make you a deal."

Brows furrowed, I asked, "What kind of deal?"

"A simple one. Come with me to the renaming." Maverick leaned in close. "As my boyfriend."

Gob-smacked, I jerked my head back. "What?"

"You heard me. I want you as my boyfriend, Aaron." He kissed me, arm wrapped around my waist. Our tongues teased each other. Not hungrily, but sweetly and needily.

"What about Connor?" I inquired, pushing against Maverick's chest. "Doesn't he hate that I ... you know ... fucked his brother?"

Maverick chortled. "Of course not. Connor only came to warn me our mother was coming to the States within the next two months. Believe me, Connor is many things, but he looks out for me."

"Oh. So, he wasn't trying to get rid of me, then?"

"No," Maverick replied. "He wanted to see who I dared stand against our mother for. I know he's ... unsettling—"

"That's an understatement. Guy freaked me out."

Another eyeroll. "About our deal?"

I decided to have some fun. "Since you demanded so nicely, sure. But I have a slight problem."

"What is that?"

"I don't have a tux."

Maverick kissed me again, more passionately. His tongue thrust into my mouth, tasting everywhere he could.

I angled my head to deepen the kiss. Neither one of us needed to say anything else. In this moment, we both felt the same.

Relieved.

"Shh, you need to be quiet," Maverick said with a hushed laugh. "Or do I need to put my hand over your mouth again?"

I squirmed against him. The tiny space left virtually no room between us. Somewhere in the distance, a door slammed shut. *Another poor sucker subjected to his partner's will, no doubt.*

"Remind me whose idea this was again," I said, barely above a whisper.

Maverick chuckled. "Yours."

"Well, I'm an idiot. Should've gone with the supermodel thing of stepping out and showing off each one."

I shuddered at the idea, but it sounded better than the current arrangement. The only reason I hadn't shoved Maverick off was because I was inhaling his cologne like a man addicted to huffing paint. That wild, musky, raw man-smell swam up my nose. The scent engulfed me, making focusing on anything else hard as hell.

"Perhaps, but then I wouldn't get to see you in your under-wear or help dress you. Now, quit moving. I'm almost finished."

I choked back a whine while Maverick worked his magic with the twentieth bowtie. He'd insisted I wear one of those vest/tuxedo combos to the party instead of a regular tux. He said something about loving how I looked in my vests so much and having a plan he didn't deign to tell me about.

"Are you sure this suit is crucial to this 'plan' of yours?" I whined, air-quoting the word. "Because I'm not seeing any reason to subject myself or my wallet to this torture."

Maverick finished with the bowtie, backing up as much as possible and admiring his handiwork. "I'm sure. Don't worry about paying. I'll be buying this for you."

Happiness that we'd made up swelled in my heart. After agreeing to let me have my way with him—and taking me home to launch me into sexual Shangri-La—Maverick insisted on meeting me the day before the renaming and helping me pick a tux. He never said anything about buying one for me.

"No way! This thing has to cost at least one-and-a-half of my paychecks! There's no way I'm letting you cover it. I can afford it," I protested.

Maverick's eyes darkened. Lunging forward, he grabbed my wrists and pinned them over my head. His thigh pushed my legs apart. The thin material did little to protect against the friction.

I bit back a groan.

"I have no doubt you can handle yourself, but this is essential to my plans. I should be the one handling the burden. Don't worry. You can buy dinner next time. Deal?" he whispered while kissing my neck and swiping his tongue over my Adam's Apple.

With my sex-hazed brain, I'd have agreed to let him dye my hair pink.

"Fine. Christ, you're pushy." I stole a kiss when our eyes met. "For now, I'd like to get out of this monkey suit and grab something to eat. I'm starving."

Maverick's hands went to work on the buttons. "Getting you out of this is going to be much more enjoyable. Want to get dirty?"

"Are you serious? Here? We'd wind up needing your legal services," I said with a laugh.

"If not here, I know where a nice family restroom is."

"That, I can work with."

No other incentives were needed.

In half the time it took him to help me into the tux, Maverick had me out of it.

"Wait," I said, rushing out as Maverick left the dressing room stall. "Please tell me you have a condom."

We both laughed at my comment. The woman who over-heard me covered her mouth, a giggle in her eyes.

She definitely knew all about not being able to wait until you got home.

CHAPTER 30

I spent the night at Maverick's condo the day before the renaming—on Elliot's orders—getting my head sexed off with the hottest make-up sex I'd ever experienced. Maverick left no room for argument, and by the time he finished with me, I felt like I floated on a sea of ecstasy. We fell asleep next to each other, Maverick's arm thrown over my waist.

I woke to find him lying on his stomach, arms tucked under his pillow. Thick, black lashes stood out against the cream sheets. Layer upon layer of muscle rippled from his arms, down his shoulders and back. Sun-kissed skin, fitting for someone who lived in Miami, glistened with the remains of sweat from our heated night. Sheets sank low on his hips, revealing his tailbone area.

He's fucking beautiful.

Reaching out, I ran my fingers through layers of Maverick's soft hair. Carefully, I pushed the sheets down to free my legs, stopping when Maverick moaned and stirred. Once he stilled, I continued, placing a leg over his thighs.

The position gave me access to the full expanse of his back. My eyes devoured every delicious muscle as I imagined taking Maverick exactly like this.

You lie there. I want to imagine what I'm getting soon and taste this gorgeous skin.

I bent down, tracing the path of Maverick's spine with my mouth, starting at his tailbone. The scent of sun, sweat, and sex wafted into my nostrils. Every few inches, I placed a kiss on a more defined muscle.

Soft moans and shifting told me Maverick was enjoying what I did to him. He opened his eyes, a tired smile on his face.

"Good morning," I said, kissing his jaw. Stubble scratched across my lips.

"Yes, it is," he replied. "By all means, don't stop now. It feels amazing."

That was good to hear. But I had another idea.

"Turn over for me, gorgeous," I said, blowing in his ear. "I think I want to have a nice pre-breakfast meal."

I'd wanted to do this for the longest time. Dreams of pleasing him with my mouth eased the stress on the nights I couldn't see him. Backing away, I sat on my knees, waiting while Maverick rolled over. His thick cock created a tent with the sheets, muscles bulging as he placed his arms behind his head. That coy half-smile I adored made its way to his face. Its presence excited and stimulated me to continue.

"What did you have in mind?" Maverick asked, his voice raspy.

I crawled like a cat up his body and placed a kiss on the corner of his mouth. "You'll have to wait and see." A chuckle rumbled through his closed lips.

I made my way back down, pulling the sheets and freeing Maverick's massive shaft. *Fuck, I love it.* Giving blow jobs was my specialty, and the one thing I thanked Declan for as Maverick spread his legs, giving me full access to his heavy balls.

I started at the base, licking the full length of the veiny member. Maverick groaned, shuffling on the pillows. My cock twitched at the delectable sound.

Positioning myself over Maverick, I opened my mouth and took him to the back of my throat. Slowly, I slid my mouth up, sucking the salty pre-cum. The tip of my tongue teased the deep slit, chasing any remaining pre-cum.

"Oh, Aaron," Maverick purred. "Yes." He reached a hand out and gripped my hair.

My heart throbbed, confidence boosting from the slight burn of Maverick's twisted fingers. I repeated my previous actions. I took Maverick so far that I coughed.

Above me, Maverick shifted. I wasn't sure what he was doing until his hips matched each movement I made.

"Don't stop, sweetheart," Maverick begged. "Fuck, your mouth is so soft. Everything about you is so bloody soft."

Our bodies moved in perfect harmony as Maverick ran after his orgasm. To help him along, I fondled his balls.

Opening my eyes, I saw the expanse of Maverick's chest. He'd thrown his head back, his Adam's apple begging me to suck and tease it. My fingers drifted from his balls to the dark crevasse between his dick and hole.

I long to be in here, I thought upon feeling the tight entrance I probed for.

"Ah, fuck!" Maverick shouted when I dared push a finger inside him. A slow thrust of my finger was all it took, and Maverick exploded, shouting my name.

The salty taste of him dazed me. *Wow. He tastes as good as he feels. Could I have found anyone more wonderful?*

"Christ." Maverick panted, squeezing his eyes closed then opening them wide like he was fighting off vertigo. "It's like someone made you for me."

I sniffed a chuckle. "Likewise. When was the last time you had a finger in you?" *Or a dick, for that matter.*

Maverick turned solemn eyes away. "I haven't bottomed for anyone in many years. The last time was in law school." He raised his arm. "Come lay with me."

"You sure? Today's a big day." He repeated himself, so I joined him, snuggling against his chest. "Tell me," I said, my finger tracing his nipple.

"You might find this hard to believe, but you aren't the first one I've been in ... a serious relationship with," Maverick said.

He caught himself. Was he going to say he's in love with me?

"There was one other. Someone I thought I'd want to marry."

"What happened?" I asked, slightly jealous I nearly lost him to someone else.

Maverick cleared his throat, rubbing a hand over his face. "He um..." Another throat clearing. "He..."

I'd never seen Maverick struggle. Witnessing it weighed heavily on my heart. If I didn't know any better, I swore I saw his eyes tearing up.

To calm him, I rubbed soothing circles on his chest. "It's okay. You don't have to tell me. I think I get it." I scooted up to kiss his jaw. "I'm not leaving you. Mav, I..." I paused. *I shouldn't say that yet. Not when he's hurting like this.*

"You what?" Maverick asked, almost eagerly.

I shook my head. "It's not important." Sitting up, I put my legs over the edge of the bed. "We should get ready for tonight. I know Travis needs a few last-minute things set up before the event."

Springs squeaked as the bed shifted.

Maverick stood, rounded the bed, and offered me a hand, his warm eyes welcoming. "Will you bathe with me, Aaron? I could use your company."

I gasped, my eyes large as small saucers. Another of my dreams was coming true.

"Yeah," I said. "I'd love to." I took his hand, letting him lead me to the bathroom. Once there, I propped my naked ass against his vanity, waiting while he turned on the shower. "Just don't get too attached. We don't want to be late."

Maverick pressed his body against mine. Firm fingers took my jaw. "I wouldn't dream of it. After all, what I have planned for you will be worth sacrificing a little shower time." He let go and walked toward the shower.

"Oh, come on! You can't drop a bomb like that and expect me not to think about it the rest of the day!" I stepped in after him, closing the glass door. Anyone walking in would get a shock. "Mav!"

Maverick laughed, taking the shampoo from its hanging shelf. "Later. Right now, let me get us both clean. There're some remnants of our love-making last night all over you."

He had me.

After taking him inside me the last time before falling asleep, I hadn't had time to clean myself up. "Fine," I complained. "But I still hate you."

We both laughed at that one.

I thoroughly enjoyed having Maverick clean us both up. I doubt he knew his ass went right up against my very eager dick.

After a heated make-out session in the shower that ultimately made us late, we spent the rest of the afternoon helping finalize the party—gala, whatever—set-up. I enjoyed watching Maverick fix the problems Travis's uncertainty caused the caterers and organizers. He looked amazing in his suit, those tight pants hugging an extremely fine ass I couldn't wait to have.

Watching him, I let my mind wander to the possibilities of what our life together would be like. Would he want to go steady? Maybe move in together?

Getting ahead of myself. I can't help but imagine, though.

Maverick finished with another caterer, turned toward me, and waved.

I returned the wave, gesturing "come here" with my head.

Maverick held up a finger yet never made it over to me.

With the fading sunlight, guests started arriving en masse. Members of the firm and other partners who apparently knew Mr. Kimball clamored in. High paying clients shook Maverick and Travis's hands on their way through the door. Upper class music—the kind that could bore a guy to death—played from the speakers.

The whole atmosphere of the thing made me yawn frequently.

Since Maverick spent all his time talking to the guests, I found myself alone most of the night.

"Hey, babe!" Elliot called out. I turned to see him gussied up in a maroon tux. Josh was hot on his heels. The two joined me at the bar. "Some event, huh? I'd say Maverick's a tremendous hit in the New York law scene, wouldn't you?"

New York law scene. That was one thing I didn't want to think about. If Maverick had a place in New York, he wouldn't want to leave it when I left for New Orleans.

"Yeah, they love him," I replied.

"Uh oh, I know that look," Elliot said. "What's up?"

I took a drink from the Gin & Tonic condensating on the bar. "I was just thinking. You know I have that internship coming up."

Elliot rolled his eyes, shaking his head. "Please don't tell me you still haven't told him."

"Okay, then I won't tell you. What if he doesn't do long-distance relationships?"

"Has he asked you to be his boyfriend?"

I nodded. "Sort of. Not in those words, but something close. I told him I'd come to this thing as his boyfriend. Not sure if that's really official though."

Elliot smacked my shoulder, earning a hiss. "Ask him." My friend glared at me, all joviality gone. "I mean it, Aaron. Stop being such a pussy and tell him exactly what you want. Even if he already assumes it, tell him anyway."

"There you are." Maverick walked up as if cued and placed a kiss on my cheek. "I've been looking for you."

"And that's our hint to skedaddle." Elliot grabbed his boyfriend's tie. "C'mon, baby. I feel a dance coming on. Boring music or not."

"Wasn't that...?" Maverick trailed off, pointing.

"Mhm. Don't ask."

Maverick sat next to me, clasped his hands, and glanced at me. "Something troubles you."

I tried to laugh. "No one talks like that."

"I do," he replied, kissing my lips in full view of everyone. "Tell me what's wrong. What can I do to help?"

Another head shake.

Maverick cradled my cheek, moving my head to look at him. "Don't do that. Don't close me out. I want to be here for you, sweetheart. Let me."

I fought tearing up. Anytime he talked to me like that, made me feel valued, or showed genuine affection I melted. "I can't. Not here. Too many people need you—"

"I don't care for them like I do you." Maverick stood, taking my hand. "Come with me. I know somewhere we can have some privacy for a few minutes."

My pounding heart pushed blood south of my belt buckle. I let him lead us through the crowd and into the small hall connecting the offices.

We walked through the main waiting room to the door that separated our offices from the secondary reception desk.

When we got into the room with my desk, Maverick spun me around. His arm wrapped around my waist as he crushed his mouth against mine. Locked together, Maverick pushed me through his office door, kicking it closed.

"I have thought of nothing else tonight but this," Maverick rasped.

A fury of hands worked the buttons of my suit jacket and vest. They dropped to the floor in a pile.

Maverick breathed hot in my ear. "Naked. I want to see you naked."

Getting me in my birthday suit didn't take long. Maverick worked quickly. Almost like he'd rip a button or seam in a hasty move.

"Okay," I said, holding my arms over myself. "I'm naked. In your office. With a big ass window behind us. Now, what?"

Maverick stripped, his clothes falling next to mine. "That window can't see in during the night. It's made to keep out the sun. Believe me, no one will see your gorgeous body but me."

Hunger darkened Maverick's eyes. Taking my hips, he rotated me so my back faced him. With a splayed hand, he pushed until I rested my hands on his desk.

"Perfect," he murmured, placing a kiss on each of my shoulder blades. One hand guided me, raising my ass a bit. "Yes. Just like this." Maverick leaned over me, his chest flat against my back. "Spread your legs for me, beautiful Aaron. I want to see the hole I plan to fill."

If my heart beat any faster, I'd faint. Sweat beaded on my forehead and back. Some already started dripping down my spine. I loved when Maverick's more dominant, wild side came out to play. I spread my legs.

"Please tell me you have lube," I said.

"Of course, I do."

In seconds, Maverick was on me. Lubed fingers probed my entrance. *Wait, when did he...?* I didn't have time to finish the thought as two thick digits pushed past the ring of muscle. The sting was brief, but the intense pressure Maverick's demand created made it hard to stand.

Maverick cradled my throat, asserting light force, not enough to choke me, but enough to tell me I wasn't going anywhere until he was finished with me.

"Have I told you how much I adore you?" Maverick asked. A third finger joined the others in an erotic euphoria I couldn't get enough of. Each thrust ordered my body to take all three, and I fucking loved it. "No, it's more than that now," he said, panting. "I'm in love with you, Aaron."

Between the pain-mixed pleasure of the finger-fucking and the slap of the statement, I couldn't form a decent thought. Trying to keep from falling forward became harder.

"Time for me to take you. Fitting the first time I fill you should be in my office, yes? I told you I'd fuck you here," Maverick said.

I whimpered at the loss of his fingers. My disappointment didn't last long, though. I soon felt the thick tip of Maverick's cock nudging my already sore hole.

"Be ready, sweetheart," was all the warning I got before Maverick thrust inside me to the hilt.

"Ah! Fuck!" I shouted. Burning pain erupted inside me.

Falling onto my forearms, I couldn't hold back my whimpers and moans. It wasn't until I opened my eyes that I realized what was going on.

He ... he's taking me bare.

Maverick began a gradual thrust. "Let me make love to you," he mused.

Pain dissipated with each careful withdrawal. My body held him when he retreated, swallowing him when he returned. Every thrust searched for that perfect spot to send me further into sexual heaven.

"Ah!" I gasped when he rubbed against my prostate.

"There it is," Maverick said darkly. "That's what I wanted." He took my shoulder and pulled me to stand straight. "Aaron, tell me what's troubling you?"

I'm supposed to form a thought?

"I..." I said, more of a squeak than a word.

"You?" Maverick prompted, never breaking his rhythm.

Damn, his control is crazy. "I want ... ah ... I want to know if I ... hah ... what I mean is..." *God, this is torture.* "What do I mean to you?"

"You mean everything to me," Maverick said bluntly. "I love you, Aaron. More than my next breath. More than my next day of life. Why do you ask?"

Tears broke free. Not from the pressure or burning in my ass. Not even from the fear of losing Maverick to my dreams. But from the honesty I heard in his tone.

"You ... gah ... really mean that?" I asked. Tingling in my lower spine warned me of my oncoming orgasm.

Maverick sucked my earlobe into his mouth then released it with a pop. "Every word. Now, why do you ask?"

I let my head fall to his shoulder. "Fill me, and I'll tell you."

"As you wish." Maverick pushed me flat against his desk. His thrusts increased in speed.

Soon, Maverick pushed all the way inside me, his balls against my ass as hot streams of cum shot into my body. He remained inside me until he grew soft enough to withdraw.

I stayed where I was, falling to my knees.

Maverick joined me beside his desk, where we sat together, not bothering to go after our clothes yet. "Before you tell me, I have to ask. Will you be my boyfriend, Aaron? In front of everyone. I don't bloody care who sees or knows."

I didn't hesitate to respond. "Yes. Officially. Yes." My chest heaved. Sitting hurt like hell. "Now it's my turn. Mav, I ... I have an internship at a restaurant in New Orleans."

He pulled me close, so my head lay on his heart. "Sounds like a good plan. I've been thinking about starting a personal practice, anyway."

"Wait, what?" I asked, looking up at him. "Just like that? You'd leave a firm you've barely started at. One that took your name only tonight? Just like that?"

Maverick smiled. A few sprigs of hair fell over his eye. "Just like that. I told you. I care little about anyone else." He brushed the backs of his fingers over my cheek. "I searched for you and told myself I'd never stop until I found you. I'm not letting you go, my love."

More tears fell. Not caring if anyone came looking for us or not, I embraced Maverick's mouth with mine, moving to straddle him.

"Fill me again?" I pleaded.

Maverick chuckled. "As many times as you want."

As we readied to have more sex in Maverick's office, I could only marvel at the swelling happiness in my heart.

A final thought crossed my mind.

Maverick Waylan. Definitely a yes.

STORMIE SKYES

More books from
4 Horsemen Publications

Romance

Ann Shepphird
The War Council

Emily Bunney
All or Nothing
All the Way
All Night Long: Novella
All She Needs
Having it All
All at Once
All Together
All for Her

KT Bond
Back to Life
Back to Love
Back at Last

Lynn Chantale
The Baker's Touch
Blind Secrets
Broken Lens

Mandy Fate
Love Me, Goaltender
Captain of My Heart

CPSIA information can be obtained
at www.ICGtesting.com
Printed in the USA
LVHW110339191022
731049LV00013B/103